REINCURSION

RYAN HARDING &
JASON TAVERNER

DEATH'S HEAD PRESS

an imprint of Dead Sky Publishing, LLC
Miami Beach, Florida
www.deadskypublishing.com

ISBN: 9781639510146

First Edition

Cover Art: Alex McVey

Book Layout: Lori Michelle
www.TheAuthorsAlley.com

BEFORE

ON OCTOBER 25, 1978, dressed in military garb replete with a gasmask, Vietnam vet Richard Dunbar embarked on a killing spree in the campgrounds of Morgan Falls and the surrounding town which ended with fourteen victims dead, plus Dunbar himself after the intervention of law enforcement. No cause was attributed to his rampage, though accounts from men who served with him detailed a certain delight Dunbar showed for the horrors of war . . . and a flair for expanding them.

On May 9, 1980, impossibly, Dunbar returned to Morgan to resume his wetwork upon campers and assorted Morgan citizens. Killing him this time proved much more difficult, with twenty-six people claimed before the nightmare ended again. In the wake of the murderer's return, he became better known as Agent Orange. This was only the first of many times. After a year, a matter of months, sometimes only weeks, Agent Orange resurrected— always in Morgan—until stopped once again by police, military, or private citizens, increasingly harder to kill each time.

After another night of terror on November 9, 1984, the government opted to evacuate the dwindling populace and erect a thirty-foot wall around the area to contain Agent Orange. Military patrols guarded the wall to keep citizens away and neutralize the recurring threat when needed.

On December 20, 1996 Orange managed to escape the walls of Morgan to besiege the neighboring city of Sandalwood in the worst massacre to date. Another evacuation mandate followed, with a wall established around Sandalwood's perimeter. A further wall expansion occurred on October 29, 2004 when the government annexed the nearest town of Westing for unknown reasons and erected a third barrier.

This territory of a walled-off city and towns is known as the Kill Zone, and in the ensuing decades has become the most feared and, to others, the most exciting and mysterious locale in the United States. Theories abound on the explanation for Agent Orange's resurgence and the potentially mystical properties of the land within. A group of people known alternately as Stalkers or Prowlers have become adept at infiltrating the Kill Zone to lead curiosity seekers and exiles inside to experience the forbidden area, while avoiding both military and the traps and attention of its resident slayer.

I.

TODD PULLED CINDY across the moonlit field to the trees. They giggled as they ran, shushing back and forth with greater exaggeration. Once within the cover of the woods, they traded their shushing for moaning, kissing hungrily.

"We have to be quiet," Todd said when it ended. "He'll hear us."

"'He'll hear us,'" Cindy mocked. "He's not even real, stupid."

"Maybe, but there's some reason they want to keep people out of here."

"I'm more worried about who I want in *here*." She pointed down.

A grin threatened to split Todd's skull in half. "I can't believe we're doing this."

"Are we? You seem awfully scared."

"I'm all about it, baby. I just don't want to get butchered by some dude in a mask."

"That's what I like about you, Todd. Most people go their whole lives wanting that, but not you."

"Ha ha," he said dryly.

Cindy slowly dropped to her knees in front of him. He looked around a bit anxiously, but soon expressed only delight at the sound of his fly unzipping. He slipped his fingers into her hair, surveyed their surroundings one more time, then shut his eyes as he lost himself in the pleasure of Cindy's bobbing head. She clenched her hands around his rump as she took him in.

In seconds his whole body erupted in spasms, like a puppet bounced on its strings. Cindy jerked back, startled.

"Not alre—" Her eyes widened in shock as she looked up to find a pair of garden shears jutting through Todd's eye sockets. She screamed. The shears snapped shut, meeting at the bridge of his nose, and the top of his head slid away like the stalk of a carrot. His body slumped and collided with Cindy as though to embrace her, knocking her to the ground and revealing the figure holding the shears. A clown mask emerged from the darkness, blood-spattered in the same shade as its eternally grinning mouth. The killer took a step, crunching Todd's skull toupee under a booted heel.

Cindy sobbed, trying to free herself from the dead weight as the figure bent toward her—

"A clown mask," Bryce said. "Come on. Why would a soldier wear that?"

"People are scared of clowns," Erica said. She never looked up from her tablet, barely paid the movie any attention at all.

Bryce shook his head. "That doesn't look scary. And no clown could survive a nuclear strike like Agent Orange. Not even Silly Jackson."

Erica smiled faintly. "I wish they'd let him do a show in the KZ. How awesome would that have been?" She swiped her screen to scroll down a message board forum. He didn't have to ask which one.

She settled on the image of a couple in front of a crashed helicopter with the caption GET TO THE CHOPPA! At the edge of the frame stood a pole with a severed head. The couple made cartoonish faces, trying to mimic the frozen horror of the dead man's face.

Classy.

"You remember which stop this is in the Gauntlet?" Erica asked.

"The last stop for that guy."

"No extra credit for jokes. Come on, which one?" She angled her chest toward him. "A button for a correct answer."

Bryce grinned. He'd seen behind the pink blouse several times in the past two months but it made him no less eager, even if the subject unnerved him more than he cared to reveal to her. This tease would be all he'd get for now, too, so better make it count.

"The helicopter is in Sandalwood, obviously, which means one of the last nine."

"Wow, you narrowed it down to just over half of them. So impressive." She rolled her eyes, but playfully.

"I'm building suspense. The helicopter is Gauntlet Station number eight."

"Very good. You can do the honors." She gestured to her blouse.

Bryce chose a button to expand the valley of already plentiful cleavage he'd admired from afar in their psychology class, before scrounging up the courage to talk to her—thanks to Sigmund Freud for the assist, her opinion on "anatomy is destiny" the perfect icebreaker. She proved more receptive to the concept than the instructor, and also bought it when Bryce claimed he purposely mispronounced Karen Horney as a joke.

You sure that wasn't a Freudian slip? Erica said.

A Freudian slip about Karen Horney (Hor-nay, as it turned out)? Mind blown.

Her research aside, he liked having her to himself tonight, away from the withering glares of other guys and the way they openly ogled Erica. He sometimes imagined getting in someone's face about it.

Hey, man, what are you staring at?

I was staring at an ass that won't quit. Now I'm looking at one who should have.

It was in the fine print, though—guys resented you dating a goddess like Erica and weren't shy about volunteering to take your place should circumstances necessitate.

On TV, a bloody slice opened in Cindy's palm as she tried to ward off the shears. She drew her hand away and a lingering close-up showed the blades glide in and carve a rift in her throat with an exaggerated gargling effect. Blood erupted from the four valves rigged by special FX guru Sergio Grueletti, as shown in the BluRay exclusive featurette "Orange You Glad He's Back?" Cindy's head bobbed as she choked and gasped, not unlike the oral antics she performed on Todd a minute ago. Crimson gushed between her lips.

"Not bad," Bryce allowed.

The soundtrack hit a stinger note as the scene switched to Todd and Cindy's friends back on the other side of the wall.

"They should have been back by now. Maybe we should go look for them."

"Yeah, maybe you should do that," Bryce said.

Erica joined in. "They're just playing a trick on you."

One of Todd's bros said, "Man, they chickened out and they're just trying to scare us!"

"But what if . . . what if Agent Orange got them?"

"Oh, come on. You don't believe that fairy tale, do you? I hope we do find him. I'll kick that little bitch in the face. Come on, let's go!"

Erica swiped to another picture. A Chicken Exit—one of the emergency lines to call the military to bail your stupid ass out of the Kill Zone when you realized you were in over your head. The couple from the helicopter picture yukked it up again, terror from the girl straight out of an old monster movie as the guy pretended to shout into the phone for evac, pronto.

"That's not part of the Gauntlet," Bryce said, hoping for another button.

She didn't acknowledge him, sweeping past more pictures. "I can't believe we're going to do this!" An ominous echo of what Todd said before his transformative Pez dispenser surgery.

"I can't either!" Bryce made sure to say it with a smile, but he really *couldn't* believe he agreed to it.

He was content to imagine sneaking into the KZ while conveniently escaping the orange dragon's wrath within. He entertained no illusions about actually doing it in real life.

So naturally after five weeks of dating when Erica suggested they participate in the Kill Zone Gauntlet, Bryce heard himself say, *Fuck yeah, baby, let's do it!*

It had been the nearest thing to an out-of-body experience, but that was hardly surprising. His whole life seemed like one since meeting Erica.

The movie continued. Bryce wasn't even sure which one this was. *Kill Zone Massacre 7? 8?* Whichever came after the maligned found footage entry.

"I don't like this, boddy . . . that looks like blood to me."

"Bullshit, man! I'm telling you, they're just trying to scare us. *Hey, come out, Todd, you asshole! This isn't funny!*"

"Trent, did you hear that? It sounded like—"

"Jesus Christ, it's just Todd, you retards! Watch this, I'm going to scare the shit out of him."

Trent brushed aside tree branches as he pressed into the copse of trees, an expectant grin on his face. The Agent Orange suspense theme played helpfully for the benefit of the three or four people in the audience who might not know what was going to happen to the intrepid explorer.

Bryce grimaced. A silly movie, of course, but the carnage it depicted was a real possibility for anyone who went inside, no matter how the colloquial term "KZ" swept fatality under the rug. So much friendlier than Kill Zone.

When it's your time, it's your time, Erica once said to someone who echoed Bryce's own privately held views on the insanity of trying to go in there. *You can crack your head open in the shower.*

True. You didn't necessarily have to jump in the bathtub on roller skates to exponentially increase your chances of tragedy, though.

Trent's face froze in a rictus of horror as the camera panned across the mutilated remains of Todd and Cindy, posed like headless bodies (or half so in Todd's case) before an invisible TV. Cindy's head dangled above her neck stump, long brunette hair knotted around a branch and swaying softly. Trent turned to run back to his friends, abruptly and predictably stopped in his tracks by the tall figure with the clown mask. A gloved hand seized his throat to cut off a cry of alarm, followed by a smattering of cracks as the arm vibrated and bones shattered in his neck.

Bryce tried to distract Erica. "Lame. All those weapons and he's strangling him like an old black and white movie. Remember to buy war bonds!"

She looked up long enough to smirk, but went back to the tablet and furrowed her brow as she kneaded her chin, lost in concentration and strategy. The hottest girl on campus by far, and probably the entire world, too. Even the cheerleaders looked like the offspring of cousin-fucking bumpkins side by side with her, at least to Bryce. Shoulder-length blonde hair, nearly white. Perfect body—supple, athletic, just busty enough. An ass that filled out her jeans to ideal proportion. Pouty lips that made simply kissing her as exciting as the more triple X-rated variety activities.

It wasn't just that, though. It was the fever intensity he felt upon seeing her, the certainty that his life had been a twenty-year journey to put him in the same psychology class. Actually talking to her convinced him she had everything he wanted— exciting, spontaneous, and damn near fearless. His brief time with her revealed she was perhaps *too* exciting, spontaneous, and fearless, and as he charted the appreciative looks and leers she received around campus, he began to worry about competition should he be exposed as timid, unadventurous, and cowardly. He didn't think of himself that way, but what if she did?

The Gauntlet offered both conundrum and solution. It began in 2006 with a man who went by the user name EXTREMEDEAN69 and an unnamed companion. He uploaded pictures he took from fifteen places he charted on a map, all purportedly from the KZ. They spanned over ten miles from Morgan to Sandalwood, images indelibly attributable to the restricted area. Many believed them fake or at least the product of multiple visits rather than the longest, luckiest day for anyone who ever dared entry, but believers were inspired to duplicate EXTREMEDEAN69's success.

In ten years, alleged completion occurred six times, but half were done in multiple visits (the die-hards dismissed those out of hand) and one condemned as a masterwork of Photoshop. The Kill Zone made many an armchair botanist and zoologist ready to call out discrepancies in the color of foliage, the absence of foliage, certain plants and trees, and fauna. Of the remaining two candidates, only one seemed legit. Numerous posts discredited the other as a single visit with research minutiae as impressive as that which revealed the actual dates of Ferris Bueller's day off and Ice Cube's good day.

There weren't hundreds of attempts since getting inside in the first place was no given, but still several.

REINCURSION

People uploaded their photos to OSnap when possible (electronic devices were highly unpredictable within the walls) to chart their progress, and often the pictures stopped with no subsequent posts on the account. Ever. So the Gauntlet had the dubious reputation of being the Mount Everest of Kill Zone endeavors. Cynics believed EXTREMEDEAN69's Gauntlet to be a government fabrication which offered up easily impressionable lambs to the slaughter. EXTREMEDEAN69 himself conveniently disappeared after announcing plans for a second Gauntlet.

A lot of troubling history, but if Bryce did it with Erica, he'd never have to prove himself again. If he didn't do it, she'd eventually bail. The former might kill him. The latter most certainly would, as a witness to the torture of her gutting loss. She wouldn't leave him because of the Gauntlet, of course, but it would all start there, a wound through which infection could thrive. She talked about it every day since she happened upon it in the rabbit hole of KZ lore. It captured the imagination, much like the snare trap on *Kill Zone Massacre Whatever*, which just strung up Trent's girlfriend and launched a tree trunk into her face.

THUNK.

It swung back to reveal a misshapen clump that looked like raw meat fed through a grinder.

"Trunk or treat!" Bryce snickered, momentarily forgetting his anxiety. Come on, there weren't really traps that elaborate, were there?

Artistic license.

Erica ignored the pun. "You're sure about Adrian, right?"

Oh yes, Bryce was "sure" that Adrian posed a threat to him as someone grooming for an actual "career" as a so-called Prowler—a mentality Bryce found idiotic and suicidal, but Erica might find courageous and somehow romantic. As for Adrian's "prowess" as a Prowler, though, he only had two things to judge by—Adrian's word and his continued existence outside of a coffin.

"Yeah, I mean, I've never known him to make shit up before, especially not something that wild."

Erica nodded. "I trust him. You've known him longer, though."

He grimaced again. Adrian saw her first at a party Bryce missed because he stayed in the dorm to cram-read Lawrence's *Lady Chatterley's Lover* for an English exam—the softcore film adaptation swiped from a torrent provided *zero* help. Thank God Adrian wasted the opportunity, but it was a closer call than it had any right to be. The introvert found the balls to talk to her, but she said she couldn't leave her friends. He didn't push for a phone number. Bryce resented the implied personal history when he thought he was introducing them. *Oh, wow, yeah, the mixer that time!* Two ships passing in the night; who knew what might have happened if not for the Bryce-berg.

"Adrian the Stalker," Erica said, as if trying out the words. Bryce's stomach sank through a hole in the couch.

"Make sure you say Prowler. I got a lecture when I called him a Stalker."

"Oh, right. You told me that."

He doubted Adrian would mind anything Erica called him at all, but when Bryce made the mistake of saying "Stalker," he got a condescending lecture. Although borrowed from a Russian movie of the same name (from the source novel *Roadside Picnic*) and an accurate allusion, many couldn't separate "Stalker" from its literal meaning. Thus, many now preferred "Prowlers."

There's only one true stalker in that domain, Adrian told him, holding up one finger to illustrate in the final annoying touch to his impassioned speech. Bryce shared a finger with him too and told him to "stalk this," something so nonsensical it defused the tension and they laughed about it. Bryce bet it had its roots in jealousy over Erica.

She mercifully set aside her tablet and turned to him. "We're really doing this, baby. Three days."

"Three days," Bryce echoed.

It echoed in his mind like a death sentence.

II.

EVAN SHOULD HAVE known they would display The Picture. Most times he saw it and felt the boy a stranger, but every now and then it became a portal back to That Day. Strange to be associated with something so iconic, although thankfully somewhat tangential; "the aftermath rather than the math," he often joked to deflect any deeper inquiry.

Black and white, like so many wartime chronicles, a boy carrying a heavyset Persian cat with the backdrop of a military checkpoint. A bulb flashed above one of the cautionary signs (ABSOLUTELY NO UNAUTHORIZED ACCESS). A wisp of smoke from the cigarette of one of the soldiers, the fog of another's breath in the punishing cold, a third soldier carrying an M16. Trees behind them, skeletal and gnarled from the more natural cruelties of winter. A black and white beam cut off the road, tiny icicles on the underside. Impeccably symmetrical framing, everything emanating from dead center like a still from a Stanley Kubrick film. The photographer won an award and the *Life* magazine where it featured on the cover still fetched top dollar in mint condition. The weariness and sorrow etched in the boy's face suggested permanence, as did the sense that his eyes glimpsed a future of frightening uncertainty and a world off its axis.

For his own part, Nigel looked indifferent and bored by the whole thing, although he'd been overjoyed when Evan first showed up to rescue him. The subsequent trek through uneven terrain in crisp January cold soured his good will after a couple of miles, though. The cat gave him puzzled looks at each rest, as if to say, *Why are we doing this? Home is back that way.*

Part of Evan wanted to stay and believed he could avoid detection by military patrols until they quarantined Sandalwood with its own blockade wall like Morgan. But then he would be trapped alone when the horror came back, because it would; it always did. What little resolve he had on the matter vanished in his house, though. No crime scene tape or body outlines since the military took the reins immediately after the breach, but the mural of bloodstains slashed across the living room wall cured him of the notion. Death still hovered in the atmosphere. If Nigel hadn't meowed inquisitively from upstairs he might have fled right then, run into the woods without a look back and not stopped until he hit the checkpoint.

"Poor taste," someone opined beside him, pulling Evan back through the portal to Now. A taller man with glasses and blond hair. "The reunions are weird enough without throwing that in everyone's face."

Evan checked his name tag: BEN GILLIAM. He remembered an Alec Gilliam from Sandalwood Middle School, who sat in Evan's row in social studies. Alec bragged about Reebok pumps his parents mysteriously wouldn't let him wear to school. They almost fought when Alec threw pizza on a dressier shirt Evan's mom made him wear. Alec asked if he was going to cry about his "pussy shirt." Evan, thinking about the brutal tirade he'd face at home when his mom saw the stain, said at least his shirt was real, unlike Alec's bullshit Reeboks. *Meet me after school if you want your ass kicked, queerbait,* Alec proclaimed (amongst much *Oooooooooh*ing from the others at the table) but when Evan stormed out for battle, Alec promptly hopped on his bus at 3:32. Never mentioned it again and never threw food again, either.

He spotted a resemblance in Ben Gilliam's face; an older brother, perhaps?

When Ben sauntered off without waiting for Evan to reply, he thought: *Yep*.

He studied several snapshots from school activities ages past—homecomings, dances, basketball, football, pep rallies, proms, band performances, yearbook signings, graduation ceremonies. An almost dizzying array of rituals superimposed from one year to the next on other students. When everyone in Sandalwood became refugees—or "relocaters," as the media euphemized to foster a more positive spin on "fleeing home because some supernatural nutcase slaughtered several people"—it both comforted and disturbed him to find the same events and expectations in his new home. This made for a smoother transition, but also left him thinking the same thing could happen again. Move a hundred miles, build a hundred walls, but someone determined enough could break through them all to find Evan and destroy his life once more.

Other pictures showed scenes around town, which he examined with wonder. The Pitford Center, the tallest building in town, years before its makeover as the Pitfall! Center. The Sandalwood Seven Theatre, where he and his dad saw *Last Action Hero*, the auditorium otherwise completely empty. He did a double take when he noticed the word LAST on the marquee, but it was LAST MAN STANDING. He almost expected to see himself in line with his dad.

A full color picture of Barker and Electric from twenty years ago seemed downright surreal. These days the same angle would show heavy deterioration of the concrete with trees growing up through the cracks and kudzu on the walls . . . not to mention a crashed helicopter.

He glanced at a collage of remembrance photos, victims of the Sandalwood Slaughter. So many faces. As more people crowded around the display, uneasiness spread through him as it often did with too many people around—an occupational hazard of sorts. Evan slipped away before anyone commented on his picture or before he saw familiar faces in the tribute.

As he entered the banquet area, cameras flashed like strobe lights. Media always turned out for the reunions, but the feeding frenzy reached a new level of bloodthirst this year: the twentieth anniversary of the Sandalwood Slaughter.

The school colors of black and gold decked out the gymnasium. Streamers, balloons, tablecloths, even some school banners with the leopard mascot.

What, no cheerleaders?

WELCOME BACK, SANDALWOOD! read a banner stretched across a stage. Below that: THERE'S NO PLACE LIKE HOME.

Evan wasn't sure whether to laugh or groan. A rather ill-advised sentiment to express to a bunch of people exiled from Sandalwood for twenty years. They were like evacuees from Chernobyl, except radiation didn't hunt anyone with a machete. The committee could decorate with school colors, display pictures from yesteryear, and bring back hundreds of people from the old gang, but nobody would forget they were in Marshallville.

He usually wavered on the reunions, but not this year. The big 2-0. Funny how such an arbitrary number mattered so much more than eight or seventeen, but the ten-year anniversary held the previous attendance record and he expected this one to surpass it. He didn't dwell too much on who might show up, although he hoped for a few. Even so, he wasn't here to rekindle old fires. This was strictly business.

Evan actually almost convinced himself of that.

He wasn't the only one here with that objective. Carlson toasted him with a red plastic cup from a table of refreshments, favoring Evan with a goofy grin as he strolled over like they were best buds. He'd opted for a powder blue suit with a ruffled shirt, perfectly chic if this was a prom where someone planned to dump a bucket of blood on Sissy Spacek.

"They already have a band tonight," he said.

Trademark Carlson, an introduction by way of non sequitur. He assumed everyone received the new pages from the script of his life.

"What are you talking about?" Evan said.

Carlson gestured to a stage beneath the WELCOME BACK, SANDALWOOD banner. Drums, guitars, a bass, amplifiers and microphones waited for someone to use them.

"No hay banda," Evan added, knowing Carlson wouldn't get the reference.

"What?" Carlson looked annoyed to have a rogue element attempting improv in his carefully scripted scene. "I mean you're out of luck if you came here to drum up business."

Then you should have said they already have a drummer. *Idiot.*

"No hay banda," Evan repeated. "I'm solo."

Carlson remained confused, then looked relieved to have a deflection prop in hand. He raised the red cup. "Well, Evan, looks like I already beat you to the punch."

It sounded like the sort of phrase police would give an undercover operative if things went south. Just to screw with him, Evan said, "Are you wearing a wire?"

"You're giving me nightmare flashbacks to geometry," Carlson said. "Obtuse much?"

"Just like the old days at East Sandalwood High, right? . . . Except you didn't go here." An inner voice admonished Evan for falling into the trap that "here" was Sandalwood because of a banner and streamers.

Carlson smirked. "Didn't see any pictures of you tossing your cap in 1996." He sipped from his cup, swished it in his mouth like a wine connoisseur, and grimaced.

Evan shrugged and gave his tie an adjustment it

didn't need. Black and gold stripes, of course. To prevent the topic veering toward the checkpoint picture, he parried with, "Any prospects?"

They looked around the banquet area at everyone dressed to the nines, the majority graduates from classes of the 90s but some several years earlier judging by age. They'd be retired if the economy didn't necessitate punching the clock until incontinence and senility.

"They're all prospects," Carlson replied, a born salesman. "I've had a few serious inquiries."

"Nothing like a little nostalgia to loosen the purse strings, eh?" Evan said, but not critically. Despite his attachment to Sandalwood, he too came here primarily with financial motivation, a chance to speak to potential customers and gauge their body language. Emails, forum interactions, and a credit report couldn't always reveal which "tourists" from the internet might try to entrap him or do something stupid at a critical moment in Morgan and Sandalwood.

"Any others?" Evan asked, meaning Prowlers.

"Oh yeah. Everyone's scouting for draft day. "

Evan noticed someone standing off to the side watching them. The man held the stare for a few seconds, then looked away to track a cluster of people billowing through the doorway with synchronized gasps over the decor. Maybe a fellow Prowler who didn't believe in a competitive market, or he just thought he recognized Evan and Carlson from school.

Carlson followed Evan's eyes. "Wow. If gaydar was radioactive, I think my hair would be falling out."

Evan looked at him doubtfully.

Apparently someone delivered new script pages in the preceding seconds because Carlson switched gears again. "You know, it really is worth a try."

Evan knew he didn't mean radiation poisoning, but otherwise had no idea what might be worth a try.

"We're both consummate pros, boddy. Double the experience, double the clientele."

Now Evan knew. He should have expected it— Carlson campaigning to join forces. Prowlers rarely sought a partnership unless they hurt for business. Or they made a deal with the government to roll over on other Prowlers for a reduced sentence, and discussing the operation added a conspiracy charge to the rap sheet. Maybe he *was* wearing a wire. Did desperation lurk behind that devil-may-care confidence? Well, you'd see that in about anyone if you looked hard enough.

"Double the greensleeves too," Carlson added.

"Yeah, and double the exposure, the risk, and the volume. Not interested."

Carlson deployed another smirk. "Well, the offer stands. For now. But don't let it get away. Full disclosure—you should know Bennett is giving it a long look."

Evan managed not to laugh. He didn't know Bennett, but heard from other Prowlers that he'd lost two tourists. Any dipshit off the street would probably lose ten times as many, but it inspired the same confidence as an anesthetist with a few wrongful death claims.

It seemed like a reply was required, so he offered, "Well, I'm sure you two will be very happy together."

The smirk became a scowl. "Have it your way. I'm

going to make the rounds and put out the vibe." He tossed his cup at a trash can ten feet away, banked off the rim and dumped half the punch on the floor. He mouthed *shit,* but made no move to redress the spill. He turned one last time to Evan. "Don't jack," he said.

Evan nodded. "Be seeing you."

Scattered applause drew his attention to the stage where a guitarist finally picked up his instrument. The sight of Josh Korzhakov, a.k.a. the Mad Russian, tightened Evan's necktie into a noose. He heard Noztalja lost the gig after the mercurial frontman attacked a fan at their last show. Apparently they signed an ironclad contract. Korzhakov played a repeating chord sequence while his bandmates took their places.

Seven years ago Evan "stole" Korzhakov's girl, even though Danielle left him months prior. The Mad Russian remembered things his own way and didn't let a petty hindrance like reality stand in the way.

"Saw these guys at the Fall Festival, they're great!" said a guy who sounded like Tony the Tiger.

After a minute of guitar intro, the drummer joined the act. Collective Soul's "Gel." With a wide grin, Korzhakov swept his eyes over the appreciative audience.

Evan turned his back when Korzhakov looked his way. Danielle succumbed to cancer two years ago, and Korzhakov blamed Evan, as if his excursions in the Kill Zone affected her like radiation poisoning; a case bolstered when their daughter Bella also developed a rare cancer. Right now her prognosis was good—provided her treatments continued. Expensive treatments that made his attendance tonight mandatory.

Carlson returned to the punch table where he chatted with a blonde, probably regaling her with tales of near misses in the KZ. If things went well he'd give her his business card, "Rod Carlson, Trail Guide" [wink-wink], complete with his potentially confusing email address, Rad.carlson@yahoomail.com. *What could I do, boddy? Rod.carlson was taken!* Evan couldn't see her face, but if he knew Carlson at all he'd targeted someone way out of his league. Let his struggle be mighty.

"Hey! Evan, right?" asked a heavyset man with a receding hairline and no nametag, extending a hand. Either the years had been rough or he was at least a decade Evan's senior, likely both.

"Fritz MacArthur. My little sister was your classmate."

Evan took his mitt. "Oh, Patricia—Patty!"

Patty held the distinction of final addition to the official death toll in early 1997. Weeks after sustaining what should have been survivable wounds she'd succumbed to complications. Media invariably linked her passing to construction updates for the Sandalwood Wall as if to reinforce its necessity. This didn't stop angry "relocaters" from challenging the government's right to exercise eminent domain over an entire city. It was a battle where they had no allies. *The rest of the U.S. sympathizes with your loss, Sandalwood, but shut the hell up, the wall is for* all *of us.*

"Great girl," Evan said, but she was just a blurred face in his mind, unraveled by time. Would he have remembered Patty tonight if not for her brother? Probably not. It reminded him of the Stalin quote,

"One death is a tragedy, one million deaths is a statistic."

"She always liked you. Said you took up for her on the bus." Fritz sniffed back tears. "Thanks."

Evan nodded humbly, but he'd always walked to school. He liked to think his agreeability was the path of least resistance, not because he saw Fritz as a potential mark.

They talked a bit longer but none of the stories resonated with Evan, who ended up in a distant burg in the Class of 2003 while Fritz graduated Sandalwood High, Class of 1993. It became clear that Fritz's interests lay entirely within this building. Every Prowler in the room studied Sandalwood faces for a certain expression and he didn't have it. Fritz noticed someone he actually knew and excused himself.

Evan saw a Prowler named Miller with a forty-something gentleman in a navy jacket. He crossed the guy off his list the same way other Prowlers dismissed Fritz when Evan let him walk away. In an Easter egg hunt you didn't search the spot where someone else already found nothing.

Evan sought another potential client, hoping Carlson missed his exchange with Fritz. He and Carlson shared a KZ entrance which couldn't accommodate Patty's brother. Another possible motive for Carlson's alliance—Evan's other KZ entrance(s) would instantly expand his business opportunities to clients above one hundred and eighty-five pounds.

Fat chance, Broseph.

Noztalja's repertoire included country songs of the late 80s and 90s, too. Korzhakov might be a total prick but a versatile one, and the band provided a soundtrack that kept things light apart from a cover of "Don't Come Back Unless You're Ready." They wound down a spot-on cover of Dwight Yoakam's "A Thousand Miles from Nowhere" when Evan spotted Carlson's blonde across the room alone.

Yes! Oh, God, yes!

He almost fist-pumped.

Elizabeth Rheingold . . . Billie. Visits to her page bookended his Facebook research of old friends before the reunion. Truthfully, she'd been the reason he went to the site but he looked up others to feel less self-conscious; less like the endeavor would be a waste if she missed yet another reunion.

Evan lost sight of her. Momentary panic. Had he only imagined her?

"Show of hands," Korzhakov requested onstage, now strapping on an acoustic guitar. "How many from the Class of '84?"

The bassist adjusted her microphone as she prepared to take lead vocals.

Evan found Billie again, closer now, talking to a tall man.

"That's it?" Korzhakov shrugged. "Guess this is for the three of you."

Evan expected the song to mean nothing to him as a child of the latter half of 1984, but despite the acoustic setting he instantly recognized "Time After Time" by Cyndi Lauper. His mother's favorite song, a gut-clencher every time he heard it. His mother wouldn't be here tonight. Agent Orange saw to that.

The military recovered most of her body from the upstairs bedroom. Fast sweep. Collect what could be verified through dental records or DNA, bag it, tag it with an address. Leave the rest. Orange crushed her skull against the dresser hard enough to crack its polished surface. When Evan found desiccated chunks of brain matter and pieces of skull, long lengths of hair still attached, he averted his eyes—straight to three fingers scattered on the floor. Enough of her to fill a shoebox which he'd buried in the back yard.

Leave it to Korzhakov to ruin a moment.

You are not a baby. Get your shit together. You've seen worse.

Wallowing in emotion and dredging up the past weren't his style so naturally he'd thought himself immune to all of this. Could a gathering this large have enough collective anguish to spread heartache like a contagion? Had they created a sort of Grief Pentecost?

Nah, you're just a baby.

"Evan?"

If not for the hand on his shoulder he might have pretended he didn't hear her to rebuild some composure. He settled for hurriedly wiping his eyes and facing the person he'd waited almost twenty years to see again.

"Like the first time we met," she said, reaching to his face.

As a seven year-old mama's boy who didn't want to be left with a stranger while his parents went out—well, that night he'd been a little . . . emotional. Billie, all smiles and consolations, quickly won him over.

She waved a hand to give herself air. Everyone spoke the same language at Grief Pentecost.

"Sorry, this isn't the reintroduction I'd aimed for," Evan said with a belated smile. The wave of sorrow passed, perhaps now sweeping through the room to hit each person in turn with their own remembrances of those awful days and nights.

Their first embrace in two decades was a reversal of the last, with his chin atop her head.

"This better?"

"Much, Billie," he said, though she'd become "Liz" since then. She didn't have a nametag so he went with what felt right.

Stunning in her knee-length black evening dress with sheer sleeves, she appraised the crowd while many of the men therein surreptitiously appraised her. Evan included.

"All these people here, but it still feels so incomplete, doesn't it? Like a puzzle missing most of its pieces."

"Because he took so many."

"Or they're too scared. Stacy, Trevor, and Dawn wouldn't come. Trevor . . . " She paused to ward off the emotion. "Trevor said this many people he'd missed in one place might draw him here . . . that he'd feel us."

"I'm glad you didn't listen to him." He stopped there, overwhelmed by the presence of lost years and fear he might unload on Trevor.

"So you live here now?"

"Soon as I graduated." He came to Marshallville to take his home back. In truth, he shared Sandalwood with Agent Orange. Joint custody, but a stilted arrangement where the other parent held all of the power, which echoed Billie's situation with her ex-husband. You could learn a lot online.

Korzhakov interrupted. "Special request time! For Sandalwood's own Cat Boy. There you are, Evan!" Near the stage Carlson laughed like this was the best thing ever. Ensure Cat Boy was mobbed the rest of the night; destroy his business prospects with an endless cavalcade of autograph-seekers and inquiring minds.

"Is he talking about you?" Billie asked.

He gave her a look and implored her to move with him. An evacuation among the evacuated.

People nearby were already talking. "The kid with the cat." "On the magazine?" "Which one?" "I think it's him." "Where?" "He charged for autographs at the ten-year reunion."

Hey, I did not, liar!

Evan and Billie grabbed cups of soda and moved toward the back of the room.

When Billie heard the first few lines of the song her face lit up and she leaned close. "They wrote a song about your cat?"

"No, XTC had a song called 'Making Plans for Nigel' and he hijacked it."

Billie's presence made Korzhakov's provocation feel distant and trivial. Soon the songs bled into each other with Evan only vaguely aware of the ballroom of aching souls. The whole world receded. The conversational equivalent of her life's greatest hits kept him enthralled, and it didn't matter it was the sanitized, social-media version of events because Billie talking meant Evan could search her updated profile. His eyes wandered every contour of her face, the luxurious curve of her smile, the lack of smoothness around her eyes so refined, so womanly, so sensual. Billie left town and come back a woman. The mind beggared.

Bradley Hudgens, who looked like a member of the Class of '89 or earlier, inserted himself between Evan and Billie and asked her, "Aren't you?" He snapped his fingers several times, less to prompt his memory than a rescue from Billie. "I know you. You're . . . "

"No, I'm not."

"Thanks for playing," Evan added. "Your consolation prize is at the bar."

With a smirk, the guy ambled away. "Wear a tag, then."

She leaned toward Evan's ear and said, "I haven't had this much attention in ages."

"I doubt that."

"Seriously. A year ago I was several sizes larger."

He noticed there were fewer pictures in her timeline prior to the last few months, but it never dawned on him she'd been too self-conscious to post them.

"I'd be mobbed if I wore the tag," she said.

"Oh?"

"Orange wounded me, remember? I'm a *survivor*. I still get calls about it. They beg me to come to reunions, conventions, special events. Bet they call you, too."

He laughed. "Of course, I'm Cat Boy."

Billie raised a brow mischievously. "Too bad we didn't walk out of Sandalwood with our secret identities intact like The Newlywed."

The mythic survivor The Newlywed escaped Sandalwood Motel room 10 that fateful night. Orange swept through the place like the Tasmanian Devil, creating adjoining rooms out of 8, 9, and 10 (and unjoining the limbs and heads of the occupants in 8 and 9). When he reached room 10 he had a hatchet for the honeymooners. The bride wore red, but survived unscathed—physically, anyway—and became known thereafter as "The Newlywed" because she and her lover signed the registry as "The Newlyweds." The twist—the man recovered from 10 had a wife back home in Poughkeepsie who definitely hadn't been in Sandalwood and probably passed through the five stages of grief like shit through a goose.

Evan and Billie found a vacant settee in a quieter hallway. Large enough to seat four comfortably, yet Billie positioned herself close enough that her leg settled against Evan's. Leaning forward she flipped her hair over her shoulder. Her neck became a temptation.

"I feel like I'm monopolizing you, Cat Boy."

"Not at all. I'm disadvantaged, though. I only know your secret identity."

"My superhero name would be Gut Girl."

"Cat Boy and Gut Girl."

She extended her right arm and flexed. "Strong enough to stuff bulging intestines back inside and escape from Orange with a backside full of shattered glass."

"Impressive. Well, I'm clearly the sidekick since I'm only in it for the pussy."

She laughed. "That's awful. Major cringe. I'd have sent you to bed early for talking like that."

Evan decided not to push his luck despite the "bed" comment.

With strangers distant they could now go wherever the conversation led. He learned of Billie's bouts with depression leading to too much drinking, too much eating, divorce, the loss of her two kids in a nasty custody battle where David assassinated her character for the sake of their children (he actually said, "You'll thank me some day"). What happened twenty years ago changed her forever and David understood that. Until he didn't. Apparently her trauma should have an expiration date. He could handle the nasty scar on the outside as long as there were none inside.

"In my worst moments, I'd remember her. The Newlywed." Billie leaned close to Evan as if imparting secret knowledge she'd never told a soul. "Elaine."

"Seriously? How'd?—"

"During the massacre her husband ended up in another room. They tagged him 'Snow Hater' when the military seized the registry to help with identification—hey, it was one of those kinds of motels. They never looked for a Mrs. Jensen."

"No, I was going to ask how you knew her name," Evan said, envying the ease of the assumed identities at the Sandalwood Motel. Nowadays you practically needed a birth certificate and character references to check in somewhere without a reservation. He put in a lot of early hours and extra drive time for any non-residential clients, making sure they used out-of-the-way motels to better discourage paper trails. In 1996, someone annoyed to be waylaid by the blizzard simply became Snow Hater, paid his forty-five bucks, and checked into his room to eventually become one of the most popular motel fatalities since

Marion Crane, albeit in the Newlyweds' room instead.

"We were in the same truck in the evacuation," Billie said. "God, she was beautiful. Only about twenty, but elegant. Like a princess who'd visited on the day of our destruction and came out without a scratch."

"How? Did she clean herself up?"

"Oh yeah, she did. She saw her husband . . . ruined. Everyone in the truck saw something like that and they were all sharing it, almost confessing it. Maybe just because I was on an IV by then and they were trying to keep me awake. Was it like that on yours?"

Evan shook his head. "Deathlike silence."

"I was thinking how strange that seemed, her especially, wanting to disappear but still talking. Like we all knew none of us would share those secrets."

"Welllll . . . ." He gestured to himself.

"Oh, you know what I mean. With anyone who didn't go through all that. You'd have been in the secret club. She had his wallet and pulled out a Polaroid taken at the court house when they married . . . remember instant cameras?"

He smiled. "Sure." He mimed shaking a picture around to speed up the chemical process.

"She said they used the timer and you could tell, like they weren't quite set in the picture, you know? Or they were trying to leave the frame. Funny how a picture can sometimes show you the opposite of what you're seeing. The husband was nice-looking enough, but I don't know. Hard to picture them together . . . even with a picture."

"Love is blind," Evan said.

"I don't know what became of her. I imagine she married again. Someone like her, I bet even David would have endured all the PTSD. So I tried to be like Elaine, cope the way she would have coped. But it made no difference. Some of us aren't as good at dealing, you know?"

"That's supposition," Evan said with a smile. "She was able to sink into obscurity and avoid the media hounding, and all the armchair Orange enthusiasts. You don't know how she dealt with it. Maybe not as well as you think since she let an innocent man take the fall for an infidelity just because his body was found in the wrong room. The media were sharks, but that's still cold."

Billie elbowed him. "Stop shattering my illusions, Cat Boy. Elaine was a rock; *she* never gained forty pounds . . . probably."

Evan talked about Danielle, her fate, and Bella. "Yes, Danielle took the name from *Twilight*. She was a big vampire fan. I couldn't say no." He briefly touched on Bella's cancer, but took the conversation elsewhere because he didn't want his hand held out of sympathy.

Five minutes past the difficult topic, Billie's right hand still nested in Evan's left. As he wondered at the implications she asked a question on a matter he meant to bring up himself.

"You know Carlson?"

Evan laughed softly. "Yeah, I know him." It had been incredibly easy to tell Billie everything, well, everything except his "career." This could get tricky. It had to be done right.

"I asked him the best ticket into Sandalwood and he pointed me your way."

Clearly nervous, she released his hand, ostensibly to fiddle with the straw in her drink.

"He did not."

"No," she said with a grin, "he didn't."

What a disarmingly coy smile, but it couldn't defuse the bomb she casually threw into the conversation.

"How did this come up?"

"He couldn't name any teachers so I asked if he was a Prowler. He choked on his punch. Then he asked if I was wearing a wire."

"How cautious of him."

"What's with the cloak and dagger? Doesn't the government turn a blind eye to you guys crossing the walls?"

"*You* guys?" Evan laughed. "Sometimes there's enforcement and sometimes not, but they never say when or why. Theory is, they target competent Prowlers so the amateurs will fill the void." He sensed her confusion so he added, "More likely to keep Agent Orange happy with sacrificial lambs."

"That's so cynical. And probably so true."

Evan grinned. "Still wondering how my name got thrown into the mix."

"He thought I lied about the wire so he eagerly pointed me your way."

"I'll have to thank him."

"You *could* get me in there, right?"

"Are you serious about going in?"

"For over a year I've been hiking, jogging, conditioning, researching. This isn't something I decided last week. Evan, I need to go in there, to my house. I *have* to go back."

Ah, here it was. What every Prowler sought tonight—the look. Ubiquitous enough to have its own name: the Sandalwood Syndrome. The aching need to return. For something. For nothing. Although many wanted to go to Morgan or Westing, not one of them ever had the Syndrome. Always Sandalwood. Always exiles. He'd seen it for the first time in late December 1996. At a gas station overflowing with refugees a young boy whispered "Nigel" to a bathroom mirror.

He thought of Carlson cornering her at the punch table. Assessing her. Fucking outsider. He may know what the Sandalwood Syndrome looked like, but he could never know the other side of it. Thirteen times the strength of an unrequited first love. One hundred percent pure, irrational need. The idea of Carlson taking Billie in there was anathema.

"Please? Will you do it? It has to be you."

Still reeling from the implications of a dream come true—seriously, how many times had he wished Billie would show up on his doorstep or at one of these stupid reunions and ask him to take her home?

On verbal autopilot he heard himself issue his standard response. What he asked them all.

"What's your MacGuffin?"

"Huh?"

"The thing you need. The reason you've gotta go back."

She'd have an answer. Most of them did. Sometimes it was as real as a cat.

He held up a hand. "Never mind. It doesn't matter. I'll take you."

Carlson hadn't seen what was right in front of him. These were the best, safest clients of all. In their desperation to go back they'd pledge their life savings. Once inside they wouldn't do anything to jeopardize the journey. For them, going back wasn't for profit or thrills or experience; it was a profound longing. A spiritual need.

"Thank you. I'll pay you."

Evan looked at his cup. His hand shook.

"No pay. Do you have a couple of days?" A winter storm dropped three inches of snow the previous week. "The last of the snow will melt within a day or two. We can go then."

"I'm free for several days. As long as I'm home by Christmas Eve."

Evan nodded.

"Oh, there's something I left out."

"Yeah?"

"I'm with the Department of Homeland Security and you're under arrest."

"I knew I should have searched you for a wire."

She grinned. "So, you want to head back in there? Feel like you're missing out?"

"Not at all. You hungry? I've still got two hours of coins in the babysitter meter."

She abruptly stood and extended a hand. "Let's see what kind of trouble Gut Girl and Cat Boy can get into tonight."

III.

FOREHEAD AGAINST THE concrete wall, Shelly's breaths came quick and shallow. She stared at Bryce with vacant eyes, an animal trapped in a crawlspace.

"It's okay," Bryce whispered. He tilted his head so the mounted flashlight wouldn't blind her. "You're fine. Just rest a minute."

In her panic she managed to work her right arm backwards to reach toward him, but to clasp her hand would create significant overlap of their bodies. She'd have to settle for Bryce's hand on her ankle. He did it as much for himself. With no room to turn around in here, the tunnel seemed like a coil which could knot up to seal them in individual membrane prisons while the weight of the world pressed in above.

And when—*if*—they made it through this, the true danger began. Oh joy.

"Hang in, Shell," Tina stage whispered behind him. "Almost there."

"We were 'almost there' thirty minutes ago," Shelly replied miserably.

Their voices sounded muted, hollow, discorporate.

Per Bryce's phone, actually forty minutes passed

37

since they were "almost there," and sixty-five minutes total of crawling minus a "break" when they passed through a small chamber at the midway mark. It gave Bryce a much-needed chance to stretch and adjust his kneepads. He would have loved to actually stand, but the small concrete box did not allow him to do anything more than squat and stretch body parts one at a time.

When not bemoaning the rigors of the crawl, he regretted his suggestion of Adrian. He had little choice, though. Erica found a Prowler through a KZ forum on the dark web, but he turned them down with a terse explanation: *Too young.*

Her: *What the hell? People our age go off to fight in wars!*

When she downloaded a pamphlet called *Over the Wall: Get In and Out of the KZ Alive* (derided in some circles as *The Dumbass-ist Cookbook),* Bryce worried she'd try it herself, with or without him. Against his better judgment, he said he knew someone who might get them in. The nagging worry he made a mistake found confirmation when Erica and Adrian discovered they met before. Too late to back out then.

Too late to back out now too, unless Tina led the way in reverse.

At five-thirty that morning Bryce, Erica, Tina, and Shelly joined Adrian in a Walmart parking lot. Adrian arrived with a friend, too, some local kid named Dustin or Dusty he never mentioned to Bryce before. Dustiny played designated driver because you couldn't leave a car parked anywhere near the KZ or the cops would be waiting when you returned.

Meeting at Walmart wasn't just to give Erica and

Tina an inconspicuous place to park their cars, either. They had to purchase knee, elbow, and forearm pads, amidst all the predictable jokes about oral sex. Adrian didn't trust an oath of silence and blindfolded them in Dustiny's car—an unnerving reminder to Bryce of hostage soldiers eventually beheaded. The drive lasted approximately forever, though only half as long as this crawling nightmare.

Trying to center himself, he leaned toward the darkness beyond Shelly and called, "Erica, you okay?"

She began to answer in the affirmative but Adrian talked above her. "We need to be quiet now. We're close to the Zone."

Bryce's lips mimicked the words. At the outset Adrian gave each of them a number, which would be their traveling order from start to finish. Obviously he would be number one as the Prowler. Erica as second didn't seem ominous until Adrian designated Shelly as number three.

No way, Bryce said. *Erica and I go together.*

Way, Adrian said, and the self-righteous *I'm a* Prowler, *not a* Stalker tone returned with a vengeance. *I'm picking the best order to get us through a tight squeeze, not a package deal for a fucking kickball team. You don't like it, go back and play the home version on your Xbox.*

Bryce's face burned but he offered no reply. A middle finger and "Xbox *this*" was the best comeback concocted in the subsequent hour, long after the moment passed. Not particularly devastating, though it beat his only candidate at the time of *I've never owned an Xbox, dickhead.*

So now Adrian wielded the cachet of a special Kill

Zone entrance and he effectively separated Bryce from Erica for an hour. At this rate, Agent Orange wouldn't be Bryce's biggest worry today.

Tina and Shelly didn't appreciate the order either. They were the friends Erica couldn't leave behind at the mythic party where Adrian met her, even though they turned out to be a couple and would have been fine without her. Maybe it was Erica's polite way to let Adrian down, but something else scratched at the back door of Bryce's mind. Not so much Shelly, a default friend, but Tina, Erica's "bestie." It didn't matter that in a comparable situation—Bryce with a homosexual best friend—there would have been no temptation. The thought lingered: *Had Tina and Erica done something before?* Erica certainly seemed adventurous enough to do it if she wanted to. Had Tina been some girl she hadn't seen since high school, it wouldn't matter. It would be a pretty hot story, even. But they texted and hung out a lot *now*. Tina jumped at the chance to come with them, apparently dragging Shelly along.

Maybe it was nothing. Many would consider this a "once in a lifetime" opportunity and would go with Adolf Hitler and Ted Bundy for the chance. He just hated the reminder Erica had viable options, people willing to rush into something like this. Bryce preferred to look both ways with everything before he crossed the street.

"Fuck it." With a grunt, Shelly attacked the tunnel with renewed vigor. Bryce didn't bother telling her to pace herself; his whispers would be lost amongst the echoes her body made. He slowly lost ground behind her. Given his bigger size, he had a harder time using his elbows and toes for leverage.

Following ten more grueling minutes where he tried to focus more on Adrian's shady tactics than the horrifyingly cramped space, Bryce heard low voices. An increase in beautiful, albeit dim light, almost made him laugh with relief. He pressed ahead and Adrian's face greeted him. Adrian put his hands beneath Bryce's armpits and eased him forward. Bryce planted his hands against the concrete floor.

"Careful," Adrian said as he backed away.

Bryce crawled out to the exit chamber, nothing more than a slightly rectangular concrete box with an iron gate at one end and the smaller drain opening at the other. Enough space inside for one person to squat, unlock the heavy duty padlock, and open the gate. Bryce turned around and helped pull Tina through the hole.

"Thanks. Don't look forward to *that* again," she mumbled. "I just knew I'd get stuck with the wall right above me."

Yeah, seventy-five more minutes of storm drain hell. Maybe Shelly wouldn't have another mid-pipe freak out. She cost the group ten minutes—possibly more. Bryce hoped Adrian and Erica's bodies muffled her initial screams, but who knew? Orange could be running through the woods right now to intercept the visitors, or guards might be waiting for them when they climbed back out. With Bryce up to his ass in student loans, he didn't need a black mark. Anyone could access the website with a registry of all the people busted in the Kill Zone.

It's like the Mutant Registration Act, but with less adamantium, Adrian once joked.

Shelly removed her forearm and elbow pads and stuffed them into the backpack Adrian brought.

"I thought we were done with these after Sioux Falls," Erica told Shelly with a playful wink as she slipped her own pads, a reference to their recent volleyball championship.

Bryce enjoyed the feel of the chilly morning air, heavenly to breathe again after the premature burial. The unseasonable warmth of yesterday would progress until almost sixty by midday. He still felt overdressed in his jeans and the black hooded sweatshirt sticking to his back.

A thick morning fog reduced visibility to ten yards max, limiting initial impressions. It enhanced the feeling of crossing over to another world, everything still except the slow drift of the white mist. He imagined their movements created unseen ripples in the fabric of the KZ like flies vibrating a spider web.

Adrian took the loaner flashlight and pads from Bryce, stuck everything into the backpack, and took it to the tunnel to stow in the pipe.

Bryce joined Erica. She stood with arms outstretched, feet together, head tilted back. She looked incredible in her black mini-skirt and thigh-high leggings, a half inch of exposed skin between them—more when she reached for the sky. Her black sweatshirt rode up high enough to expose the skin of her midriff.

Tina massaged her sore arms and shoulders. She opted for the recommended black shirt, but chose one with sparkles. Adrian gave her wardrobe a contemptuous look, as if to say, *You don't wear sparkles into the Kill Zone.*

Shelly's eyes glistened, bloodshot and horrified as though someone pushed her face into the jaws of a lion. She wore a dark turtleneck sweater that added some phantom bulk to her delicate frame. Noting Erica's pose, her vacant fear receded somewhat as she removed her phone to document. Bryce could imagine this shot as the cover of a brochure, *Kill Zone, it's where you want to be.*

Their sim cards were confiscated at Walmart, left with Dustiny, but Bryce anticipated the move and handed a decoy. Just in case. Plus he relished putting one over on Adrian and his "my way or the highway" approach to tour guide. *There's only one stalker in here . . . but at least one sim card now too.*

"You gonna make it?" he said to Shelly, who gave him the least convincing nod ever. Erica told him about Shelly's passion for photography, though he hoped she had a real camera at home because taking pictures with a smartphone seemed like a car enthusiast who only collected Hot Wheels.

She angled for a shot of the tunnel as Adrian worked a padlock through the bars. Some sixth sense kicked in and his head swiveled around, almost owl-like. He shook it curtly. Although doubtful, others in Adrian's business might trace the entrance, and more importantly, a Prowler never wanted to be pictured in any fashion. *We're like the ghosts of the Kill Zone,* another tenet in his GlowerPoint presentation.

"Won't pictures in the KZ cost your scholarships?" Adrian asked Erica. He probably overheard Shelly on the way, murmuring about being only slightly less scared of losing her volleyball scholarship than her life. Those things must be more cutthroat than Bryce realized.

Tina laughed. "Shelly can blur faces before posting. Duh."

"Blurred or not, don't take any of me." He turned back to his business at hand, not very ghost-like in his gray and black flannel jacket and black jeans.

Bryce slid an arm around Erica and she melded into him, a perfect fit. The moments like this were worth all the self-doubt and grim prophecies.

She smiled at him. "This is too cool," she whispered. "Thank you for doing this with me. You're the best."

The temperature spiked twenty degrees. "Anything for you, baby." For a moment at least, he felt happy to be here.

Shelly took their picture, then several of Tina.

Adrian succeeded with the latch and snapped the padlock shut. He jangled to test it, and satisfied with the result, he turned to face them again. Bryce's good cheer soured.

We're locked in.

He didn't see the sense in padlocking them out of the hatch. If they had to leave in a hurry, it could be the difference between life and death. Orange would have to gnaw off both arms to fit through that tunnel.

Adrian covered the drain entrance with creek rock and a thick log to complete the subterfuge. Large stones scattered the area just like the other end a quarter of a mile distant. The military buried the drain pipe back when they constructed the wall. Maybe a Prowler who lived in the original Sandalwood knew of its existence and later uncovered it, perhaps even Adrian's mentor for Prowler stuff. His parents footed the bill for an expensive education while their son hedged his bets on a secondary trade.

"Before we start, does anyone have second

thoughts?" Adrian whispered. Maybe he should have asked before he covered the stone entrance.

They all looked expectantly at Shelly, Bryce trying for a facial expression that said *There's no shame in quitting, we're all behind you.* Her lip quivered, but she didn't speak.

"Where's the wall?" Erica asked and Shelly took a picture: *Erica's first question in the KZ.*

"Tenth of a mile that way." Adrian pointed past the pipe entrance where the limbs of pines broke through the fog. "Wall selfies on the way out."

When Shelly heard "on the way out" she closed her eyes, surely envisioning the bliss of a world far from the slings and arrows of the Kill Zone.

Adrian closed the distance to the group so he didn't have to raise his voice. "Remember, don't step in mud or snow. We don't want to leave a trail. We keep the same order from the tunnel." He pointedly stared at Bryce as if daring dissent. "Don't lose sight of the group at any time."

Bryce tried to remember the likable Adrian of freshman year, a more awkward, amiable version. You could still find him as long as the subject didn't involve the KZ. Unfortunately he liked to steer conversation to that topic like a reporter whose questions always returned to scandal.

Adrian 1.0 would never approach Erica in the first place, but Adrian 2.0 fancied himself something of an alpha dog. Erica thought they could steamroll him to lead them through the whole Gauntlet no matter what, but it wouldn't happen that way. That was comforting—yay for safety—but then came the bastard fantasy. *I can take you back in there*

*sometime, Erica. Your own private tour. Free of
charge, unless you can think of something you'd like
to donate. Heh heh.*

Erica bent down and unfolded a crude map of the
area from her bag. All the Gauntlet stations were
marked as X's with a yellow highlighter. "What's
closest?"

Adrian frowned at the crumpling of paper and
covered her hand so she would stop. "He's probably
nowhere near us, but you need to act like he's just
twenty yards away. *Always.*"

Erica returned his frown with something of an *oh
no you didn't* expression. He carefully folded the map
shut and reached toward his own bag, like a teacher
confiscating a comic book in class. Erica firmly
yanked it away by pincer grip and put it away as
quietly as a breeze stirring the grass.

Adrian blinked. "Well, uh, the G9 station is back
past the tunnel . . . " He gestured flippantly as though
it were the Ringo Starr of Gauntlet stations. "But the
C-S-X-X-X is much closer, a mile that way toward—"

"Sandalwood," Erica finished, almost religious
zeal in her eyes. "Yes, take us there."

Bryce grimaced. Oh, that was just grand. Of the
fifteen Gauntlet destinations, C-S-X-X-X came ninth
. . . the outlier, the single point most distant from all
the others. The stupidly named station 8 of Chinookie
and the absurdly named station G9: The Tower of
Sexual Power (Bryce preferred its short and sweet
nickname the G-Spot) were closer to each other than
the one "between" them. It also annoyed him that a
place called G9 wasn't the ninth station but the tenth.
Dumb. Not that anyone had to do them in any

particular order as long as they did them all, but any backtracking would be less than ideal, especially several miles of it.

Trainee Buzzkill might insist they call it a day when they came back through, which suited Bryce fine except for the G-Spot's status as the place for partners to consummate their journey at checkpoint 9.5, a room in the tower. He understood Adrian's soft pedaling—two couples in tow with him odd man out, "the Bummer" probably seemed like the second deadliest presence in the KZ next to Agent Orange— but not Erica's ready dismissal. She hyped it to him big time before, framed it as his reward to sweeten the deal. Maybe she just didn't want them to shoot their wad right off, so to speak, but he couldn't help take it a little personally that she slammed the door on it.

Adrian pointed into the gnarled branches of a tree. "Take note." A faint, silvery glint fifteen to twenty feet above them served as a marker for their starting position; a deflated balloon with a few inches of yellow string dangling below it. Shelly took her most useful picture yet, but all the trees would look the same soon enough.

They fell into a single-file line in the preordained order. Picked last by Adrian, Tina looked into the fog perhaps wondering if Agent Orange would pick her first.

Slowly the group made their way along a creek bed that frequently required climbing fallen trees. Far easier to travel here than through the woods where there were sure to be more traps, although Adrian did a brief once-over with every obstacle and implored them to step exactly where he stepped. He caught

Erica's exasperation at one point and gave her a dose of the GlowerPoint presentation.

"This isn't some video game where you can make the same moves each time, Erica. He can set traps in here 24/7. We're going to be sure every time."

Adrian spoke quietly but intensely and held eye contact for an awkward amount of time until he saw what he wanted. Bryce wondered if all of Adrian's comparisons eventually led back to video games.

He drew even with Erica and stepped ahead of her as a human shield.

"Calm your tits, Ades," he said, adopting a nickname he knew Adrian despised for obvious reasons. Damned if he'd let Amateur Hour get an attitude with his girl. "Don't worry, we promise not to sue you if we skin our knees."

"I know you won't, Bryce-T." Adrian smirked. "You can't sue Prowlers for liability. *Cunningham versus Miller.*"

"So? You sure you even count?" He tensed in case *Bryce versus Adrian* became the next case on the docket.

"I *count* you second in line now. Back your ass up to fourth or we can all go home. How's that sound?"

Like a little boy threatening to take his ball and go home, but the imploring and unmistakably threatening look on Erica's face kept that response safe inside his vocal cords. Bryce backed up to his assigned spot in the rotation behind Shelly, hands held up like every athlete ever called for a penalty. *I didn't do nothin'.*

He read Erica's lips: *Cool it down.* He nodded, satisfied to have stepped up to the plate as well as by

Adrian's poor showing at ingratiating himself with Erica so far.

They resumed course after Adrian provided the all-clear once more.

Bryce begrudgingly saw the sense of the order as they walked. Clearly the weakest link, Shelly needed to be safely tucked in the center, between Erica and Bryce. Light, quick, and the smallest of them at only five-two, Tina would have the easiest time traveling backwards in the tunnel if they needed to reverse. She also carried Adrian's spare padlock key from the outset and locked up the entrance as the last one through. Should something happen and the group split up in the KZ, Tina would be the alternate focal point for a second group.

The shadow world afforded by the fog added an extra layer of eeriness, although Bryce's anxiety leveled off as the minutes passed. The lack of visibility was a two-way street. Agent Orange needed to be on top of them to know they were here—certainly, he couldn't catch a glimpse from some distant ridge. Any rustling and crackling within the grayness seemed to be the activity of common and decidedly non-homicidal woodland creatures, and the group shared fewer uneasy glances deeper in. Aside from the threat of federal sanction (and total bodily dismemberment), it seemed almost disappointingly familiar.

Black shapes appeared, a latticework of thick beams. The legs disappeared into the gray swirl far above, like the bones of some extinct race of giants.

Adrian paused, a fist held up to head level. He hadn't run through hand signals, but everyone halted. Satisfied with what he did/didn't see or hear, he veered toward a rocky incline and waited for everyone to huddle up.

"We're going up. Take your time and watch your step. It's a long way down if you miss one. Keep the order and be ready to help the next person."

Bryce tilted his eyebrows at Erica. She smiled, but faintly. This was beginning to feel like a school field trip with his best friend on a different bus.

Adrian cracked his knuckles theatrically and began to scale the steep rocks. They all used the damp surface of the wooden beams to steady themselves. Bryce smirked at how Adrian's insistence on order deprived their fearless leader of a prime view up Erica's skirt, tight ass in glorious motion. The G-Spot seemed so impossibly far away.

He soon paid particular attention to Shelly, who might enjoy Erica's show too and could bowl him over if she slipped, but she seemed steady on her feet, having pocketed her phone for the climb. Tina kept pace behind him, sparkles and all. It took ten minutes before the underside of the bridge appeared through the mist. Tree trunks and exposed root systems clung to the top of the valley so it became easier to negotiate the steep incline. Near the summit a tangle snapped off in Shelly's hand and she pitched ever so slightly backward. Bryce thrust a hand out to brace her, which instinctively went to her backside. It did the trick and she oriented herself. Her thank you crossed with his apology, both mumbled with embarrassment.

It became a moot point a moment later as they joined Erica and Adrian on the train tracks. Bryce intended to help pull Tina up but totally forgot about it when he saw what grabbed their attention.

Agent Orange had been working on the railroad. Three stakes were driven into the ground between the rails, the three skulls adorning them old, mostly devoid of flesh. None of them retained lower jaws, but probably because Prowlers claimed those for the reward money. The non-profit Victims of Richard Identification Project (a.k.a. V-R.I.P.) paid a minimum of five hundred bucks for a mandible they could match to dental records or DNA. Some families pitched in extra for the peace of mind that came with a proper identification—and the resulting classification of "deceased." Sometimes insurance payouts, although KZ exclusions abounded in policies these days.

The age of these artifacts encouraged Bryce a little. Grim relics, to be sure, but they may as well have been found on the *Titanic*. They offered solemn assurance of Orange's absence.

Even Adrian lightened up a little bit, showing polite interest when Erica said, "Could you imagine making a million off a jawbone?"

Everyone knew about the biggest payout ever. A Japanese multi-millionaire bereft over the disappearance of his suicidal, KZ-obsessed daughter paid seven figures for proof of death, provided when a Prowler returned with her mandible. The Prowler could have retired, but for a second million he went after the rest of the head. Two months later a different Prowler returned with *his* jawbone.

Adrian laughed. "My mentor scored the rest of her head, but that gazillionaire dickhead canceled the reward after the first guy got snuffed. Brah was so pissed he punted her head off the door of the limo."

Bryce would feel like a douche talking about a

mentor, but Adrian perfected those anecdotes over the past few months. He sounded like he'd jump off a bridge if the dude told him to.

"Why didn't the first guy take the whole head to begin with?" Tina asked.

"Oh, there's a special tool for cutting off the jaw. It's a lot easier than trying to pry the head off a stake, and risk him catching you screwing around with his trophy. Intense reek, too, like you can't believe. It's over if you get pulled over and cops get a whiff. Heads are also heavier than you'd think. My mentor broke two toes when he kicked that head. Security chased him down before he could limp to his car and they kicked the shit out of him."

"That's hilarious," Erica said.

"Right? The jaws are also easier to conceal. You don't want to have to explain to a cop why you're lugging around a head."

"You carry a Jawbreaker?" Bryce asked. He thought the terminology would impress Erica, plus make Adrian sound like a disgusting ghoul if he admitted it.

"Haven't used one, but we keep an eye on the wanted list."

"Wanted head or alive?" Bryce cracked.

Adrian frowned at him. "You just need the jaw."

Right, because wanted jaw or alive would have been hilarious.

Shelly snapped some photos of the head triad. Then several more still. Bryce understood they were powerful images, but it began to seem excessive, like paparazzi catching a celebrity at the grocery store without any make-up.

"*Okay*, Shelly," he said.

"What? They keep showing up blurry." She proffered the screen. No mistaking what the image showed but it came off as shaky and fake, the last thing you wanted when forum users questioned authenticity for the most arbitrary details.

LOLZ, sure, that blurry head is a confirmed kill. Cool story, bro!

"Step back from it," Adrian suggested.

Shelly backed away a few feet, hit the zoom, and tried a couple more pictures. She inspected them. "Hey, that worked. What gives?"

"Don't ask me. This place is just weird." He swiveled his head as if evidence lay all around. Bryce thought he would elaborate on this but instead the pitch of his voice dropped back to stealth mode. "We better get going."

The levity apparently passed for the moment.

"We have to cross the bridge now, don't we?" Erica asked.

"Right. The incline was easier on this side. It's not far after that."

Bryce dutifully waited for Adrian, Erica, and Shelly to get ahead and fell in line. His calves ached from the climb. The tunnel crawl and incline were arduous enough and they hadn't even hit the first checkpoint yet.

Guess that's why it's called the Gauntlet and not the Kill Zone Cake Walk, moron. Just keep going. Someone will give up.

He'd thought about faking an injury on the climb for about half a second, but he couldn't disappoint Erica under false pretenses, even when it seemed like the only sane move left. He agreed to it, she was happy, and they were here. Best of all, this area seemed like an unpopular hang-out for Agent Orange. Unfortunately it wouldn't remain so. Every now and then a KZ prospector found a phone and uploaded the images of unfinished Gauntlet exploits for internet posterity. He'd have to hope the checkpoints they covered today weren't among Orange's favorite slaughtering holes.

They gained a little more visibility across the bridge. The mist hovered near the other side, allowing them to see the expanse of tracks and the long drop-off. It revealed tree tops but only little pockets of the actual ground. Tendrils wove between the trees, impenetrably thick in some places. Bryce estimated a hundred foot plunge, at least.

Patches of rust spread through the rails which meant medical care back in civilization for anyone who cut themselves. A tetanus shot . . . or worse. As Adrian said, this was a weird place and Bryce read so many rumors, it was hard not to be a little paranoid. Some believed in an area called Sector 8 where the government took people with basic afflictions like poison ivy or insect bites contracted in the Kill Zone because they developed horrifying complications and had to be quarantined (and by extension studied and experimented upon). The arm of a guy who cut himself on a sticker bush supposedly swelled to the size of a tuba which started to grow its own set of internal organs. Bryce laughed when he read this months ago, but after crawling for over an hour to get into this abandoned world, so mist-shrouded and mysterious, it became easier to believe different rules applied here. They already did for one person.

REINCURSION

The unreliability of Shelly's pictures confirmed some of the lore. There were several places here where gadgets acted up with no discernible pattern. Electromagnetic anomalies spun compass needles endlessly. A group known as the Hybridians theorized Agent Orange the result of alien technology—a human/alien hybrid—and a ship which came to collect him crashed, somehow "activating" him. Thus, bizarre electromagnetic activity, a man who came back from the dead over and over, and the government conveniently evacuating and quarantining thousands of acres while they researched the debris. Someone who claimed to see the ship proved conveniently unable to photograph it because of "some kind of interference." Another had no problem taking pictures and posted proof that aliens apparently modeled their ultra-advanced spacecraft after a defunct line of toys from Zirnco called GalaxyMasters ("They're out of this world!").

The tracks seemed to elongate and the other side of the bridge drifted away like a permanent horizon. The procession had moved much more quietly below. Up here, the ties groaned or clomped under their feet, distressingly loud.

Shelly turned to him at about the quarter mark and whispered, "Do you think it's safe?" She appeared on the precipice of panic again. Had they been plunging to their deaths this very second, Bryce wouldn't do a thing but reassure her after her tunnel histrionics. Those would probably be audible past the International Date Line out here.

"Sure," he said. "This isn't like the shitty suspension bridge from *Evil Dead* or something. It held up trains weighing several tons. We're fine."

Unless he trapped the bridge. But Bryce wouldn't put that thought in her mind and wished it never entered his own. It would probably have to be an explosive device, though, and not the sort of thing Orange could easily come by without a PO Box for *Soldier of Fortune.* Adrian showed more concern crossing the fallen trees through the creek bed than this bridge, considering he'd be the one to trigger any surprises as the first in line.

There was no save point back by the stakes.

Bryce nearly bumped into Shelly and stopped short. She stood tallest of the girls, so he craned to see around her and past Erica where Adrian held his fist up again, ten yards ahead.

Tina broke the protocol and drew even with Bryce. "Now what?"

His senses were alert. They only had one escape if danger lay ahead and he'd have to make sure he wasn't separated from Erica while also keeping up with Tina and her back-up tunnel key.

"Do you hear anything?" Shelly asked over her shoulder.

At first he didn't, other than the beat of blood in his skull. Gradually he heard past it, but everything sounded alien, as if rendered unrecognizable by the fog. He felt something like a current of electricity humming through his body, the tension sickening as he awaited the appearance of that thing he dreaded since Erica proposed this adventure; since then and several years before. As inevitable and unstoppable as an actual train, but one that could leave the tracks no matter where he ran.

"Listen," Tina whispered.

Cold blood rushed through Bryce. Now he heard something beyond the natural movements of the woods, the insects and animals within the gray curtain. Branches rustled in rapid succession like lashing whips with the delicate thunder of footsteps.

Adrian turned around so fast he should have snapped his neck. Bryce recognized the look on his face—helpless horror. The immediate terror for which no amount of training truly prepared him. Adrian seized Erica's wrist as he drew even, his other hand batting the air.

Bryce understood the significance—*go go go*—but felt rooted in place. It was as suicidal an impulse as he'd ever entertained. Some irrational part of him resisted the fight or flight imperative, some twisted obligation to witness a legend, even knowing what it meant for an already frail hope of survival.

Erica lurched a few steps, towed by Adrian. She seemed possessed by the same madness because she repeatedly turned back to see the end of the bridge. Shelly and Tina likewise held their positions.

"Run, for Christ's sake!" Adrian urged. In an impressive display of his training, he did not raise his voice. As he joined Bryce's trio, he pushed at everyone with his free hand, still dragging Erica. They ceded a few backward steps but without true momentum; more like hitchhikers hoping for a ride.

The lurking mist could have been smoke from the mouth of Hell. Someone burst through the haze, far more diminutive than expected, a black man. A redheaded woman followed, holding the hand of a bald man with a bushy black beard. They both looked back into the murk, noticeably slowing, reluctant to gain too much ground. Not exactly the panic-stricken sprint Bryce expected from someone pursued by Agent Orange. Either they had the same ill-advised compulsion to behold the slayer or—

"It's not him," Erica said matter-of-factly.

"Adrian," Tina said, "there's people."

Adrian ceased his pushing and dragging efforts and turned around a little hesitantly, as if it might be a joke. *Bro, we so got you! It's really that guy who mutilated a metric fuckton of human beings and we're all gonna die!*

The metronome of footsteps subsided as the first one through the fog noted Adrian's group on the bridge. He approached cautiously. The couple behind him stopped altogether and watched the mist. Rustling sounds continued in the void, less rapid but suggestive of more power, before someone else emerged. Had he been first, Bryce would have hauled ass, certain of Agent Orange. He couldn't help but think of this giant as Thor because of his blond hair, although a Norse god wouldn't be caught dead in that sweater with horizontal red and green stripes.

"What the hell?" Erica asked. "Do you see . . . "

Bryce didn't understand her reaction at first. The couple blocked his view other than the blond head towering above them and a shoulder that could crash through a fire door. Male voices quietly conferred, then the bald man faced forward after accepting something from Thor.

Adrian must not have seen the strange thing either since he began a lecture. "You guys are lucky it wasn't him. You can't just stand around . . . " His voice trailed off.

"Holy shit!" Tina and Shelly almost harmonized.

Now Bryce saw for himself—Thor handed a child to the bald man.

He watched the small figure, waiting for something to return this picture to some semblance of sanity. Maybe it wasn't really a child—a doll, perhaps, or a midget (either would be creepy as hell, but still better than someone bringing a kid in here). Instead, the redhead kept pace with the bald man and lifted a hand to the child, who reached out to squeeze it. Definitely not a doll.

It looked to be a girl with long black hair, too old for parents to lug her around. Bryce guessed seven years old, certainly in grade school.

"What dumbass would bring a kid in here?" Tina asked.

"Be sure to get their names," Shelly said. "I'm calling CPS on their asses."

Bryce laughed. "Great idea. Be sure to tell them where you found out."

Shelly sneered. "Asshole."

The other group advanced, checking behind them intermittently. Bryce bet they weren't searching for another member of their party so much as its dismemberer. The black man led the way. He looked to be in his thirties, grimacing as if battling a splitting headache, wearing a gray shirt soaked by several patches of sweat as well as patches of unmistakable deep red near the bottom. His chest heaved as he fought to get his air back.

Bryce looked to Adrian, who appeared to have as good an idea on how to handle this as he did. You only ever expected to see your own group in here, minus the misfortune of encountering Orange himself.

The man cut off Adrian's greeting. "We need to keep moving the way you came. He could be here any minute."

It made no sense that hearing this seemed more chilling than the rustling a moment ago, but Bryce's group didn't need to be asked twice. The way his specter haunted even a simple pronoun, they knew exactly who "he" referred to without further inquiry or introduction to this new group. They spread out on the tracks and reversed direction, allowing the new arrival to take the middle with Adrian.

"I'm Omar. You guys on your own? We really need a Stalker."

"Wait, so you actually saw *him?*"

"Look, kid, no time for fucking explanations, okay?" Omar held out the bloody end of his sweatshirt as if it were explanation enough. "You on your own or not?"

Adrian threw a bewildered look at Bryce. *What do I do, man?*

Bryce shrugged: *Don't say anything about an Xbox.*

Adrian tried again. "Sorry, I'm Adrian. I'm a Prowler."

"He's training," Bryce said.

Adrian scowled like this admission was tantamount to betrayal.

Omar fixed Bryce with a hard stare, something granite would have envied.

"He really does know some things," Bryce finished weakly. He felt better when the hard stare swiveled back to Adrian.

"Okay, you've still got training wheels. But do you know a way out?"

"Out?" the redheaded woman echoed. "We can't leave yet, Omar!"

The bald man holding the child said, "Megan . . . "

"We are *not* leaving." She held her hands up. "We can't!"

Adrian turned his attention from the couple back to Omar after another look at the child. He visibly steeled himself for his next words, as if gravitas were something you could pull on like a cloak. "If you want to get out of this alive you need to listen to me. Every fucking word."

The profanity seemed a cheap way to prove he didn't need to sit at the children's table; a kid testing the limits after his dad gave him a sip of beer.

Omar lifted a brow, half-grinned, but said nothing.

"Now, where's *your* Prowler?" Adrian asked.

"He's a couple miles back," Omar said. "What's left of him."

IV.

AN HOUR AGO, Omar felt good about their chances. He'd been here four times before, three in this capacity, all without incident. Noel led one of those expeditions. Omar preferred Daman, but he wouldn't be stateside until March. Megan, Clark, and their daughter Sarah couldn't wait that long. Noel seemed trustworthy, and if he did little to distinguish himself from Daman, he'd at least not done anything stupid.

. . . Until an hour ago, when he managed both simultaneously.

He tried to walk while reading a map—a simple mistake where he might have skated in the vast majority of acreage, particularly on the outskirts of Westing where Agent Orange tended to lose enthusiasm for the game of anti-personnel devices.

"Okay, we need to go through here a ways, and then—"

And then came a loud snap that made them all jump, except for Noel himself; jumping was off the table for him. Metallic jaws burst from the undergrowth, their teeth clamping into the meat of Noel's ankle. His knee buckled in tandem and his body twisted to the ground as if directly wired to the pained contortions of his face.

Omar's mind seized on the words *through here* in his mental playback of the moment. They seemed to take on a whole new meaning, like *we're through, here*.

Clark hurried forward. Omar grabbed a fistful of his shirt. "Not so fast. There could be another one."

Four trips and he'd never seen a sprung trap. Thirty-four minutes into trip number five already offered a new perspective.

Noel redeemed himself a little. After his initial cry of pain and anguish, he dialed down the volume. He still writhed on the ground like Ric Flair caught him in a figure-four leg lock, but limited himself to gasps and groans. Omar ruled out other surprises in the tall grass; Noel would have tripped them too.

"We'll need your help," Omar said to Grant.

Grant nodded from fourteen inches above, though he seemed reluctant to relinquish Sarah. He carried her the entire time, so far with no signs of fatigue. Good thing, too—they brought him for his strength and durability. He'd been the transporter for three other trips, including the first, where circumstances were quite different for Omar.

"I can do it," Doug said. He would play auxiliary transporter when Grant needed a rest, but mainly handled grunt work. He carried a shovel for later, although Omar doubted there would be a later now. He tried to mute the roll call of ramifications speeding through his mind and focus on the next thirty seconds.

He and Doug approached.

Mist hemmed them in since Noel took them through today's entrance, a tunnel dug beneath the wall. He excavated a few of these for access. Unfortunately, gatecrashers sabotaged the entrance nearest their destination, necessitating this outlier plan B. Noel used remote security devices to tip him off when this sort of thing happened, an inherent risk with accesses so close to the wall. Earlier this week two black-clad saboteurs entered the best tunnel and collapsed two sections, likely more. Months of reconstruction thanks to rivals or busybody anti-Stalker activists.

Omar deemed the tunnels reckless as hell. Military groups swept the more covered roadsides all the time, and they didn't simply pour concrete down the tunnel if they found one—they watched until someone tried to use it again, then dragged their asses off for sanction and censure. If Orange found one, the Kill Zone would go from thousands of acres to thousands of miles, like some kind of raw land deal for Native Americans. He rejected the conventional wisdom that Orange shirked the walls to avoid snipers taking cheap shots thirty feet up. People weren't parachuting in here when military had authorization to use anti-aircraft weaponry on any craft, so he had to know there were hidden exits.

Noel's head tilted back, his body braced several inches up where his backpack boosted him off the ground.

"Bear trap," Doug said. He sifted through grass with the shovel to reveal the steel jaws embedded in Noel's ankle as well as a trailing chain staked to the ground

Noel looked at it miserably and then away, a sheen of sweat on his face. "I can't believe this. God, that hurts like hell."

Omar patted his shoulder, wanting to slap him upside the head. Megan and Clark looked no less sick. They footed their Stalker a princely sum to get in here, only for their Stalker's footing to become their biggest impediment. It would be foolish to carry on without Noel, but they wouldn't want to hear that, despite seeing the dangers firsthand.

"How bad is the bleeding?" Noel's tan complexion veered toward the spectrum of cottage cheese. He fidgeted with the bill of his camouflage hat, and pulled it down over his eyes so he wouldn't look at the wound.

"Not all that much blood," Doug reported.

It wasn't, but that would change when they pried the jaws away.

We can't take him back to the tunnel like this, Omar realized. *If Orange tracks the blood, he'd find a way out of here.*

Doug waited for marching orders, with Omar the unspoken second in command. Doug wasn't that impressive side by side with Grant, but few would be unless they were sent back in time to kill Sarah Connor. Grant vouched for the younger guy/Kill Zone virgin, though, and Omar liked what he saw so far. He appeared unruffled by the crisis situation.

"It might be better if we left that on him," Omar said.

"Screw that, no way! You have to take it off, it's killing me."

"You'll bleed more."

"I don't care!"

"We can take the stake out of the chain, no problem," Doug said. "But it might be trapped."

It did seem conveniently easy to limp away with the whole device, but someone dragging a chain with a crippled leg wouldn't get anywhere quickly. Even with a head start, Orange could run them down if Noel bled out a handy trail.

He decided the quicker they moved him, the better. The trap would slow them too much. Orange may not check it anyway and rely on someone screaming for help to alert him.

Worry about the next thirty seconds, forget the rest.

They could figure out how to cover their tracks or fake a trail when they had some distance from here.

The bear trap looked top-of-the-line powerful. If it closed on your hand, you were in the market for fingerless gloves. Each clamp provided room to get a decent enough grip to pull, but blood pooled around the jagged teeth to sluice and slicken both sides.

"I hope that Sector 8 shit ain't real," Noel said. He let his head rest on the ground again.

A meek voice wheezed behind them, too quiet to hear the actual words. The little girl, Sarah. Clark and Megan offered equally quiet assurances. They hoped she would sleep through the whole trip.

Omar took a last quick look around before he tried to seize his side of the bear trap. Pine trees with cones and dead nettles scattered on the ground. Birds chirped faintly several yards off. Beams of sunlight pierced the fog like lasers. Nothing moved, though a new shadow in the smog might go unnoticed.

"Watch," Omar said over his shoulder. Grant nodded. To Doug, he said, "You ready?"

"Let's do it."

"Keep your fingers out of the claw."

"Didn't plan on it."

"Noel, bend your knee."

Noel tented his leg, gasping. Omar seized the metal behind the leg while Doug took hold of the front claw. They both strained. Warm sticky blood oozed on Omar's fingers, discouraging a stable grip. It budged enough to slip a penlight between the teeth and Noel's ripped pant leg. Doug fared a little better, but still not enough clearance for Noel to slip his foot through. They each lost their hold and the jaws snapped shut again.

"*Ow, shit!*" Noel cried. "Careful!"

Omar winced. Anybody would hear him fifty yards out. "We need to give you something to bite down on."

"I'll give *you* something to bite down on," Noel said. His peaked face now bore an ugly shade of red/purple. "Jesus Christ. I'm about to puke."

"Sorry, bud." Doug wiped his bloodied fingers on the grass. "There's nuns' assholes looser than this thing."

Omar listened for a moment now that Noel alerted half the forest to their presence. Hard to tell between the labored breathing and Doug's open mic night at the Improv.

"Try using your feet," Noel suggested.

It might work, but if the trap snapped shut when Noel pulled his foot away, Omar or Doug might end up taking his place.

"Wipe it down." Omar used the tail of his shirt to

clear the blood. Doug followed his example. Crimson still smeared the jaws, but now they felt sticky instead of slick. "Okay, try again."

They pried once more. The trap rattled and protested, but they both had greater success. Omar's clearance went from penlight to flashlight size.

"Hold it!" Noel interlaced his hands beneath his left knee and pulled back. The heel of his shoe prodded the spikes before slipping through to freedom. He crawled away as if the trap could jump over and snap shut on him again.

"All right, let go on three," Omar said to Doug. The jaws stood open wide enough for someone to insert the top of their head. Omar counted off quickly and they released both sides of the trap, yanking their hands away. The jaws clapped shut and tipped over on the grass, the world's sharpest set of chattering teeth.

Noel worked his arms through his backpack and unzipped it. He removed a red bandanna and cinched it tight above his wound. His face remained etched in a sick grimace of pain.

"Better?" Omar asked.

"I'm not ready to hit the dance floor, but yeah, beats fifty thousand pounds of pressure on my freaking leg." He wiped his forehead with his arm and zipped up the backpack.

Doug stooped to pick up the map, a superstitious eye fixed on the dormant teeth.

Had they gone through Noel's original entrance they may have encountered no trap at all and no need to consult the map so frequently in the first place—probably not at all, though erosion and unchecked growth necessitated altered routes in optimal circumstances. Orange also removed and switched road signs around like a homicidal Wile E. Coyote, so you went without a map at your own peril. Today Noel demonstrated the reverse peril of having a map.

Such a little thing to sabotage the whole expedition.

"What happens now?" Megan said.

They all knew what she meant. The show must go on, but how, with their guide effectively crippled?

"We can't go back," Clark said, as if to preempt the argument.

"I'm sorry," Noel said, shrugging on his backpack again, "but there's no way I can go on. Look at me."

"Clark's right," Omar said. "We can't take you back when you're bleeding out. If he follows the trail to your tunnel . . . "

Noel waved a dismissive hand. "Bullshit. He could have dug his own path out of here a long time ago if he wanted to go near the wall."

"It's too big a risk."

"And it's not too big a risk if he picks up our trail and butchers us?"

Omar left that unanswered. Their safest play didn't involve Noel with them, period.

"We should take the tunnel and call an anonymous tip from town," Noel said. "They'll stick someone on the wall to make sure he doesn't get out. I'll lose the tunnel, but it's my own fault. That sounds fair."

"And what if he finds the tunnel before—"

The words died instantly as something happened to Omar he'd never experienced before. The closest comparison would be the sensation of icy fingers tapping along his neck one at a time when he turned his head at the wrong moment, but this was like hundreds of those fingers caressing his entire body at the same time, each one as cold as the grave, a second shuddering skin.

Despite never knowing this idiosyncrasy before, he implicitly understood its meaning—an ancient warning system, something buried deep in the evolutionary vault. Somewhere in the nebulous gray where Noel led them, a darker shape moved, its imprint solidifying the nearer it grew until it emerged from the mist. It might have been born from it, an idea coalescing into actual color and form, incarnating from the imagination into their horrified reality.

Doug stood nearest by virtue of retrieving the map, apparently lacking the fortune to dial into the universal warning system frequency like Omar. The map compromised his attention as it had Noel's, with a potential for greater consequence.

"Doug," Grant warned. His tone didn't portend the scope of the peril—couldn't—but Doug heard something in it anyway and looked up sharply.

The lack of a true face made him seem supernatural, inevitable. He possessed merely the approximation of one, black rubber superimposing his head with goggled, almost insectoid eyes. The gas mask became cylindrical below the visor, terminating in a round valve from which a black coiled line connected somewhere in his camouflage garb. Behind the coil, a necklace bounced back and forth, fashioned with grisly ornaments Omar didn't need to see up close to recognize. Ears. A nasty habit of mutilation he picked up in Vietnam in his life as merely human.

His surprising lack of a weapon didn't slow Clark, Megan, and Grant with Sarah in tow. They took off through a break in the trees to the left, away from both Agent Orange and the path they took to get here, pine needles shaking in their wake. A solitary cone dropped and rolled.

Omar didn't cut and run with them. It wasn't courage. They stood to lose their guide and their map in the next thirty seconds. They might survive without the former, but probably not the latter.

Noel looked on helplessly, hands held up to fate as if to question either why me or what about me.

"Come on!" Omar shouted to Doug. The distance between them might be fifteen feet, and only a third of that between Doug and Orange, who knelt beside the bear trap.

Doug lurched into motion, the encumbrance of the map downright comical, like a cape somehow twisted around to his front. The bear trap chain rattled behind him and appeared in a looping arc as it unfurled toward the back of his head. Omar heard a hollow thump and Doug collapsed in an abrupt home run slide, the map fluttering beneath him.

Orange had yanked the chain from the ground. Quite business-like, he stretched the bear trap open again with gloved hands. It flipped open effortlessly for him.

Noel found the shovel, maybe to use it as a crutch, but Orange launched into action the moment he identified the potential threat. He twirled the chain overhead one time, lasso like, the open mouth of the trap sweeping past before he released the slack. As if magnetically drawn to Noel now that he shared his blood with it, the trap swung right at his head. He dropped the shovel and tried to scoot back, in his panic pushing against the ground with the foot of his wounded leg. He stopped short, mouth agape to scream, and the bear trap swallowed his face.

Omar rushed to Doug, sparing one quick glance to see the steel claws hugging Noel's face like that thing in *Alien*. The resultant scream carried a strange echo through the mechanism, which Noel fumbled to extract as he pitched over on his side.

Orange charged him.

"We gotta go, now," Omar said, trying to pull Doug up by the arm. A trench traversed the crown of Doug's head, blood pooling through his brown hair like oil. Every instinct told Omar to forget it and run then and there, while he still could. Somehow he ignored this and scraped under Doug to free the map. It moved a few inches but stayed caught. If he bolted with only a fragment of Morgan's layout, it wasn't much better than fleeing empty-handed.

He whipped his head back to verify Orange remained preoccupied, in time to see him midair, descending. Noel struggled with the jaws, oblivious, the trap like some kind of horror of the Inquisition, instant confession guaranteed. Orange's boot struck one thick manacle with his full weight behind it. He dropped to the ground in a crouch, punctuated by a sound like someone crushing a pillar of Styrofoam.

Orange turned to them, the damage revealed through his wide-legged stance. The trap lay once again separated from Noel, having taken his face and part of his skull with it. A hollowed cavity of grisly pulp and stringy brain matter gaped back at them, the widest of silent screams. The chin survived intact, a surreal counterpoint to the otherwise complete decimation of the rostral section of the head. Incredibly, nauseatingly, the head continued moving as if seeking Omar with its missing eyes. The hands continued their why-me/what-about-me petition to the sky, his body flailing in a spasmodic death ritual like the first primordial creature to pull its way onto land only to discover it didn't have the lungs for the next part of the evolutionary gambit. A mangled clump of shredded meat protruded from the jaws of the discarded trap. Noel's feet kicked a couple more times, and at last lay perfectly still.

As if waiting for this cue, Agent Orange crouched to grab the handle of the fallen shovel and advanced. Doug sluggishly crawled off the map and withdrew a knife strapped to his boot.

Omar started to shout *no*, but realized the futility. Brandishing a weapon obviously determined the wrecking order, and he never considered taking out his own blade; may as well use it on a tornado. He folded the map in half, intending to pick it up and run when in the corner of his eye Doug hurled the knife from his knees.

Hardly a marksman feat given the distance of ten feet, but impressive all the same to see the blade jutting just above Orange's knee a second later. He developed an instant limp. Omar's odds of escape just doubled, as if to counterbalance the disintegration of Doug's respective chances of a painless death.

Orange glanced down at the offending blade and

swung the shovel around to grip it with his other hand. Omar ran for the break in the trees, folding the map against an outstretched arm to take it down in size again. Behind him came a clang and the thud of a body.

He knew what he would see but once he had the cover of the trees, he paused. Sure enough, Doug lay splayed in cruciform, his face a mask of blood from the shovel blow. Between that and the initial strike to the head, his struggling echoed the reflexive death spasms of road kill.

Orange reoriented the shovel as if to begin digging a grave for Doug, but drove it into his stomach. The force pushed him a foot across the ground. Doug found a hidden reserve of energy, his arms lashing heavenward with a scream that tightened Omar's skin all over. Though foolish to watch another second, a ghoulish impulse gripped him, knowing he could outrun the slightly crippled Orange with the extra incentive of witnessing this carnage.

Doug's scream became more liquid, a clogged drain. He feebly clutched the shovel as Orange hoisted. Ribs cracked with a sound like knots bursting in a fireplace. The blade cleaved through more skin to reveal the cavity. Doug's insides clung to the shovel in squid fashion, mushroom-colored ropes stretching like taffy as Orange excavated a grisly heap of organs. Omar's gorge rose when something that might have been Doug's liver slithered off the side to squelch on the ground.

Orange jerked back on the shovel and the collection of viscera dropped far behind him. The gruesome bouquet hung from tree limbs like dripping vines.

Doug settled back into cruciform, motionless and hopefully dead now. Orange stood over the body, triumphant. He moved up a little, sinking one of his boots into Doug's hollowed stomach, and held the shovel guillotine-like over the neck.

Something switched off Omar's pause button and he bolted, burning through the mist like rays of sunlight. He folded the map on auto-pilot, somehow achieving a slim column as he hurtled past blurs of tree trunks. He slipped it into a zippered pouch in his pants without stopping. The remainder of the group could find their way later, but only distance from Orange mattered now.

Despite the eternity of memories Omar would carry from the attack, it hadn't lasted a full sixty seconds. He adjusted course and caught up with Grant, Clark, Megan, and Sarah quickly enough once he heard the sounds of disturbed branches and panicked footsteps. He took the lead, angling them to the left. There were no pauses to strategize, only the most reluctant intermissions of spirited walking in place of all-out sprinting or jogging, ever onward, somehow not duplicating Noel's unluckiness with any traps. The bulk of conversation came from one brief exchange, their first time slowing below a jogging pace.

"Is Doug . . . " Grant left it at that.

"Doug hurt him, stuck his leg with a knife, but . . . " Omar trailed off, powering through a hot stitch in his side. "Him and Noel both."

Grant looked worn down, but Omar would have passed out five minutes ago carrying a first grader like that.

Clark traded doubling over for arching his back. "What'll we do without Noel?"

"I managed to get the map." Omar patted the pocket of his pants.

Megan brightened at that and gave Clark a tilt of her eyebrows.

"For now," Omar continued, "we move and we don't stop."

Which is exactly what they did, until the better part of an hour later they happened to find their way to the bridge and Adrian's group.

V.

WHEN OMAR APPROACHED with the two groups' last best hope of getting out alive, Clark saw little to inspire confidence. Adrian opened his mouth to speak, but paused to quietly clear his throat. Self-doubt covered his face as clearly as a newly inked tattoo.

Adrian made brief eye contact with Clark before looking away. "We should, uh . . . "

"He thinks we should split up," Omar helpfully translated.

From everyone's faces—Adrian's own group included—Clark wasn't alone in thinking the kid unfit to lead someone to the corner store for an Icee, much less this place.

"And he's right." Omar's voice carried the weight Adrian couldn't summon. "Hear him out."

"Does he know the way to—" Megan started, but Grant cut her off.

"Not this time."

"But Omar has the map," she pleaded, close to tears. Clark felt the anguish, too, but the map led to the Healing Place and nowhere else; right now they needed an exit.

"We can come back," Grant said, barely audible

but very firm. And it would soothe if only Megan let it: *We tried. This is literally a dead-end if we don't reverse course.*

"We'll come back," Clark whispered to Megan. "I've still gotta get him to say 'Bones.'"

Megan glared at him; this wasn't the time to remind her of their secret game, "Put Words in Their Mouth." Each proposed a word or phrase the other had to get the mark to say. Because Grant looked like a super-sized Scandinavian William Shatner, the challenge was iconic Shatner quotes. Megan already completed hers on the way to the KZ. She called Sarah "tiny dancer" and used the nickname to segue into a discussion of Elton John songs; how fortunate "Rocket Man" proved Grant's favorite. She usually won this game. Clark once mused there must be an alternate universe where he usually won, to which Megan replied, *Yeah, the same universe where* Splinter of the Mind's Eye *was the second and last* Star Wars *movie.* Neither of them wanted to live on that earth unless its version of Sarah was healthy and whole.

"This many in one party will lead him straight to us," Adrian said, sounding more assured, as if Omar's backing conferred credibility. "Omar, the big guy and me." He pointed the opposite way. "We'll make noise in that direction. Sound travels funny through here. It should lead him astray."

Adrian tapped the shortest girl, Tina. "Leave it unlocked."

Clark didn't want to split up, but he accepted Sarah from Grant without voicing his opinion.

"You're going to be fine," the giant assured him.

"No whatever-it-is they say 'about it,' right?" Clark said.

Megan caught the subterfuge and rolled her eyes.

The William Shatner face frowned. "You mean, no two ways about it?"

"Right, that." Clark glumly branched off with the others, carrying both Sarah and the burden of another defeat in his game with Megan.

They separated fifteen or twenty minutes ago and began the trek from the railroad tracks to the valley. The path seemed dreamlike and endless in the fog. Clark imagined Sisyphus on the other side of the hill on a similar journey, rolling a boulder upward while they fled with certain death nipping at their heels in an infinite descent. Still alive but always fleeing, always moving. Never dying, but not escaping, either.

At the bottom of the ravine, Clark thanked God they made it unscathed. One slip might have turned ugly fast, no two ways or twenty-seven fractured bones about it.

Adrian knew his stuff after all. It took too long to negotiate the tricky terrain; enough time for a maniac to catch them if not for the distant distractions.

Like clockwork, Clark heard the faraway ping of metal clanging the steel I-beam of a railroad track, resonating through the woods and valley. Weaker than the last time.

"Here," Megan said as she reached for Sarah. Balanced precariously on two large rocks, she rolled her eyes when he hesitated. "Just for a minute. I know you're hurting."

Clark kissed Sarah's head and passed her to her mother, then reached for the sky and stretched his back. Experience told him nothing short of his inversion table would counter the strain in his lower spine. Seven years ago he drove his power jack from a loading dock into the rear of a trailer. *Dock lock's busted. You chock the wheels? Put the tractor in park?* Clark asked. The driver was in his late fifties and though he sported a hooked nose and a half-ring of badly-dyed black hair surrounding a bald spot—in effect, the appearance of an evil Smurf-chasing wizard—Clark believed him when he nodded and said, *Sure enough.*

As so many times before, he entered the trailer, slid his forks beneath the pallet and backed toward the dock with his load. The familiar bump as prelude to a rise didn't happen. Instead he felt an odd dip, followed by a metallic racket as the portable dock plate slipped through the developing chasm between rolling trailer and dock door. The yelling and cries of *Clark! Wait!* came too late. His trajectory took him backward and down. He next remembered awakening in the hospital with a fractured skull, broken ribs and cracked vertebrae. He'd heal, but his back would never be the same. When he finally returned to work several months later his mishap earned him the nickname "Papa Smurf." Several witnesses claimed as he drifted in and out of consciousness he'd said, *Looks like Gargamel got us this time.*

As expected, stretching didn't help. He imagined the ache in his lower back as a twisting of his spine, like someone wringing water from a wet cloth—a little more torsion and the moisture would be tears. Despite this he would reach for Sarah anyway; Megan needed to stay fresh in case Orange came for them.

Only Clark could buy the group time if/when the moment arrived. He didn't trust that Bryce guy to do anything but help his own.

"Not far now," said Erica, adjusting her miniskirt. She seemed self-conscious about her wardrobe since Megan explained why they came here with Sarah, as though worried she were profaning a holy place. Probably didn't help that Megan initially gave her such a long look at the group introduction, either.

Careful where you point those eyes, buster, Megan warned him, maybe not entirely kidding.

I'm spoken for, he promised.

He couldn't help wondering what brought Erica here, though. Was it simple thrill-seeking furthered by the youthful misconception of immortality? Something about her resisted rote pigeonholing but he couldn't say why. Her friends suggested nothing so remarkable. The boyfriend in particular belonged no more than a man streaking naked through a soccer match.

Erica smiled at Sarah, who stirred awake once more in Megan's arms. To Clark she said, "You're sure about taking her out now?"

He shrugged. "We wouldn't know what to do if we got there. But we can try again. It doesn't have to be today."

No, not today, but terribly, unfairly soon.

"There's more to it than just finding the Healing Place?"

Clark remembered the shovel Doug carried in. "Yes, there's a process." They didn't know the ins and outs of it because Doug, Grant, and Omar were tight-lipped to preserve the secrecy. It didn't inspire much confidence in their original pitch.

Megan: *I want to believe it . . . but can we?*

Clark: *They said it didn't happen overnight. It took years of trial and error, a lot of research.*

Research? You call fooling around with superstitions and voodoo rites research?

Oh, they didn't say anything like that and you know it.

No, you're right, they didn't. Didn't say much of anything at all, which is worse. Why do we need three of them and a guide?

It's a bigger body count if Agent Orange catches us. That bought him rolled eyes.

Erica nodded thoughtfully now, but he saw her doubt. He shared it in the beginning. Yes, with their child at death's door, a miraculous healing spot in the KZ offered the legitimacy of three magic beans, but Erica hadn't heard the testimonials of families who swore to its efficacy. His and Megan's fear went from "what if it doesn't work?" to "what if it does?" because as awful as their helplessness had been, it absolved them. If she died when they had the power to save her after all, though, how could they live with that?

And if the whole thing were some elaborate hoax, they would surely concoct an easier object to carry around than a shovel.

Here, Doug, you hang on to the mystic ice cream scoop. Don't drop that puppy, whatever you do.

Bryce waved them forward.

The formation shuffled. Tina led the taller Shelly with Erica right behind, then Megan and Sarah followed by Bryce and Clark. He cringed with every step. Keeping pace with healthy kids nearly twenty years his junior hurt like hell. His sciatic nerve shot sharp complaints down both legs. The pain inspired the flotsam and jetsam of his mind and the title *The Agony and the Ecstasy* floated to the surface. A biographical novel of Michelangelo, something he read in medical waiting rooms in recent months. Particularly cruel mental joke, in the Kill Zone it was just *The Agony and the Injuries*—no telling how many Orange could inflict before you succumbed. Clark would happily volunteer if it meant survival for Megan and Sarah. Besides, if Omar didn't make it out, it would mean they failed with their only chance. So maybe his selfless act came secondary to a selfish one: dying meant not living to see Sarah breathe her last.

Shaking the thought from his head, he found a solid place to stand and waited for the procession to cross a logjam created by a fallen tree. It brought several others with it and three trunks blocked the creek, capturing a clutch of smaller limbs amongst the rocks. He took Sarah from Megan so she could use the smaller trunk to climb onto the larger. She waited her turn behind Erica, frowning at the inadvertent show Erica provided from the higher vantage point. Clark turned away before Megan inspected his line of sight.

Sarah pressed her face against his beard. Sometimes she ran her face across the wiry hair because it felt weird to her, but he heard her whisper a question into his ear.

"Does she know her panties are in her butt?"

Clark grinned. "Some panties are made that way, Sugar Bear. Don't ever wear that kind."

"I won't. That's silly."

Sometimes he forgot for little pockets of time she might never have the chance to make those choices.

Once Megan stood atop the log he passed Sarah to her. Erica offered help from the other side of the obstruction, a warm smile softening her features as she accepted Sarah.

Megan waited for Clark to cross. His back objected to every movement, turning what should have been an easy climb into a major undertaking. This wasn't the sort of thing Megan signed on for when they'd married. He went from a full head of hair and fit body to a prematurely balding, overweight guy with the vertebrae of an octogenarian. Megan looked at least a decade younger thanks to the vagaries of Clark's life. She'd been thirty-three when she'd had Sarah and snapped back to her pre-pregnancy weight in about three months. There were practically no signs she'd ever been pregnant aside from some stretch marks on her breasts. Sarah looked like her mother. Clark's only contribution to her genetics seemed to be dark hair and a predisposition for rare cancers.

Maybe because she sensed his despair Sarah smiled, which drew one from Clark. Her added weight compressed the discs of his spine, but he didn't let it slow him. With Sarah in his arms it was easier to ignore his own pain if it meant carrying her far from Agent Orange.

The next ping somehow seemed louder than the last. Sound really did travel in odd ways here; in fact, it sounded like it came from in front of them. If the others were still alive, where was Orange? Had they failed to draw him away? Had he followed Clark's group instead? He gave the woods and creek behind them a quick survey but saw nothing.

None of them talked for at least ten minutes. Their

only sounds came from the occasional clash of shifting rocks beneath their feet or an errant splash when someone stepped in pooled water. The gurgle of the creek might drown their collective sounds, but Clark had a hard time believing they'd be so lucky.

A small stream trickled beside them.

"Thirsty?" Clark whispered.

"Uh-uh," Sarah said weakly. "I'm okay."

"Love ya."

"Love ya."

The pings gradually stopped altogether. It seemed miraculous Clark's group made it so far, which could only mean one thing: Adrian's plan had worked. Unfortunately, Omar had the map. If he and Grant died, their knowledge of the Healing Place died with them. There was a back-up Stalker, but Clark couldn't remember his name and didn't know how to contact him anyway. Not for the first time, he wished he knew each man's role in the healing enterprise. As forthcoming as Sarah's doctors were regarding treatments and expectations these guys were the opposite. Lots of positivity and assurances, but no explanations.

The longer the trek stretched, the more doomed to Orange they seemed until, finally, someone whispered excitedly. Clark heard it repeated. "The balloon."

He saw it. Deflated and withered, dangling high in a tree, its silver veneer long dulled. A yellow string with a frayed end dangled. Traces of sky peeked beyond the tops of nearby pine trees.

"Here!" Bryce tossed aside an old log.

Tina skipped across several rocks to him and

stumbled when a loose one shifted. Bryce caught her and mumbled, "Don't break an ankle *now*."

Tina stopped short of the exposed iron grate and reached into her pocket. She dug so deeply Clark had a nightmare vision she would withdraw an empty hand, the key lost.

But she *did* have the key.

"Hurry!" Shelly said.

Bryce made way for Tina, heaving a rock out of the way as he gave her the space she needed to reach through the grate.

Clark put Sarah on a boulder, an array of pine trees on the raised ground behind her. She dropped a good deal of weight this year to where he sometimes swore she must have lost half her former mass, but she seemed plenty heavy now and setting her down provided such blessed relief. Bending over, he put his hands on either side of her and arched his back as much as he could to offset the incredible needle-ache. He merely replaced one pain with another, but the variation offered some solace—this new movement hurt less. Given the size of the compartment, the escape would require crawling. He didn't look forward to it, but it sure beat the alternative.

"This is the way out?" Megan moved to take a closer look. She hated tight spaces and would automatically worry over how Sarah would deal with the confines.

"Yeah, it's a tight fit, but you can make it," Erica said, though her eyes lingered on Clark long enough to cast doubt the assertion applied to him. "Can Sarah crawl?"

Tina slapped the grate with a palm. "It's a different lock!"

Erica: "Whaddayoumean?"
Shelly: "This is not happening, this is not—"
Bryce: "Give it here, you're doing it wrong!"
Megan looked as horrified as the kids sounded.

"I'm not a fucking idiot, Bryce!" Tina said as she relinquished the key. "It's not even the same fucking brand!"

Megan motioned to Sarah to cover her ears with her hands, which Sarah dutifully mimicked. Like Saturday night with potty-mouthed Uncle Tim. Would they ever see him again? Thirty seconds ago it seemed like a possibility. Not so much now.

Clark couldn't bear to look at them as they fussed over the exit that slammed shut in their faces. Just before they split at the bridge, Shelly asked Adrian, *What if we can't find it?* Adrian assured them they would find it, perhaps his most confident statement. Still, they worried they would overlook the exit or lose the key or Orange would catch them first.

No one had considered this eventuality.

"Then we're cut off from the rest of the world," Megan said in a low voice. "This is why we shouldn't have split up. What now?"

"I don't know. This was their way out. Maybe they know where to find a Chicken Exit."

The fog mostly lifted in the direction they came, but still hung thick beyond the tunnel where they'd have to flee. The creek shifted to the left. They couldn't exit and they couldn't go back because of *him*. Which left them exactly . . . where? Lost. Without a guide. Adrian might know an alternate exit, but he'd be miles away by now.

"Our stuff isn't there, either," Bryce said.

Clark looked through the bars at the sturdy padlock—sturdy for anyone not named Agent Orange. The metal bars wouldn't be much of a deterrent, either, but the drainage tunnel itself was too small to be an escape route for someone his size. Clark wouldn't have fit, either.

Probably not Omar. Definitely not Grant.

But Megan and Sarah would have fit, easily.

Clark wanted to scream.

Bryce struck the grate with the flat of his hand when he failed with his turn. Erica snatched the key from him and thrust both arms through, furiously trying to work it in the lock. *You were doing it the wrong way, GENIUS!* never materialized on her lips.

Clark heard faint scrapes echoing from the hole, only slightly more audible than Erica's increasingly desperate jostling of the padlock. "Shhh! You hear that?"

He pointed to the tunnel.

Erica listened and nodded. The others crowded close to hear their freedom scurry away, sharing frightened and stricken looks. No one succumbed to the impulse to shout threats or pleas at their saboteur. The balm of a few profanities wouldn't salve the decapitations Orange bestowed if he overheard their hollering.

Shelly wiped her glistening eyes. "Why would someone do this to us?"

Erica tapped Bryce. "Adrian wouldn't . . . would he? If he ducked the other two, doubled back and came down the hill ahead of us . . . "

"Sorry, but no way some scrawny kid got away from Omar," Clark said, thinking of how fast he caught up to their group when they had a minute head start.

"And why lock us out if he did?" Bryce said.

Erica nodded. "This just doesn't make any sense."

It seemed metaphorical of Sarah's disease course treatment—the supposed way back to a normal life which somehow never led there.

"I'd give anything to catch up to that bastard," Bryce said to the tunnel, as if hopeful the words would carry to the saboteur.

Erica hunkered down, reached to a fanny pack beneath her sweatshirt. "I'd settle for bolt cutters."

"Maybe we could find some in town," Tina said.

Clark watched Erica withdraw a folded column of paper from her bag. "Oh shit, you guys have a map?"

Megan prodded him with an elbow and gestured to Sarah on the boulder, awake, watching and listening.

"Sorry," he muttered, but felt his excitement warranted the vulgarity. They wouldn't have to wander blindly, hoping to stumble on salvation before the axe fell. Maybe literally.

"Adrian said we were close to another Gauntlet station," Erica said.

"Gauntlet station" meant nothing to Clark, but it sounded like something positive for their predicament. While they couldn't see through the entirety of their would-be escape tunnel, there seemed to be a light at the end after all.

Then a new shadow extinguished it before Erica even had time to unfold the map.

Shelly unleashed a shrill, piercing scream that devolved into a whimpering sob as she flitted across the tops of rocks, headed for the fog. Bryce and Erica became a blur of movements and Clark suddenly felt hopelessly, pathetically *outclassed*. Like the last animal in the herd to identify the threat, Clark's body instinctively moved in the same direction as the others without knowing why.

"Mommy!"

Already two yards from the boulder with Sarah in tow, Megan threw caution to the wind and let terror guide her steps. Caution would have told her to avoid the loose rock, but her foot slid, toppling mother and daughter. As Megan twisted her body so Sarah would not bear the brunt of the fall, Clark shifted his momentum toward his wife, but he was too far from her to intervene.

And then it happened.

The terror unseen pounced on the slowest animal. Clark's entire body convulsed from a hard impact that sent him hurtling toward the sloping rocks. As he spun around he saw what he only glimpsed during the Noel and Doug attack. From this close Agent Orange looked like a giant—like the NBA center you knew was big, but you had no idea he was *that BIG*.

A thousand points of pain flared like nerve endings in supernova. The shock overwhelmed him, along with the acute awareness he could no longer breathe. He could only move his eyes, which watched the downward arc of Agent Orange's boot. It struck his chest hard enough to crunch the rocks beneath him. Maybe he hovered in the space between life and death where only visual and aural input remained because he didn't feel the blow.

Agent Orange turned his head left and right,

carefully surveying the fleeing and the fallen. Beside him a spire reached impossibly into the sky, an illusion which soon revealed itself as the long wooden shaft of a bardiche, a poleaxe used in Eastern Europe in the 16th or 17th Century. Clark once penned a college research paper on European arms so he may be the only victim of said weapon to know its proper name. Such a mad serendipity.

He didn't have long to consider the implication. Orange decided his next move and, like thousands of similar decisions, it involved mutilation. Foot atop Clark's chest, Orange swung the blade of the bardiche toward Clark's face. Unable to move, he watched instant death slash the air. Only the slightest movement of his head accompanied the clang of metal against rock. The lower section of blade rose from the right side of his peripheral vision. The pole angled toward a gloved hand.

The right side of his skull erupted with searing pain as if splashed with scalding water. Orange's foot moved and Clark finally gasped. The act of arching his back to suck deep the blessed air made the rest of his nerve endings come alive—the shock of the landing merely winded him and put his body on temporary pause.

Agent Orange stepped back, wedged the flat of the blade against Clark's cheek and tilted the blade sideways. The skin of his scalp tightened as the tip of the blade scraped along the rock beneath his skull. Clark flashed back to a playground brawl when Richie "the Gooch" Felder grabbed a handful of his hair and tugged for considerably more than the little cretin was worth. His head tipped sideways from the pressure of the blade. Taut skin stretched until its elasticity gave way to the stress. Abruptly the pressure relented and Clark's head snapped to its original resting place, a crawling sensation scuttling along his skull as the stretched skin crept to its default position.

Blood dripped from the blade. Orange reached for the flat of the elongated steel with his free hand and plucked an irregular flap of skin. He let it dangle from his gloved index finger and thumb. Orange held the flesh in the air for appraisal and Clark recognized his auricle as the centerpiece of the biopsy. It looked like a piece of rubber mask a movie villain might tear from his face in a big reveal and, strangely, just as fake. The sensory terror alongside his head told a different truth.

Orange rose with his dripping prize, probably smiling beneath the mask.

Sparks flashed from the blade of his bardiche. A blast echoed through the valley. The unmistakable discharge of a firearm. Another shot followed and Orange's gas mask hose jerked sideways. A cavalry of two would-be monster slayers named Adrian and Omar emerged from the thick fog where Shelly fled. Adrian stopped long enough to steady his aim for another shot. The gun bucked in his hand. Clark's heart sank when the bullet ricocheted from a distant rock.

Agent Orange headed in the direction of Megan and Sarah. Clark rolled and grabbed for a boot but came up empty. Already a yard away, Orange closed on Sarah at her fallen mother's side. Tears streaming, she stared at the towering bogeyman.

She screamed.

REINCURSION

With Sarah at his feet, Orange successfully calculated Adrian wouldn't risk another shot. Adrian continued to approach with his gun aimed and Clark imagined Adrian making a calculation, too: *How close can I get before I risk another round?* With an incomprehensively rigid face, the kid who self-consciously stammered his lines at the bridge faced down the evil. Omar carried the metal rod they must have slammed against the railroad track so many times—a futile distraction as it turned out. Clark would have preferred it in Grant's hands, but the gentle giant hadn't appeared from the fog with them. Had he choked at the prospect of facing Agent Orange, giant-on-giant?

Clark ached at the sight of his wife and child at Orange's feet, but he didn't want to risk distracting Adrian. Then he saw her. Ten or fifteen yards beyond Orange stood Erica. Perhaps suicidal, she carried nothing but a thick stick around five feet in length.

Aware he provided the weakest link of the encirclement, Clark grabbed a large rock and hefted it into the air with both hands.

Orange tucked Clark's ear inside a pocket for safekeeping. Such a simple act yet Clark never felt so emasculated.

The monster tossed the bardiche from his right hand and caught it with his left. He grabbed near the bottom of the pole and snapped off a one-foot section. Sensing the opportunity slipping away, Adrian hopped rock to rock to close the distance. Orange slung the piece just as his target slipped. The projectile sailed through the space Adrian's torso occupied a second before.

Clark stood with his weapon, lasting two steps before the sudden displacement of blood pressure brought him crashing to his knees. His grip collapsed and he almost dropped the rock on his own head.

Agent Orange slipped the blade of the bardiche through the rear of Sarah's sweatshirt and hoisted her like a ragdoll. Dangling his human shield, he skipped across rocks with uncanny agility toward the forest across the wide creek bed.

Erica rushed to intercept Orange, who didn't deviate from his course based on this new "threat." She swung the stick at his legs. The wood snapped with a resounding crack that echoed from the pine trees. What didn't break was his stride. He bounded three more steps and leaped from the creek bed into the woods with Sarah.

Okay, now Clark had never felt more emasculated.

"Muhgn!" Clark called as he tried to steady himself on his hands and knees.

Adrian passed a black object into Omar's waiting hands and then ran toward the woods at the other side of the creek, twenty or thirty yards from where Orange entered. He stooped and didn't swing his right arm as he ran, holding it close to his abdomen as if he were wounded—or carrying something. It looked like the most telegraphed "quarterback sneak" of all time. Adrian hopped a series of large rocks and launched himself to the higher ground. Through the trees he zigzagged a diagonal path away from Agent Orange's point of entry.

Omar tucked the gun into the rear waistband of his pants as he hurried over to Clark and Megan.

"Muh?" Clark's mouth wouldn't work correctly.

The right side of his jaw felt locked, immobile. The muscle throbbed.

Great gobs of blood spattered Megan's face and sweatshirt as he hovered. To block the flow he put his hand against the jagged flesh where his ear had been. Despite its absence he still heard gurgling liquid that shifted with every movement of his head. He thought of all the times he bitched about his right earbud falling out.

"Girl, that was bravely stupid," Omar said as Erica joined them.

"Didn't even slow him down." She opened the fanny pack. Despite her assured movements, she shook like she just insulted the devil—repercussions to follow.

Megan's head wound left several small bloody trails along the rock. Awareness slowly ebbed into her glassy eyes. Clark quickly tilted his face away so she couldn't see the side of his head. The gurgling in his ear drove deeper, merging into a filter that gave him the sensation of hearing the world from the bottom of an ocean.

Erica extracted a handkerchief from her fanny pack. "Hold this against your head."

"Thunksh," he said through an ever-tightening jaw.

"You can tie it with this." She pushed down a stocking.

"Adrian thinks Orange will go after him because he's got the gun," Omar whispered. Clark had to lip-read what his remaining ear hadn't picked up, but heard the clatter of the steel bar when Omar dropped it on the rocks. He knew who really had the gun, but Orange didn't look when Adrian passed it off.

"Grant's with your friends," Omar said. "Bryce said there's a different lock?"

"Some fucker changed it." Erica removed her right boot. She tugged the stocking off her leg.

Clark pointed to Omar and then Megan: *You take her.* When Omar nodded his understanding Clark pointed to himself and the woods: *I have to go after Sarah!*

"Sorry we couldn't get here sooner."

When Omar examined Megan, Clark lifted the back of Omar's jacket and saw the gun wedged between the belt and dark skin gleaming with sweat. Centered on the handgrip was a circular emblem with three arrows. Clark grabbed for it, but Omar spun and caught his hand.

"No. Not till I try the rebar."

Clark glared, but Omar glared harder; a shake of the head left no room for compromise. Omar trotted over to the grate with the rod. He wedged it awkwardly through an opening and grunted with the effort to pry the enclosure open. It didn't budge. He switched to jabbing the rebar at the padlock, which loudly rattled around from each blow, something it would have been stupid to try without knowing Orange's whereabouts. He turned around, shaking his head.

"Didn't even scratch it. You can take this, but the gun stays with me." He passed the bar to Clark.

"Let us have the gun. We can't get Sarah back without it," Erica said.

Omar shook his head. "I got people to protect. Including Megan."

"Pleash," Clark managed. His jaw hadn't loosened

at all. It ached on both sides. Along with the pain in his head and back he felt a strange numbness in his joints and a slowly ratcheting nausea, as if the contents of his stomach were spoiling.

"Okay, shoot the lock and then give us the gun!" Erica said.

Omar smiled sadly. "You must not watch *Mythbusters*. The lock's here to stay." Speaking directly to Erica, he said, "You should come with me. He wants us to follow him. He's counting on it."

"She's a little girl."

Despite her grand plans to rescue Sarah and make the world safe from the horror in the gas mask through sheer will and spunk, Erica trembled like someone rightfully scared shitless. Omar picked up on the fear and gave her an out, but she proved strangely reluctant to take it.

"It doesn't matter if you take her back if you don't kill him too. He'll find you again. Even if by some miracle we get her out, as sick as she is . . . " He left it unfinished.

The gurgling sound now might have been Clark's rage boiling in his head. Less so at Omar's brutal truths than Orange, Fate and all the things conspiring to put his family in this impossible, unthinkable moment.

Sarah screamed, her wail echoing from the ridge above them.

He jerked rigid. The weight of tempered steel in his hand didn't make him feel any more lethal, but better than a stick. The rebar had a straight body with a point at one end; just the sort of thing you'd find in the Kill Zone. Orange probably used it to end some poor fool, then left it for the next guy to find with an option to reclaim.

"Adrian's in contact with someone on the outside."

Omar hauled Megan off the rocks. Clark grasped her shoulder one last time, wishing for a chance to say goodbye if this was a one-way trip, but his words would sound warped even without the fog of a concussion.

"If you somehow get her out, she won't get back in," Omar said to Erica in one last push to get her to abandon this quixotic quest. "Do you understand? She's terminal. Your friends are with Grant. Adrian said the creek will take us by the Morgan Wall and from there we can follow it to a Chicken Exit and get a military evac. We've got a chance. Let Clark handle this."

"I'm not going with you," Erica whispered.

Megan mumbled something, cringing from the head wound.

Clark ran for the forest before she became fully aware of the situation, as well as to abandon Omar's proclamations of doom in the seashell of his severed ear root. It carried its own symbolism, fleeing from Omar's likely last pitch to dissuade Erica: *Even if we get her out, a military evac means protective services will take her and we'll never get the chance to bring her back. The best case scenario is you rescue her for a longer death, and the most likely result is you're going to die for nothing.*

His current agony would keep him bedridden anywhere but here. Amazing how the human body endured when circumstances demanded. Outside the wall everyday aches and pains were just excuses, ways to put off what you needed to do.

He'd never see Megan again. He'd be lucky to see Sarah, but he could never leave her alone to her fate. If nothing else, he wanted to deal the bastard a blow he wouldn't soon forget. Too bad he only had a bar he probably couldn't even swing when the time came. Another David versus Goliath but this David had barely more mobility than Michelangelo's version. The Philistine could and would mete a crushing defeat to the upstart.

Adrian's ascent made the climb look relatively easy, but Clark greatly lacked such spryness. He slipped on exposed roots, jarred his back, slipped several more times, and slung a gout of blood onto the leaf-strewn ground as he clambered toward the higher ground. It took a helpful hand shoving his ass to get him into the forest. It didn't get much easier from here. The first fifty yards climbed at a 30% grade, but rose sharply after that.

Erica grabbed Clark's bloody, dirty hand for help. What did Sarah mean to her? It didn't matter. Two were better than one, although she'd be his fifth choice if he'd had a say in the selection of back-up. This called for brute strength, not suicidal determination.

"Daddyyyyyyyy!"

This one different than the others. Not mere terror. He had *hurt* her.

Sugar Bear!

Clark shouted and ran until the slope turned against him, and then he somehow overcame all odds and ran some more. Soon his forward progress couldn't match the level of his exertion and he cried from frustration—if only he were more fit—if only he'd never crashed his power jack—if only the key fit the padlock—*IF ONLY*—

He paused long enough to listen to shuffling elsewhere in the forest, cadences too fast to be human. Clark figured they were deer.

At once the cacophony ceased, leaving only Clark's tortured gasping.

He scanned the hillside. Patches of snow lingered where shadows protected them from the sun. The drape of hazy mist countered the lack of foliage that would have allowed him to see much further. The direct sunlight cleared more of the fog but Clark didn't know if that was such a good thing. What hid Orange also hid them from Orange.

Wheezing as quietly as he could, Clark used his left hand to hold a small tree. The rebar better be of use down the line considering the energy he spent lugging it this far. Somehow he made it halfway up the hill before stopping, but his ankles and shins throbbed from the brutal angle. He leaned forward to keep himself from tipping backwards at the persistent tug of gravity. His feet slid slowly on wet leaves from the pressure of his weight. Fifteen feet down the hill, Erica also rested against a tree. When he caught her eye she nodded, probably meaning she was ready to go on even though the effort to get this far doubled her over.

The thought of Sarah alone in her torment, failed by her father, pushed Clark forward once more, zigzagging from tree to tree. The sturdy trunks helped offset the punishingly steep grade. A fallen tree intersected his path, lying across the slope. At the other side of the log he saw her. A tiny shape slumped against a tree, arms above her head, fastened to the tree with old, rusty barbed wire.

Damn you! She wouldn't have gone anywhere!

Either Orange waited nearby or he'd trapped Sarah. Clark ran for her anyway. If he freed her, maybe he could delay Orange long enough for Erica.

Bad genetics curtailed decades of Sarah's potential life to scant months. He and Megan came here to reclaim those decades, only to reduce her remaining time to hours. Time to fight for every second he could get, and give Erica the chance to take Sarah beyond the wall without military evacuation, where hope to heal her yet remained.

The tree offered two feet of clearance beneath, a thin layer of snow upon the shaded ground. Erica dropped to crawl through it, but he'd never duplicate the maneuver with his damaged back. Instead Clark hurled himself on top of the log and practically rolled over it. Erica emerged beside him and wiped her hands on her sweatshirt, her lone stocking lightly torn in a couple of places.

Sarah sat only ten yards away now, more or less a straight shot if not for the merciless slope. No sign of Agent Orange. Maybe he fell for Adrian's trickery and pursued the boy after all.

Did he take Sarah's ear, too?

He couldn't tell from here. Her head lay slumped against her arm. She had passed out (he hoped), unable to see her father came for her.

There were several large trees to the right and he could use those as "stepping stones." Clark rammed the point of the rebar into the ground to provide support as he struggled toward the next tree. Erica kept low to the ground and scaled the hillside straight up the middle at Sarah. She'd reach her first—at least he thought so until Erica face-planted when her feet and a supporting hand slid through the mud. Undaunted, she shook it off and scurried onward.

Right hand hooked around the next tree, Clark pulled himself forward and tugged the rebar out of the ground as he passed it. When he reached the tree he edged around it and rested his shoulders against the trunk. His lungs burned. He might have been scaling Everest.

Orange tied Sarah to the side of the tree but the slope left her precariously balanced. Her right foot left streaks in the mud where she'd tried to keep her weight from tugging against the barbed wire. Once she lost consciousness her buttocks landed on her left foot and wedged her in place.

Clark eyed the next tree up the line, a sweet-gum only four inches in diameter, but solid enough to support his climb. Reaching it would take him diagonally right, away from Sarah, but the next tree would put him within ten feet. From there he could sidle over on his hands and knees.

Erica rounded Sarah's tree from the opposite side and used the trunk for support. She quickly assessed the wire wrapped around Sarah's hands, cringed, and gave Clark a worried look. Her eyes widened an instant later; her face became pure terror.

A movement in Clark's peripheral vision confirmed they were not alone. For the second time today the behemoth surprised him, leaving Clark barely enough time to retreat. He raised the rebar as a defensive measure. The sweet-gum snapped near the base of the trunk as a whoosh of air heralded the return of the bardiche for a second bite. The tree at his back shuddered violently and the incredible blow to Clark's waist pitched him forward. The rod landed point-first in the soil and Clark's right shoulder hit the flat end, spinning him to his back.

Bare tree limbs reached toward the sky, thrumming like vibrating bass chords from the wallop. Several loud cracks preceded a rain of long dead limbs. Big and small, they fell in a wild pattern, ricocheting off lower limbs, dropping through the wisps of fog toward Clark. He weakly raised his left arm to protect his face as small pieces of broken bark pelted him. The limbs strafed the forest floor all around him, shaking and snapping, but only a few small bits landed on his chest.

Tilting his head up and back he looked for Sarah. He saw more of Erica than Megan would have wanted as she clambered up the hill on hands and knees with Sarah on her back. Clark felt a twinge of guilt for judging her.

Go go go!

In the foreground a large branch struck the forest floor, kicking dirt and leaves into the air.

Clark quickly looked away, fearful his stare alerted Orange to their escape. But *he* already knew, right? The ground below, the trees, the water, the very air within the Kill Zone were like strands of a spider's web, the gentlest touch of a trespasser signaling the hidden sentinel. Once in his web, nothing escaped.

Clark's tentative fingers found a gaping cavity

below his waist with exposed tissue hot and wet to the touch, yet strangely painless despite this probing. Absent the feedback, he could imagine himself touching nothing more than the viscera of an animal he was field dressing. Aghast, he found confirmation still standing at his former resting spot and he remembered: to ease the pressure on his back he locked his right leg and kept the left knee at a slight bend. And there they were, no more than a yard from him, his lower extremities propped against the tree as if carelessly left behind.

A frightening numbness spread along his nerve endings and he felt exceedingly faint. His face, scalp, and fingers tingled. He couldn't keep his eyes open.

A strange, high-pitched squeak intermingled with a strained creaking. Clark's mind puzzled over the sound. Was he hearing nails on a chalkboard? Well, *that* didn't make sense.

Unless . . .

You're not in the Kill Zone!

Relief washed over him as a high school classroom coalesced on the fringes of his perception like the light at the end of a nightmarish tunnel. He sensed a large room, with desks, classmates. Confusion. He teetered on the razor-thin edge between two realities. In one, a teenaged Clark asleep in History class the morning after bingeing an Agent Orange marathon on Cinemax; in the other, adult Clark two decades into a possible future with a wife and a terminally-ill daughter. Leaving behind the REM-state nightmare was as simple as reversing course through these final stages of sleep and embracing awareness. He could go back to high school, safe, sound, and more than a little embarrassed because—*Shit, I'm probably drooling on the desk!*

Heartened by the realization, Clark felt further from the nightmare already. Salvation from the terror.

Nails on a chalkboard. Mr. Carlisle sees you asleep and he's trying to wake you. The class is struggling to hold in the laughter until the moment you look up from your desk.

A light appeared. Perhaps a glimmer from the classroom at consciousness' edge. If he merely opened his eyes the nightmare would end.

But . . . Megan. Sarah.

Clark could go toward the light and end this, but his life with Megan would never happen because he hadn't met her yet . . . and Sarah . . . Sarah would never exist.

Her pain and suffering will never happen.

The way out . . . as simple as turning his back on a possible reality.

Go to the light.

But Sarah . . . he saw her face. Remembered the tender fragility of her cries in the moments after passing from womb to world. The joy of her first steps. Her tiny hands full of Post Super Sugar Crisp, tiny legs kicking in glee beneath her highchair tray. Her first "Daddy." The time she explored Megan's makeup drawers to disastrous effect. *Look, Daddy, I'm pretty like Mommy.*

Sugar Bear!

Eyes bulging, lungs gasping for all the air they could suck, Clark rose on his elbows. Some of him bulged, steaming, into the crisp, morning air. His sudden movement jarred him loose and he began a slow slide down the hill. Next to him Agent Orange had the rebar prepped for launch, ready to throw it like a spear at Erica and Sarah.

Clark grabbed for the wound inflicted by Doug above Orange's knee and squeezed with all the energy he had left, which amounted to unleashing the charge of a single AAA battery.

The gas mask tilted and the necklace of ears swung as Orange bent toward his dying victim. Clark recognized the newest addition to the otherwise mostly dark, leathery collection. Orange hadn't idly waited for Clark's arrival; the monster passed the time stripping away the excess flesh from the scalping.

With trifling effort, Orange pulled away from Clark's flimsy grip and stomped the offending forearm; it sounded like the snapping branches. The pointed end of the rebar slammed through Clark's open palm. Orange walked away, leaving Clark to slide until his arm stretched taut.

The dealer of mortal wounds swung the bardiche so hard the blade embedded all of the way to the shaft. The diameter of the trunk had to be two feet and the weight of the tree locked the blade like a hydraulic vise. The metal squealed as Orange worked to reclaim his weapon from its grasp, the sound of fingernails on a chalkboard.

Clark tilted his head to see Sarah one last time. But she was gone. Erica reached the top of the hill, crossed over to the Flee phase of her bid for survival.

Thank you, Lord. Let her live! Let her live, please! Give us a miracle once, just this once, please!

The creak of straining wood returned Clark's

attention to Orange in time to see the bardiche handle give. The poleaxe snapped a foot below the blade, splinters flew like sparks. Orange tossed aside the broken pole and grabbed the shaft. The squeal came again. This time Orange put his left hand against the trunk above Clark's severed anatomy. A steady screech accompanied the sliding of the blade through soft sapwood. Orange jerked sideways when it wrenched free. Clark's legs buckled when the bent knee gave way. Like a mighty tower that had given him half of his former height, his extremities toppled toward him. His waist struck the ground, unleashing a glut of viscera. Several coils of intestines slapped stickily against his face and bald head. He shuddered and rolled his face away, spat a fountain of blood across the wet leaves.

Clark shook his head and screamed, but the mighty roar came out as a gasp. His excised lower half stood up again, uncoiling intestines stretched to the forest floor as if grabbing for purchase. Orange rifled through Clark's pockets and discarded everything but the pocket knife his grandfather gave him on his fourteenth birthday. He never went anywhere without it.

Orange cast aside the extremities and turned his attention to the upper half.

An otherworldly exhaustion gripped Clark; maintaining consciousness an act of superior, stubborn will. But every second Orange spent on him was a second for Sarah. Clark pulled at the rebar to free his hand, but the will to movement no longer translated to the act of moving. The thin shaft of metal might as well be a steel girder.

RYAN HARDING AND JASON TAVERNER

A black shape landed on Clark's sternum. It swam into focus long enough for Clark to recognize Agent Orange's muddy boot. The sudden increase in pressure broke through the tingling muddle of disrupted nerve endings and Clark felt his ribcage crumple like twigs underfoot. His remaining organs gushed across the forest floor like the contents of a punctured abscess.

VI.

MORNING HADN'T BROKEN when Billie and Evan reached the wall. Marveling at its imposing stature, she pressed her hands against cold concrete that rose thirty feet into the air; all that separated her from home.

All that separates him *from us.*

Her excitement over the next phase of the trip overwhelmed any fatigue from the early rise and vigorous hike. They travelled lightly, with backpacks that only contained water and energy bars, no gear, and absolutely nothing that could be interpreted as a weapon should they get caught by a random patrol. Evan assured Billie patrols were relatively rare along the mountainside. Trespassers preferred easier access than an hour's hike on the strenuous trails to the north. The most heavily guarded section of the KZ wall was its western and northwestern edges where it touched the Marshallville City Police's jurisdiction. The county sheriff department and military loosely patrolled everywhere else. In the event of a lockdown or wall breach drill the state highway patrol lent help where needed. And, of course, the U.S. military held ultimate jurisdiction over the KZ itself and maintained several small posts around it. Their helicopters daily flew the perimeter, sometimes one token trip, sometimes two or three.

From conversations over the past few days she learned Evan utilized several entrances, but preferred this one for solo trips. Unlike most clients—not that she liked to think of herself as one of "them"—Billie spent time preparing herself for an arduous journey. Many tourists showed up expecting an easy time in the place as though finding a Prowler represented the hardest part of the journey.

She liked that Evan called her Billie. Old friends still did but typically only in text or Facebook messages. She rarely heard the actual word and for him to use it in the past few days seemed like an invocation to summon the past. And here stood the portal.

The infamous wall comprised concrete panels usually thirty feet high and often topped with concertina wire. Evan stood at the junction of two panels that weren't perfectly aligned. Whether an engineering flaw or a shift that occurred over time, Evan didn't know. It extended from the wall top to bottom, a small fissure inches wide and not very deep. This is where they would enter, but probably not exit. Going directly over the top was only advisable before daybreak or after nightfall since you could be seen from a distance.

She tensed, waiting for something to stop them. Evan warned that Prowlers stayed the hell out when military fired up sirens over the course of a day. No one knew what it meant for sure, other than the worst odds for getting in and out unseen or unslain. This occurred no more than twice in the course of a year and never this late, but of course this would be the time. And then the next time they tried. And the next.

But they heard no sirens on the approach and nothing now.

This is happening. I'm really going back home.

Evan put his hand in the opening. She couldn't see in the darkness but knew he'd extended his thumb and applied pressure with the tips of his fingers to lock his hand into place. They called this technique hand jamming and he used it to scale the wall. Watching him ascend reminded her of Nathan Drake, the protagonist of *Uncharted*. She and David often played the third game in multiplayer mode against online foes. What great partners they had been, covering for each other as they advanced on objectives. Great fun until their real life objectives diverged. The fourth installment of *Uncharted* debuted last May; cue the inevitable depression every time she'd seen an advertisement for it. In June she'd picked up the kids and David asked her if she'd had a chance to play it yet. He hadn't liked her answer. *Seriously, Liz? This is one of those subjects? It's just a game.* She wanted to ask if he played with his new girlfriend, Miss Stability, Miss Well-Adjusted, but she held back lest she look like Miss Instability, Miss Maladjusted.

Evan reached the top of the wall where he clung by his fingers. He had to shimmy approximately twenty feet to get to the spot where a similar crack ran down the Kill Zone side.

Billie had the option of following Evan from the ground and waiting for him to descend the other side to get a rope ladder stowed for emergencies. She told him she could rock climb, but purposely played down her skill level.

She fed her left hand into the darkness of the crack, turned her thumb, pressed the tips of her fingers against the opposite side and pulled. Tight fit. Billie angled the toes of her shoe into the gap and hoisted herself so she could put her right hand into the fissure at a higher position. She pulled her left hand out and angled her other foot to push higher. Evan hadn't used his feet in the crack but Billie didn't want to put too much strain on her arms since she'd have to climb across while holding her entire weight with her hands for a time.

Evan did a double-take when he saw her approaching along the top of the wall.

"Well, look at you," he muttered when she caught him.

"Told you I can keep up."

When Evan reached the targeted wall joint he reached into the concertina wire and unfastened a segment. The coiled wire came away from the rest and hung harmlessly to one side so Evan could hoist himself through the three foot gap. Billie patiently hung a safe distance from him until he completed the crossover amid light grunts and the sighs of concrete scrapes.

Perched on the wall with his body on the KZ side, he leaned toward her and whispered, "You cross. I'll close it. Don't get hung in the wire."

Billie pulled herself atop the wall and flashed him a smile. She found the crack on the KZ side comparable to the one they used to scale the wall.

"Wait for me at the bottom," Evan told her.

As Billie descended she replayed the words in her mind. Had there been strain in his voice? Was he tired from hanging for so long or was he perhaps upset? He warned she might see Kill Zone Evan, his description of the dour, humorless survivalist he sometimes became. In those instances she shouldn't take anything he might say personally. *Survival sometimes supersedes sensitivity.*

When she dismounted, she put her back to the wall and breathed the air. It seemed alive with an unnatural charge. Now that she'd arrived she felt different. Everything up to this had been a flirtation that could have ended well short of consummation. On this side of the wall her home no longer seemed impossibly distant.

While she waited for him she remembered a different flirtation that hadn't ended in consummation—the first night's reunion. Afterwards, they went to the Double R, a perfect replica of the original 50's-style diner at 137 West North Bend Way, Sandalwood. The place had been hopping with former denizens seeking to relive memories so Evan and Billie made their opportunity by sliding into an uncleaned booth as soon as a vacancy presented, soiled plates and empty coffee mugs be damned. By then their shared experiences opened emotional doors she thought forever locked. They shared a closeness that left her open and willing to see where it led. Yet later, when the pivotal moment came at her hotel room door, a split second of indecision ruined everything.

"I told you I don't like surprises," he said upon descending, rubbing his hands together. She saw the trace of a breaking smile as he looked away, pretending to survey for the slayer.

"Is this Kill Zone Evan?"

He chuckled and sighed.

She remembered the look on his face that night after the aborted kiss—a semi-amused expression as if he fatalistically understood and she could imagine him thinking, *Of course, this is how unrequited love should be.* Several times since she nearly kissed him, but the moment never seemed quite right. And then there was Bella. Their children kept them anchored to different locations, but even beyond that, Bella's sickness and Evan's status as a single father made his situation more complicated. What right did Billie have to become a distraction in his life?

"No waddle here." She flicked her right triceps through her long-sleeve black shirt. "I rock climb, remember?"

"From here the game changes. No more surprises."

But she had a feeling the surprises would continue and it didn't take fifteen minutes for the next.

"Check this out," Evan nonchalantly said as he led her to a break in the woods at a mountain ledge.

In the valley below fluffy white fog nestled like a vast sea of cotton. Scattered treetops and houses along the higher points of elevation broke through the cover like tiny islands in a placid white sea. The cross atop the steeple of Hill Top Baptist arose from the snow-colored veil. An errant puff of cloud floated past the sacred symbol, giving it the illusion of a periscope rising from the depths, an unknown captain surveying for souls to save. As a child Billie attended Vacation

Bible School there; as a teen she'd probably viewed Sandalwood from this very ledge—yet, this was such a new and unique experience she might as well be visiting for the first time.

Evan looked at her expectantly but any attempt at translating what she felt would sell it short. He seemed to know what she meant and nodded appreciatively.

After a loaded silence, he said, "Some nights there's an aurora borealis."

"This far from the poles? You're not serious."

He smiled. "They've made some changes since we left."

She didn't enjoy the thought of spending the night here with Agent Orange around, but it thrilled her to consider the secret world of phenomena within which had nothing to do with him. It wasn't all death and horror.

"A lot of weird electromagnetic aberrations, like you've probably read," Evan said.

"And something like that explains him, too?"

"The Energizer Bunny with a machete? Who knows. Maybe it caused him, maybe he caused it."

"What, you don't think it was because he conditioned his body to regenerate from torture when he was a POW?"

He smiled, obviously giving that theory the same credence she did. "We'll probably never know. And if they figure it out, they'll never tell us."

Soon Evan found Hilltop Road, the main route into town from the mountain. The fog still hung thick when they reached the plateau situating Sandalwood. A section of Main Street looked as one would expect with buildings in disrepair, trees in odd places, pieces of clothing and shoes dropped randomly here and there, traces of over a decade of skirmishes with Agent Orange, and heads on stakes . . . always heads on stakes. Orange marked his territory with all the panache of a pissing dog.

Anomalies abounded as well. Some structures looked to have been abandoned maybe a few months ago rather than decades, somehow surviving the elements and the inevitability of entropy. Sometimes only half the building preserved this integrity with the other half withering like a rotted conjoined twin. Shoots flourished on random branches of otherwise dead and uprooted trees. A flock of birds flew past in a gyre, like a small winged tornado.

Evan traveled on main roads whenever possible and Billie picked up that he was more likely to use a side street when obstructions kept the range of visibility to a minimum.

Suddenly he stopped and raised a hand as if an entire garrison of troops were behind him.

Then she heard it, too, loud cracks echoing distantly.

"Way south," he whispered and Kill Zone Evan returned. An intense gaze half contemplation, half . . . anger? His head shifted almost imperceptibly at first, then more noticeably as if he were reading signals drifting through the fog.

Billie was about to ask when he answered.

"Gunfire. The shots were spread. Anyone dumb enough to smuggle a gun in here would empty a magazine if Orange found him so it isn't an engagement. Unless . . . "

"What?"

"Assuming they just didn't get a chance to fire off more than a couple rounds, it's someone who knows what they're doing."

Billie dared not ask if they should turn back because she feared the answer.

Comfortable enough to continue their journey, but clearly spooked, Evan kept them moving in the same direction. Great sign. To come so close only to turn back would have sent her into the deepest funk.

"There's a new outfit in the KZ guide business," Evan explained. "One of their representatives propositioned me last month. High paying clientele, which poses its own risks. Snotty elites mistake higher premiums with increased input." He smirked. "Bringing a full tour group of six know-it-alls in here is just courting disaster."

"Lot of people if something goes wrong."

"They've been lucky so far," Evan said. "Carlson and another Prowler saw tour groups in the fall." He paused to shake his head. "The shots could have been a distraction. They lure Orange to a different part of the KZ so the tour can enter a safe area."

Billie nodded.

"Dangerous to Prowlers, though. They might lead him to one of us instead. Easy way to get someone killed."

"Do you know who they are? What can you do? Report them anonymously?"

"We don't deal with disputes that way." His face shifted. "Well, most of the time."

Evan only mentioned Carlson by name, possibly because she already knew him. These guys had their own code, which apparently involved keeping the names of other Prowlers secret even if they had some personal animosity. The cutest thing ever was that Bella also knew this code—and Carlson. She called him "Uncle Carlson" to irritate Evan.

Billie imagined Bella someday following in her father's footsteps and Evan didn't seem averse to the idea. *The KZ is surprisingly safe if you're not an idiot,* he said. But he would change his tune later. That was a distant bridge to cross and she knew Evan hoped more than anything Bella would reach the moment of crossing; certainly an argument worth having only if you *could* have it.

"Things might get a little dicey. I doubt they're bringing a tour here if they're popping off a gun anywhere besides Morgan, but I don't want to overestimate their intelligence, either. Could be thrill-seeking idiots OSnapping KZ pics."

"That happens a lot?"

Evan shrugged. "You've seen how many heads there are."

As Billie neared her childhood home she felt a glut of emotions, mostly variations on the theme of apprehension. Would it be one of the charmed places spared the ruin of lost years? If not, would she crumble with it at the sight?

It took another fifteen minutes to reach Salem Street. Giddily, she grinned when she saw the familiar red brick in the distance. Her grandfather built the place in 1940 and from this distance it looked strangely whole, even the decorative bushes half the size they should be by now. The two gables jutting from the slanted grey roof at the front of the house were a dirty off-white, but with a trace of brown that was out of place—all the windows were boarded. This was not how her mother left it; they had no warning before the evacuation and weren't allowed to return. And if they had been, they certainly wouldn't have wasted time prepping the place as though a hurricane might sweep through. They would have grabbed all the essentials they could. Other houses were boarded like this, but not very many. She hadn't asked Evan about them, simply assumed privileged owners with the right connections were allowed to empty and preserve their abodes in the event litigation prevented the wall expansion. On her street only one other appeared braced for Hurricane Orange.

"Can we get in there?" Billie asked. "Does it mean it's trapped?"

"We can get in through the back."

"You're sure?"

He nodded.

Due to her surprise at the boards she didn't immediately notice how her home and several of those nearby belonged to the delayed entropy zone, as she'd come to think of it. Weeds overran yards in a state of winter decay, but the nearby forest hadn't overtaken this street like some of the other neighborhoods; given how it practically subsumed Park Terrace just outside the business district, she expected the worst here. The Marsten house next door to hers survived in even better shape, nary a broken pane despite no hurricane proofing.

When they climbed the steps to the back porch it disheartened her to see a padlock on the boarded door. Someone spray painted ALARM INSTALLED VALUABLES EMPTIED on the wood.

She started to ask what it meant but first saw a key dangling from his finger. Her breath seized in her throat. She grabbed the key, hurried to the padlock. The key slid home and turned. The shackle popped with a click. Eyes closed, she braced herself for what she might find inside.

"Here," Evan whispered from behind her. He took the lock and found a metal sheath that ringed the shackle. When he slid it downward it covered the gap between shackle and body so the padlock still appeared to be engaged.

They entered the dark kitchen where she saw a red glow on the wall. He gently moved past her and seconds later a battery-powered lantern filled the kitchen with light. He punched a code into the keypad on the wall and the red light turned green.

"What the hell?" she asked. "Who put that there?"

"A friend runs a security business safeguarding houses from looters. We installed this years ago. Hope you don't mind."

"No, no I don't. But how? There's no—"

"Car battery." Evan opened a cabinet beneath the kitchen sink to show her.

Make that *batteries;* at least six of them beneath the sink, but only one with any wiring attached.

"Obviously we can't monitor the houses from a central office or anything, but the threat of a blaring alarm makes an effective deterrent. In ten years only one of his houses has been looted."

"Why?"

"There's plenty of easier targets."

"No, why *my* house?"

"I helped him and he set me up with a free alarm

system," Evan said as he fastened the door. "Early on looters and thrill-seekers targeted the homes where Orange killed someone—out of morbid curiosity or to collect discarded murder weapons that could be sold on the black market. You know about all the Collectors out there, scrabbling for any keepsakes they can get just to have them or they're convinced something from here might be 'magic' somehow. My house was already trashed, yours wasn't."

"Still . . . why my house, Evan?"

Yet she knew. What hadn't been obvious in the Nineties seemed only too obvious since her return. Somewhere along the way young Evan developed a hell of a crush on his former babysitter.

"You were a good sitter?" Evan smiled. Adorable how he used only "sitter" as if the prefix "baby" could taint the relationship somehow. "And, anyway, this turns out to be the best place in the KZ to store batteries for the other alarms. They don't lose their charge here. Remember this?"

He dug a nine volt battery from his pocket. Before they started the hike he had her press her tongue against the terminals but she felt no tingle because the battery lost its charge. She nodded, but instead of explaining he merely set it on the kitchen counter next to the sink.

He handed the lantern to her. "Take a look around."

Billie gave a cursory glance to the kitchen before heading into the dining room and taking an abrupt right turn to the living room. Light reflected from the glass of the aquarium set in the wall to her left, somehow still almost completely filled with water.

She assumed it would have all evaporated by now. Another strange result of the delayed entropy?

She lifted the lantern to illuminate the back wall. The urn with her father's ashes still sat on the mantel.

You're here.

Touching the cool oak surface of the urn made it real. She ran her finger around the glass rim of the built-in clock. Some day long ago the hands stopped at 10:13, yet she wouldn't have been surprised to find it ticking.

Everything was still here. She strained her eyes in the faint light. Seeing the room was like accessing a twenty-year-old memory, faded at the edges, but otherwise as familiar as if it were yesterday. It did strike her how dated the décor had become; certainly her memories carried moods and feelings and happenings, but they hadn't conveyed the fashion of the times.

They moved her grandfather's vintage smoking table, usually positioned in front of the double window, next to his easy chair to make way for the Christmas tree. Multicolor ornaments dangled from the limbs, including the special keepsake ornaments collected over the years, so many of them handmade, one-of-a-kind. The first gifts opened every Christmas morning were personalized ornaments for Billie, her mother and grandfather. She saw one dangling from a limb, a Minnie Mouse ornament with "Elizabeth Rheingold, December 25th 1989" engraved at the base. Somewhere in the armful of wrapped gifts beneath the tree were the ornaments they would have opened the morning of Christmas 1996.

The back of her hand against her mouth, she eyed

the bannister on the other side of the room, the outline of a gaudy wire peacock on the wall of the second floor stairwell. At the far right corner a dark space, beyond it the front door foyer and between that and the stairwell the doorway to her mother's room. This was too much. Too real. She felt the power of the place.

Kneeling on the carpeted floor beside the coffee table, she reached beneath the alcove on the right side and removed a heavy book. She placed it next to a crystal candy bowl full of seasonally colored M&Ms. A slow swipe of the hand across the face of the family Heirloom Bible revealed surprisingly little dust.

She carefully carried the urn and the Bible to the kitchen table, lantern atop the Bible.

Lit by a second lantern, Evan stood at the back door where he checked his phone. It vibrated a short, quick burst to indicate he set it from Do Not Disturb to Silent. She imagined him as a silent benefactor who secretly protected her from afar. She wanted to speak to the emotion rising within her. Fearing a sentimental vomit, she kept her mouth closed.

With a shrug of the shoulders she let the backpack slip off. She set it on the table where even the lace-fringed placemats held sentimental import. Soon she would carefully pack the urn for safe transport out of the Kill Zone along with the Heirloom Bible with its genealogy and other significant markings, which would prove the legitimacy of her father's remains. Though her mother wouldn't say so, she might question ashes presented by a loving daughter desperate to grant a dying wish. The Bible would leave no room for doubt. Her mother never asked for this, she'd do without rather than have anyone risk their lives for such mawkish notions, but Billie knew what it would mean.

She retreated lest the pregnant pause birth premature words.

Lantern held high, she walked to the upstairs stairwell. Passing the wire peacocks she remembered the time she ruined one of her best sweaters by carelessly passing too closely and snagging it on a wire—a meager ten minutes before Scott Grange's arrival for their first date. *Pop, look what that friggin' bird did to my sweater!* Her grandfather hadn't bothered looking up from the paper when he said, *Change it.* Yeah, and ruin her hair after she spent the better part of an hour fixing it? A smile for her dear, lost Pop. A smile for the End-of-the-World horror that paled compared to what would come...

At the top of the stairs she turned left and took two steps before she slid on the rug draped over the slick wooden floor. Back then she instinctively knew the right pace to avoid slippage. Billie grinned at the karma; she laughed her ass off at visiting friends who busted theirs.

She opened the bedroom door and gasped at the time capsule.

Her school backpack sat just inside the doorway where she dropped it on December 20th, 1996 with her school shoes next to her bed. Like a miner entering a newly drilled shaft she moved the lantern to cast light on a different vein of memories. Her dresser blocked off the wall to her left, an ancient box TV on top of it. A videotape of *A Walk in the Clouds* with a "Be Kind Please Rewind" sticker jutted from the mouth of a VCR. At the foot of her bed, left leg pulled through with a sock still inside, lay the jeans she'd worn to school that day. Jordache. She set the lantern on the TV. She tossed the sock on the bed and pulled the leg through, folded the jeans, placed them on the dresser. A small canister on the bed caught her eye. Malibu Musk.

Her breath curled through the air as she surveyed the posters on her wall. Gin Blossoms. Counting Crows. The *Romeo + Juliet* movie. On her nightstand the book she never finished, Patricia Cornwell's *From Potter's Field*, bookmarked at page 242. She picked up a frame from her night stand, a picture of her with Stacy Watson and Alicia Smith. Her hands shook.

Alicia Smith. April 14th, 1978 to December 20th 1996.

Nowadays she'd have a hundred JPEGs of her friends, but the tangibility of the photograph in the frame resonated so much more deeply. She pressed it against her heart.

Agent Orange impaled Alicia. Billie would never forget the look of surprise on her face when she saw the pipe protruding from her breast. For the longest time Alicia wandered through Billie's nightmares, befuddled by her impalement. *Why is this here?* she asked. Her death bought Billie enough time to escape—the first of several times that night. It took far longer to escape that last glimpse of Alicia, an afterimage seared into Billie's mind.

And there were other images from that night. Images far worse.

The children.

"Stop," she implored herself with a whisper.

Stirred dust tickled the back of her throat as she took the Malibu Musk to the dresser. She depressed the plastic top. Tiny droplets spurted through the air and bubbles foamed at the opening, but the weak spray died after a second. As if she performed a mystic ritual, the fragrance unlocked a door to the past, awesome in its intensity. Overwhelmed, she sat on the bed, eyes closed. A strangeness washed over her and she fell back to soak in the ambiance of all she'd lost, found again. She opened her eyes; her peripheral vision captured the trappings of a past life scattered along the walls. The still blades of the ceiling fan cast long, ominous shadows. It felt like she wandered into a place where time could not exist, a moment of stasis where December 1996 lasted forever. Outside these walls time passed as normal. She reached out and rested a hand on her alarm clock, fingers sliding along buttons with functions she'd once known by touch. It didn't have power, but if it did it would flash 12:00 always.

But time didn't stop—it didn't even slow down. Eventually she would have to leave, but this time it would be her choice and she'd depart knowing she could get here again. The place she thought lost for all time remained exactly where she left it and how she left it.

Thanks to Evan.

He's why it's in one piece. He's the sitter now.

And because of him she'd gotten her father's ashes back—her mother's greatest regret. If her mother and Pop hadn't gone to the hospital because of her they would have rescued the important things.

Billie's guilt left its own scars.

Her mind flashed to Evan and the almost-kiss. The surprise on his face as she looked away at the last moment, unable to complete a connection she herself wanted only seconds before. If he was embarrassed he hadn't shown it.

Loose fabric stirred beneath her head and she smiled because she knew what she found. She put the peach-colored nightshirt against her face and tried to tease out the scent of her former self, but not everything remained. It smelled neutral, like nothing.

Evan probably would have let her stay in her room all day. When she returned to the kitchen she found him seated at the table like a guest too self-conscious to relax, lamp extinguished, waiting in the dark.

"How is it?" he asked when he heard her bare feet whispering on the kitchen linoleum.

A subtle shift in his face when he saw she changed clothes.

"Feels like a new morning for me. I even found my old nightshirt."

"Breakfast can wait." He grinned and she knew he probably referenced a song. When he made jokes like this in front of Bella she sometimes began singing.

"Here." He gave her the battery and she knew the drill. When she pressed her tongue across the terminals she felt a light charge.

"How?"

"We don't know."

She remembered her upstairs clock, it ran on a nine volt, and the clock embedded in her father's urn used an AA battery. "The other batteries in the house . . . "

"To keep it secret the guys who discovered the

phenomena removed them. Here and in all the other places that aren't aging like they should."

She put the battery on the table with a nod.

"Words can't describe. I feel . . . " She knew the right word and, curiously, perhaps sadly, she knew the implications. She felt healed. Years too late to save her family, her marriage. The cure always awaited here like a prescription to be filled but she hadn't known the way to the pharmacy.

She settled for a "Thank you" imbued with such emotion and power she resolved to never use those two words lightly again.

It had been a long time since she felt awkward in front of her father so she whisked him to the dining room table and returned. She turned a chair toward Evan and wiped the seat before sitting down. Cold against the backs of her thighs.

"If I'd known you wore that around the house I'd have delivered your newspaper."

She smirked. "Old Jim Bob wouldn't have given up this route easily. Besides, you'd have been out of luck. The last year or so I didn't wear this downstairs. Pop lived here, you know. Nowadays they call this kind of fabric 'distressed.'"

"I'm glad it still feels like home for you."

"It's like *Fringe*. Did you watch it?"

"Yeah, but not sure I follow."

"The place is frozen in amber." She scooted towards him, clasped his knees between hers. "Just . . . without the amber."

"Cold?"

Twin confirmations answered through her nightshirt.

"Warmer than I've been in a long time, actually."

His hands went to her knees, gentle. Feigning surprise he said, "Sorry, that shirt, these legs—I'm a guy, this is how I'm programmed."

"Bad Robot."

He smiled, clearing the lingering traces of Prowler Evan. "Damn, I really like you."

"What do you feel when you come here?" she asked.

"Like I'm living Tangerine Dream's *Zeit*."

"Is that one of those symphonies inspired by the Zone?"

"No. *Zeit* anticipated the KZ, with each side like a horseman heralding the Apocalypse. Maybe no one else gets that, but I do."

"You'll have to play it for me."

His fingers left slow motion heat trails along the tops of her thighs.

"There are moments, like looking over the cloud-filled valley, with bits of a lost city poking here and there, I can close my eyes and hear those first moments of 'Origin of Supernatural Probabilities,' the sublime seduced by the sinister. You can hear the throbbing of a heartbeat and you know it's the beast and you can do nothing. Either it's seen you or it hasn't."

Her heart thrummed. His fingers moved so slowly the suspense made her ache.

"So now I know the secret soundtrack."

Gradually he leaned forward, his movements like the passage of time here, practically imperceptible. Fingers slid beneath the fringe of her shirt. She could feel their charge.

"Cellos, organ, the VCS3 analogue synth, Moog, cymbals, guitar, noise, the whispers of the dead. It's a soundscape." Elastic hooked. She felt his hot breath on her cheek. A whisper in her ear: "What do you hear when you close your eyes?"

"Breathing. Heartbeats. Skin sighing against skin." Her hands pushed against the seat. "A rising crescendo," she lifted to let fabric slide beneath her, "to a sensual symphony?" She put her feet on his knees and her own knees briefly eclipsed his face. Thin cotton up, over, down—she lifted her feet—away.

"I hear it, too."

The ancient seat creaked beneath her shifting weight. Leaning forward, she took his face in her hands, her lips lightly touched his as she whispered, "Now you've done it—gone and made me wet."

She discarded her chair, straddled his legs. Easy to imagine the house acting as a conduit to the sexual energies of a distant, younger self, channeling a raw power she felt but once, decades ago and three miles to the south in Gary Bolton's basement. Trembling, she lifted the nightshirt over her head and tossed it on the table, tipping over the small battery. Billie had never made love in this home. Perhaps, given time and the opportunity, she would have before today.

Evan's lips were a feathery touch high on her chest, drifting, floating, sweeping down the slope of her left breast to its peak.

The table vibrated loudly as his secret KZ phone rattled, its light showing through the nightshirt. The only ones who had this number were a select few Prowlers . . . and Bella.

"Check it," she quickly said, more so he would

know he had her approval to press pause than because she actually wanted him to do so.

Please don't be Bella.

And she didn't think it in selfishness, for if Bella were to text it meant something bad happened.

"Sorry." He grabbed the phone and quickly said, "Damn you, Carlson."

"Everything okay?"

"No, there's a problem in the KZ."

Billie stood to give Evan space to type a reply. Unfortunately, it seemed she channeled the entire Gary Bolton Event, including its spectacularly anticlimactic ending, at least for her. Through the mists of time came the echoes of his whiny voice: *You went too fast! What did you think would happen?*

She "thought" more than twenty seconds of passion would happen, silly her.

Billie self-consciously put her palm against the puckered Agent Orange scar even though Evan would be the last person in the world to have a problem with it.

He set his phone on the table.

"What's this mean?" she asked.

"It doesn't—"

A new message cut him off.

Shit.

She picked up her panties with her toes and slid them back up her legs. As her internal heat dissipated the room temperature nipped at her edges so she fetched her nightshirt from the table, too. She pushed her arms through and let it fall over her shoulders. When the fabric dropped away from her eyes, Evan still stood there, but not the tender version of a moment before. Like a magic trick he became the Prowler once again.

They lost their moment irrevocably to a cruel logic. They found a portal in what Sandalwood became, but its reality encroached again. It restored her to be here and see it the same as she left, to have it again, but it offered only a fleeting cure. Like a dream of a lost loved one, a temporary escape with a bittersweet awakening.

"Is it military?" she asked. A frightening prospect, particularly with her and David's already volatile custody situation.

Panic threatened to consume her. *How could I risk everything for this?* But of course she knew exactly how, and it could be no other way.

Sadly, a military sweep might be the best case scenario.

Evan looked up from texting. "No. It's him."

A black hole opened in her stomach, not coincidentally centered behind the scar Orange gave her twenty years ago.

"Carlson is grooming some kid as a Prowler. The boy took a group in without Carlson's say-so, and really wishes he hadn't now."

"Oh, no." She rubbed her arms. The temperature seemed to plummet. Ninety seconds ago she felt much warmer in nothing, but things here had a way of changing instantly. "Is this a problem for us?"

That black hole in her guts continued its inexorable pull because he wore the expression not of a seasoned pro aware how easily these expeditions could end in tragedy, but someone trapped inside his own.

Evan met her stare. "He wants us to make it one."

VII.

THOUGH NOT THE first thing his uncle taught him about Prowling, it encapsulated so much of the discipline that Adrian considered it the most important concept: *Remember, when you're in there . . . don't jack.*

Infamous for the ever-shifting nature of his conversations, Uncle Rod rejected the concept of communication as a medium of understanding and delighted in the confusion of his audience. Adrian assumed this pearl of wisdom to be another frustrating segue. It wouldn't be the last time he would ponder whether "Rad Carlson" qualified as the best teacher for this profession, but not like there were other options. This was Prowling, classified, top secret, burn-after-reading type shit, not taekwondo classes at a strip mall.

Don't . . . jack?

Never.

So . . . like, having your head lopped off because you're jacking off in the Kill Zo—

No! He looked disgusted, more so by his nephew's lack of comprehension than the embarrassing specter of self-gratification. Their blood relation also fostered his uncle's impatience and aggravation, as though the knowledge should be downloadable through a sort of genetic telepathy.

Jackers are what we call the clowns of Prowling. They're like little kids playing doctor. They know where to look to find the good stuff, but they don't know what to do with it. Then they mess around and get everybody hacked to pieces.

Not like any game of doctor Adrian ever played as a little boy, but he received the point loud and clear now.

Okay, so you mean an amateur Stalker—

Prowler, Uncle Rod interjected, finger pointed for emphasis. *There's only one true stalker in that domain.*

Right, sorry. So an amateur who gets his group killed, that's jacking.

Jacking is cause and effect. It's one mistake leading to another and another until everyone who trusted you has his head on a stake. There's no Yelp page for Prowlers but word gets around. They'll avoid your shitshow like the plague.

Adrian knew every tour counted toward repeat business and word of mouth, which held the utmost importance when you couldn't publicize your service.

You have to be prepared to act and not react. Jacking is reacting. Act. I've gone in there forty times and never seen him, but I've been ready every time. I would not have jacked.

Adrian prided himself on his maturity, accepting the gravity of this lecture with no temptation to laugh at the jargon. This was life and death, no joking matter. Something he would never disclose to Bryce for his predictable juvenile reaction.

REINCURSION

It's called "jacking"? Oh dude, that's awesome. Well, you've had plenty of practice! Hey, try not to jack when Agent Orange shows up!

Yeah, he wouldn't share *any* of this with Bryce.

So in summary . . . His uncle trailed off, waiting for Adrian to supply the big finish.

Don't jack.

Rad Carlson nodded. *Exactly. Don't jack.* Then said something cryptic which turned out to be part of a Kill Zone anecdote he shared the week before as a "teaching moment." Because Adrian, born a couple of years before the PlayStation 2 hit the market, apparently should have recognized an allusion to an Atari game called Pitfall!

Thus continued the sometimes confusing process of indoctrination to the Prowler ranks, which too often seemed like relying on World War II history from an Alzheimer's patient. But *don't jack* made for a helpful foundation.

As Adrian trudged up the hill now, he felt confident in his actions. The training took over, much like it forged a new and better version of himself throughout the past year. It gave him the courage to talk to Erica at that party a few months ago. He'd walked the world of Agent Orange seven times by that point, and while he couldn't tell her that, it still fortified him.

If he had today to do over again, of course he wouldn't take the group in. It seemed like the perfect chance to prove himself at the time, though—to Bryce, who didn't take him and his training seriously; his uncle, who seemed reluctant to hand over the keys to the family business and needed a push; and Erica, obviously.

So Adrian acted, just as he acted now.

He tried to mind his flock, provide them a clear path and take Orange out of the equation. It didn't work, but at least they escaped the first attack and now he could buy them some more time up here as a distraction. Much as he wanted to play hero and save the child, it would require a miracle.

Heroics seemed far more feasible on level ground. The grade absolutely punished his calves, with fatigue and a twinging ache seeping in that adrenaline could not counteract. He resorted to pulling himself up with branches whenever possible. Anything to put less of a burden on his legs, although he welcomed that distraction versus the overwhelming horror of his responsibility in the event any of his group lost their lives.

Another distraction—weird shit was afoot. Bryce clued him in about the change of locks before they split up. Maybe military, but he never heard of such sabotage before. They liked to catch infiltrators and parade them to prove to the world they had control of the Zone, no one in or more importantly out without their say-so. Adrian felt more inclined to perceive it as the work of another Prowler. It made for a cutthroat business strategy, in the potentially literal sense. The easiest way to phase out competition. Sinister indeed.

He let himself rest a moment, clinging to a branch as he stretched his calves to try to loosen them up, all the while listening.

Footsteps above to the far right, closing in. They would intersect if he ascended another fifteen yards. The tread sounded too soft to be Orange. Adrian checked behind him for the safest path if he needed to book it.

The shape which first emerged through the limbs looked bulky, but then he saw skin too, and blonde hair. Adrian sighed with relief.

"Hey," he called, as much above a whisper as he dared. He crept forward, ready to throw himself behind a tree. Uncle Rod claimed military rarely patrolled inside the walls, but surprising somebody could be a costly error. Not everyone followed the edict of no guns inside.

Another of Carlson's catchphrases, *Armed is dangerous.*

Adrian couldn't believe that at first. *You go into the Kill Zone without a gun?*

You bet your ass. He's out for blood no matter what, but if you go back there with a pistol or some kind of elephant gun, you're waving a red flag at a bull. Make no mistake, little boddy, he will fuck you up. Don't jack, don't pack.

(Clarification on the origin of "boddy" never came.)

By Rod's logic Orange should have attacked Adrian below in total berserker mode, but he went for the child instead and departed as if on a leisurely Sunday stroll. Like *Yeah, I stole your kid, so what?*

The figure fought through tree limbs to emerge in Adrian's plain sight, now ten yards off. She saw him before he called out again.

Erica's eyes popped, though less so than Adrian's when he saw her carrying Sarah.

Okay, that's one miracle accounted for.

"Holy shit, you got her?" Adrian whispered.

"He used her as a trap. Clark . . . " She shook her head, not wanting to reveal his fate with his daughter in tow. She needn't have worried; the girl was out like a light. Her bloody, lacerated wrists looped Erica's neck, dripping down her sweatshirt.

"Jesus!"

"I took her and ran," Erica said. "We haven't stopped since. I thought he'd look for us downhill so I kept going across."

"He didn't follow?"

She shook her head. "I think he wanted—" She mouthed the word *Clark.*

"Sit down and rest a minute," Adrian said. She looked exhausted. He helped her maneuver Sarah into a better position so they could both settle onto the tilted ground. "Let's get her wrapped up."

He tore some strips from his shirt to band around the girl's hands and arms.

"You took an insane chance." He poured some water from his canteen onto Sarah's wrists to clean out the wounds a little, then cinched a strip of his shirt around one.

Sarah's eyes flickered open slightly. "My arms really hurt, Daddy." She mumbled something else but slipped back into sleep and did not stir as a teary-eyed Erica tied the other arm. Maybe shock as much as her illness. She looked alarmingly pale.

"I'm just glad you made it," Adrian finished. He smiled. "That was pretty awesome."

Erica smiled back weakly, a ghost of her usual self, but still something that hit Adrian right in the chest. A cruel universe indeed, to give him a window to someone so alluring while she pursued a relationship with Bryce instead. He came so close. If he only dared beyond his breakthrough of connecting with her at that party and proposed later contact...but he jacked instead, in every sense of the word.

How satisfying had it been, though, when Bryce came crawling to Adrian about the KZ because he couldn't give Erica what she really wanted? Bittersweet, yes, but a glorious moment.

One that would get her killed if he didn't step up to the plate.

Erica's brow furrowed as something occurred to her. "Hey, we're locked in—"

"I know. Br—" He cut himself off before he invoked the name. "They told us by the tunnel."

He thought she'd pursue the topic more but they lapsed into a momentary silence, Erica watching the rise and fall of Sarah's chest. "Do you think this place can help her? Have you ever seen anything like that?"

Adrian shrugged. "I haven't, but I've heard stories. We call it the Fairy Pond . . . like Zelda, you know, where you restore all your life? The stuff that turns out true here sounds just as crazy as the lies."

"He couldn't be the only one changed, could he? Maybe there's others."

Adrian grinned. "Like a secret group of X-Men?"

She shrugged. "Maybe they never find out, because they're not psycho assholes shot down by the police. Or there's something else they can do besides coming back to life. Something hidden from everyone . . . maybe even themselves."

He nodded. "It wouldn't be fair if the only one was somebody like him."

"I always wondered about the G-Spot," Erica said.

Adrian's dropped jaw helpfully allowed him to say, "Oh?"

"You know, someone who got pregnant there. Or just anywhere in Morgan or Sandalwood. I bet it's happened."

"I hadn't thought of that." Having sex with Erica at G9, sure, but not her getting pregnant and giving birth to Professor X or something. An intriguing premise, provided the expecting couple's little deaths weren't trumped by larger ones before they made it out. Lore had it that despite the absence of radiation, no Kill Zone conceptions were ever carried to term, although tabloid claims abounded of special Kill Zone Babies, some even fathered by Dunbar himself.

He said, "You think Sandalwood too? I always figured it had to be Morgan Falls, whatever 'it' was."

"I do," she said, shrugging again. "Just a feeling."

He remembered how she steered them away from the tower earlier, toward Sandalwood. He wondered why the place would interest her so much.

"Well, I don't know if Omar can help Sarah," he said, "but I'm sure Orange isn't the only impossible thing here."

Erica nodded.

While far from an optimal "picnic" scenario, he couldn't help enjoying the alone time with Erica. He imagined it many times since the party, obviously fraught with far less peril and fewer children, but this still involved the core element of him and Erica with no interference. Best not allow a decapitation to spoil it.

"We better keep moving," he said reluctantly. "Here, give me Sarah for now and you take the point. Just keep an eye out for any wires."

She wouldn't be as adept at spotting potential traps but Adrian could hardly lay claim to any true expertise there. His uncle showed him a couple of active traps well off course from their usual paths, but it was like a word scramble in a foreign language—you may know *zapatos* but there was still A through Y and the rest of Z out there, many words you never knew existed.

As Adrian accepted Sarah from Erica, he noted something else she wasn't carrying. "Did Omar keep the gun?"

"Oh, yeah. Clark begged him for it but he kept it. Where'd you get it?"

"I grabbed it from a hidden box after we left the tunnel."

"But you wouldn't let anyone else bring one."

"No. Anyone gets caught outside the wall with a gun, that's a federal weapons charge and automatic prison time. We call them Lurkers. They crack down hard on them because they don't want anyone arming Orange."

Carlson had additional reasons. *People know Agent Orange is the ultimate bad-ass, but they don't understand it, not really. You put a gun in their hands and they think they have an equalizing force. You and I know that's like trying to stop a truck with a throw pillow, but that gun's gonna bail them out, no doubt about it, so they're not smart. Or you get some tool jumping at shadows, emptying a clip because a squirrel dropped an acorn. No one hit, not even the squirrel, but now he knows you're there . . . and where to find you.*

They resumed their trudge on the hill, a much

more grueling climb directly up from the tunnel than where Adrian led his group this morning, and doubly so with Sarah in tow. When Erica offered to take her back, he wouldn't put up a fight.

"Would he really set traps out here?" she asked. "The odds of someone walking through this exact spot . . . "

Adrian voiced that same skepticism in training, and Carlson gave him a strange comparison between Agent Orange and Johnny Appleseed and told him to mind his step at all times.

"Probably not, but I'm sure a lot of people felt the same way before they stepped in one." He attempted to adjust Sarah. The discomfort receded by about 0.00001%. Grant was a beast. Whatever he made as transporter, it wasn't enough.

"Sorry about the Gauntlet," he said to Erica.

"Me too—sorry I ever heard about it. We wouldn't be here."

"No, but Omar's group still would. Sarah's alive because we're here and because you went and got her. You took her from *Agent fucking Orange*. That's certifiably bad ass."

Erica laughed quietly. "Not really. He let me take her." Her voice hardened. "How could he do that to her?"

"To split us up," Adrian said, leaving the *first figuratively, then literally* unspoken.

"And now he can either pick us off or just follow until we find the others."

"Possibly."

"See? Not so bad ass."

"You still risked your life." Adrian tried to simulate the scenario in his mind. Would he dare the rescue if he found Sarah? He believed so, despite it being a pure jacker move. It lent a disturbing dimension to the psyche of Agent Orange, this deployment of moral quandaries.

He added, "I'm sorry if I was kind of harsh when we first got in."

"No. I get it now, all of it." She held a limb aside for him. "So what can we do?"

"Hopefully keep him away from Omar. I texted someone who might be able to help us, if we can just hang on long enough." The ground felt spongy under his shoes.

She released the branch and clasped his arm. "Wait, can you text Bryce too?"

Fortunately the effort etched in his face from carrying Sarah hid his reflexive wince. "Maybe once we get to the tracks. I know a couple of places where you can always send, but it's unpredictable everywhere else. Oh wait, I took his sim card so it wouldn't matter."

"Well . . . you took *a* sim card," Erica said sheepishly, stepping past him again.

"Oh." A rookie mistake on his part, though her complicity in the deceit stung a lot more than his lapse.

The Gospel According to Rad Carlson: *A Prowler who takes a tour group of his friends into the Zone doesn't have a tour group.*

Adrian understood that all too well now. How humbling to see so many of those lessons borne out, though in his defense they came from a man who called a tourist's motive to enter the Kill Zone a "McMuffin." The jury was still out whether he meant it as a joke or he didn't realize the correct term "MacGuffin." He'd claim he knew all along regardless, so Adrian never pressed him.

Erica wanted to move on from the awkwardness of her confession. "So they really can't track that?"

"I mean, you'd have to be an idiot to use anything but a burner phone in here," Adrian said, unable to pass up a little dig at Bryce, "but they can't always trust a ping in the Zone. There's a spot in Westing where you can pick up Wi-Fi from a McDonald's a good fifteen miles away."

"Weird."

"Remember the Graham Incident?"

"Sure."

The Graham Incident became big news two years ago. A disembodied voice manifested in a state park in the town of Graham, nineteen miles east of Sandalwood. Most dismissed it as a hoax but many prepared for evacuation, believing it to be a sign of an Agent Orange invasion. Seeming to blow in from Lake Zito, campers heard a male voice saying, *Agent Orange is coming! You have to come get me, please, Oh God, someone help—*. End transmission. One camper did a live stream on Facebook while goofing off and caught the whole thing ("how convenient," many a YouTube critic said after the video uploaded; fifteen million views in a matter of hours).

"My contact thinks it came from here," Adrian said. "Some kind of acoustic phenomenon, like one of those rooms where you whisper something in the corner and someone hears you way over on the other side."

"You believe that?"

"I don't *dis*believe it."

"I always thought it was fake."

Adrian pictured Agent Orange with an ear cocked half a mile away, hearing their strategy plain as day. "Let's hope so," he said.

He watched Erica as she forged ahead, focused on her backside as much to distract himself from the building ache in his arms as any carnal interest, although the latter went without saying. Her lithe frame negotiated the terrain with ease. He could only shake his head. Bryce groped that splendid ass probably every day for the past few months. To his credit he didn't brag much. Only in the beginning had he been a little more forthcoming with details. *You wouldn't believe that body naked, son*—Adrian hated when Bryce called him "son," a vivid reminder his father passed away—*it was perfect . . . the Sixteenth Chapel.* He swallowed back the bile. The most gorgeous girl who might have gone out with him now locked down with a guy in for one hell of a surprise on an art history pop quiz one of these days.

Bryce wasn't a bad guy, though. Obviously he cared or he'd blab every explicit detail about her like his prior girlfriend—sociology major, freshman, whose butt he allegedly ate "like cake frosting." He came off comparably tight-lipped and almost scared when he talked about Erica, as though she were vanishing before his eyes a little more each day. He would never disclose it any more than Adrian would admit he begrudged his friend's good fortune, but it probably weighed on their minds equally. He'd been positively lightheaded with relief when Erica requested they veer *away* from the G-Spot, almost laughing at Bryce's pouty expression.

Fresh out of McMuffins today, son.

"Oh thank God," he muttered, once more lightheaded, maybe from relief but probably sheer weariness. The last steps to the train tracks were like walking through wet cement. He sat down as carefully as he could. It couldn't have been less comfortable under his ass but still a slice of heaven.

"You okay?" Erica asked.

"Oh yeah. Let's do it again."

She smiled and Adrian's lethargy immediately improved. He became aware of a strange sensation—the beating of Sarah's heart right against his own, overlapping and not quite in sync in a continuous inner rapping. He felt more protective of her now and empowered by the resolve.

He'd brooded the past few years over his father, helpless anger over such a senseless death that overshadowed the lifetime before. There were moments of closeness like this. They were easy to forget when you fixated on the final truth—fathers died. His stupidly, Sarah's bravely. But it had to be more than the end result.

Erica remained standing. "You want me to take her?"

He did and he didn't, but he arose and gently handed her over. Sarah wrapped around Erica comfortably, like they had been doing this for years.

Adrian took his phone from his pocket and checked the screen, stretching his legs. "Damn. No signal here. I'd just tell you to go ahead and go back that way with her, but—"

"Yeah," Erica interjected, "fu . . . eff that. You said we should lead him away, so let's lead him away."

Adrian nodded and began the hike toward the bridge where they met Omar's group this morning, calf muscles pleading for a longer rest. "I was just going to say he might have circled back to intercept you anyway," he said. Which was true. More importantly as long as she had someone with her, Orange would be less likely to target her and Sarah. If he caught them alone, they were dead for sure.

He kept his cell held in front of him like a compass, waiting for a signal. Sometimes you'd get one for a quarter mile, other times a single step then right back to a dead zone.

Adrian listened beyond their steps on the tracks, swishing of fabric, labored breath. To the trees and the flutters of limbs, blankets of leaves rolling across each other like desiccated membranes, something small scurrying through dead pine needles, a bird skipping along a branch overhead and singing.

More of the Gospel According to Carlson: *Never hear what you want to hear.*

Everything seemed to belong, but he couldn't help thinking *what if I'm wrong?* Simulating stakes of life and death provided no substitute for an actual Agent Orange sighting when he knew you were in his domain.

And speaking of stakes, there were some up ahead. More of the withered remains they found this morning.

Beside him, Erica showed some strain from carrying Sarah but hid it well. "Do you know who could have locked us in? That guy who showed you the way in here, would he do it?"

Adrian almost laughed. "No, no way."

"You're sure?"

"Positive. He's . . . just trust me." As a Prowler Carlson maintained a solid reputation, apart from one tour group member complaining about "all the non sequiturs" in a forum comment. Carlson ranted to Adrian in a fashion that essentially proved his accuser correct, but inquiries actually spiked after that.

And speaking of spikes, more heads were spiked in a cluster to their right. Adrian assumed they were the same ones encountered this morning upon attaining the summit of the hill.

"If he didn't do it, did he have enemies who would?" Erica pressed.

"No, I doubt it."

"You said he kicked that girl's head when the zillionaire wouldn't pay the reward."

"He did, and the zillionaire's security kicked his ass on the spot. He pissed blood for three days. That was the end of it." Adrian found it a little ominous they were back on that topic at the same spot where he first related the tale, like one of those horror stories where something horrible happens and it turns out to be a nightmare, but the same things occur when the character wakes up.

Maybe that was why she thought of it to begin with, though.

"Oh hey, is this where we came up before?" Erica peered closely as they passed the tiers of heads.

Or not.

"Sure is," he said. Everything looked different before with the fog shrouding so much of the landscape.

They would need a contingency for this situation

in the future. Maybe stash some bolt cutters near the exit. It seemed crazy they never planned for it. Even if they couldn't imagine someone would lock them in, they relied too much on the spare key. They'd have faced the same predicament if the key snapped in the lock, which required no great leap of imagination.

But fathers died and keys broke, and he and his uncle unknowingly jacked together for all these months.

And I must never, EVER repeat that sentiment to Bryce.

"Still no signal," Erica said. It wasn't a question.

"We're due for reception. I'm hoping for an update."

"And we can text Bryce."

Ugh.

"We will. Just remember he might not get it until the Chicken Exit. The reception is better there."

Bryce's group would be closest to the wall. Unfortunately, the other side of that wall wasn't freedom but the original Morgan area. If Orange didn't back down, they were as good as dead.

Adrian clung to the hope of a rescue with no repercussions where Sarah still had a chance to be healed, but even if Carlson guided him out, he had the others to worry about. Their rescue depended upon the Chicken Exit. Under questioning Bryce and the others were sure to crack and rat their Prowler, possibly even Erica and Sarah.

He splintered from the group thirty minutes ago by his calculation. If they stayed the roughly parallel course they'd be a mile away by now, at least. The creek bed meandered through the valley, probably swollen in places due to the snowmelt.

"Anything yet?"

"Nope." He noted the slight slump of her shoulders. "I can take Sarah."

Erica shook her head. "A little further. You got her up the hill."

They crossed the bridge without incident. Adrian's phone vibrated almost the instant he reached the other side from a text received. When he tried to recreate his exact footsteps, the signal did not reappear. He held the phone out overhead, walking in a semicircle beside the tracks and back, but came up empty.

"Damn it." He gave up the hunt for the signal to check the text from "Rad C." His uncle sent it an hour ago.

calvary on way pick up at station

He held the screen up for Erica to see.

"Rad C?"

"Don't ask."

She frowned. "Calvary? I thought that was where—"

"Yeah, he meant cavalry."

"What about the station?"

"Up ahead. I was taking you there this morning for the Gauntlet."

"Any idea who it'll be?"

"One of his Prowler contacts, I guess. You ready for me to take her back?"

Adrian received Sarah in exchange for the cell phone. She seemed lighter now that he knew they were close to the signal with help on the way . . . maybe already there by now.

"You're sure we can trust them?" Erica asked.

"Yes. Whoever locked us in is long gone."

Weren't they? Someone wanted them trapped with Agent Orange to let "nature" take its course, though if they showed up to kill Adrian and his group, who could say differently? *CSI: Kill Zone* wouldn't sweep in to point out forensic inconsistencies.

It made no sense to put themselves in Orange's path to potentially distract him and likely end up dead too. Still, Carlson shared the entrance with at least one other Prowler and you had to know about the tunnel to lock it up in the first place.

Am I leading us into a trap? Am I jacking?

Adrian tried to time his breathing with Sarah's, slow and measured against his chest. He managed to calm himself a little. He had to consider all the angles and each choice felt like a ticking bomb in an action film—*Do I cut the red wire or the blue one?*

About fifty yards past the bridge another set of heads awaited them like an interstate mile marker. Adrian grew accustomed to the "decorations" during training but these stirred the initial queasiness when he first entered the forbidden zone.

Wait, that wasn't here before, was it?

The heads along this stretch always showed advanced stages of decomposition. It satisfied Uncle Rod that Orange didn't patrol the tracks and also didn't care enough to lug fresher heads here as a warning or trophy or whatever sick motive resulted in the stakes. It always struck Adrian that they would most likely end up the newest additions if Orange ever did decide to ply his trade out here again, so not such a reassuring barometer.

In that respect, it made him marginally happy to

be proven wrong. Otherwise he felt only stark horror and such a renewal of fear it was like his body forgot his prior fatigue and became some quivering shell he found his mind abruptly transplanted into.

"Jesus Christ," he said.

"Make sure Sarah doesn't . . . " Erica left it unfinished.

Ten feet from the stake they already knew. The surreal obfuscation of such a displacement—someone's head at eye level with 85% of their body replaced by a thin pole—could not delay the identity of one of them because of the beard.

Clark provided a fresh face to the menagerie. Adrian hadn't seen the conclusion of Orange's bloody handiwork before, only the artifacts from long ago. He'd thought of them like mummified remains at a museum—real people, but from a time so distant as to not seem human. He had no coping justification for this, a bearded face that moved and talked this very morning. Now it held one expression, the silent horror of eternal death, eyes open, lips parted, and parallel blood trails from the stumps of his missing ears.

The face on the stake behind wiped Clark from his memory completely for several seconds. The others in the set remained more or less intact in their limited fashion, but the third looked mangled to the point that an academic curiosity diminished some of the shock. Its face hung disconnected from the head, somehow sheared off to retain enough bone and tissue to be pinned to the rest of its skull with a stick rammed through the back of the head. The sharpened point protruded from an empty eye socket to allow it to hang side by side with the remnants of the head. Although the exposed workings of the skull bore no resemblance to a true face, the juxtaposition reminded Adrian of the comedy and tragedy masks of theater. Only the presence of the neck allowed any opportunity for this piecemeal "head" to be staked, and its point protruded through the meat of the mostly uncovered stump upon which this person's face formerly sat, like a lone tooth in an empty mouth. Ears also removed.

Sarah whimpered in his ear and he tightened his grip around her, ready to clamp a hand on the back of her neck so she didn't swivel her head around, but she merely rubbed her face against his shoulder as if trying to find a more comfortable spot on a pillow. An overwhelming moment for Adrian, this window to a traumatic horror she would never forget a yard behind her with only him to hold it at bay. He backed away from the configuration with a cursory glance at the third head, as awful in its death repose as Clark with dependent viscera from the neck. He didn't want to look, but had to assure himself he did not know either of the others.

"The ones from Omar's group?" Erica suggested.

Adrian nodded, dry mouthed. "Has to be."

Either that or it's Everyone and Their Fucking Brother Day in the Kill Zone.

Miserable timing remained a potential error, with no coordination between most independent Prowlers. Multiple groups might show up the same day all over the Zone. When Adrian asked why no one undertook some kind of schedule, Uncle Rod scoffed. *There will never be a union of Prowlers. Think about it. Who wants to be the only target?*

Adrian assumed nobody wanted to be part of a burgeoning siren song to a kill-crazy maniac either, but the logistics were easier said than done regardless. His uncle knew a few other Prowlers but hardly all of them, and withheld any he did know from Adrian—a brotherhood of secrecy, minus the brotherhood.

He continued to walk backwards, keeping Sarah turned away even when he thought Clark should be unrecognizable. Her breathing never altered, undisturbed by the hell unfolding around her. Adrian faced forward again.

Erica guided the phone back and forth, up and down in a fruitless search for a new signal, as though trying to take a picture of a bird she couldn't quite frame on the—

Erica gasped.

He walked out ahead of them from the trees, twenty yards away. No subterfuge, at first no indication he even noticed them until he took his place on the tracks and about-faced, as if following the orders of a drill sergeant.

Agent Orange planted himself in their path. Several inches of metal appeared like a magician pulling flowers from a wand as he withdrew a machete from a sheath on his belt. Adrian stopped watching the *Kill Zone Massacre* series after part four, but it was enough to know that despite his use of almost every tool in the woodshed (and a few unlikely methods such as a folding chair, umbrella, and meat thermometer), they considered the machete the gold standard of his mayhem.

Orange stood still, head cocked slightly.

"Back up," Adrian said. "Slowly. Start moving to the trees."

Erica looked at him doubtfully but edged away from him to the right side of the tracks.

Orange mirrored the move to keep her in his direct path.

Adrian stepped off the tracks to his left. Orange did not turn his way.

"Keep backing up. Don't run yet."

"Easy for you to say," Erica muttered, but didn't bolt.

Orange matched each of her steps backward with one forward, keeping the twenty-yard distance like some stalker mocking a restraining order.

Adrian went by pure instinct here. If you ran scared from a dog, it would chase you. Agent Orange wouldn't magically desist but perhaps Adrian could at least conduct the terms of which one he chose.

He's targeting her because I have Sarah and I'll be easier to catch up to.

Adrian crossed the tracks to Erica and held Sarah out to her. He whispered, "He'll come for me now. Go to the Gauntlet point. When you're able to text, reply back to Rad C. Don't use any names."

Erica stuffed the cell into her fanny pack and took Sarah. Orange stayed rooted to the spot, back in scarecrow mode. A deeper chill seeped into the air which Adrian did not entirely attribute to the loss of Sarah's warmth.

A slight glare on the plate of the gas mask obscured his face, like a beam of light hitting the point of a blade. The ears on his necklace looked fresher than before, six of them.

Sarah relinquished, Adrian stepped back to the other side of the tracks, trying to decide if he should enter the woods or go back across the bridge when Orange pursued him.

Except Orange didn't move an inch. Adrian might as well have handed Erica a purse or a selfie stick.

"Hey!" he shouted, waving his hands over his head, jumping up and down. "Hey! It's me you want, you child-killing pussy!"

Orange still did not look his direction. Erica gave Adrian an uncertain look and backed up, Sarah in tow.

Orange advanced a step.

No!

Adrian shoved a hand under his shirt, index finger extended to form a point at stomach level. "You got a gun, dickhead? I do!"

Lo and behold Orange actually did tilt his mask his way, for roughly one second. It was like something out of *Robocop*.

Threat assessme—nope, threat dismissed, back to slaying the adult female and girl child and ignoring the puny male.

Erica continued to reverse, Adrian and Orange both keeping pace with her from their respective sides. He stooped to grab a rock from between the railroad ties and chuck it. He sacrificed velocity for accuracy and struck his target in the shoulder, but Orange showed no interest in the assault, belying years of accepted Prowler wisdom. The necro-challenged weren't above tunnelvision, it would seem.

Adrian cupped his hands for a megaphone effect. "Your mother sucked war protesters' cocks and let draft dodgers do it in her ass! She 69'd Jane Fonda!"

No reaction, at least not from him—Erica looked mortified by the outburst.

Oh God, it's not working.

They drew even with the three heads now. If he woke up Sarah now and she saw her father displayed . . .

Heads.

"Switch with me," Adrian said.

"This isn't working!"

"It will. Get ready."

She passed him across the tracks. Erica's mirror image followed suit twenty yards away.

"Sorry about this," Adrian muttered. He queasily grabbed the stake with the facially extracted head, not quite able to desecrate Clark's even if it would spare Sarah the sight for sure. He ripped it from the ground. The dangling flesh slipped off the stick like a shirt from a hanger and "face-planted" on the ground. He shook free the rest of the head, where it rolled into the trees and apparently kept going, judging by subsequent thumps and cracks.

"Come on, you motherfu—oh, shit!"

Orange broke into a sprint before Adrian spit it out. He took off as well, opting for the bridge. Downhill momentum would be too much to stay upright, although as fast as Orange rushed him, staying upright on the bridge might take some miracle work too.

Adrian glanced back quickly to ensure Erica vanished into the tree cover and Orange ignored her. The good news was he seemed to have forgotten Erica existed, so mission accomplished. The bad news was pretty much the same thing.

He ran beside the tracks as long as he could, but

the drop-off came quickly and he had to drift back to the rail ties and hope he didn't stumble. Orange never strayed from them, the thud of his boots heavy upon the treads.

Adrian ran much faster than seemed possible moments ago but not fast enough. Those footsteps closed in with terrifying speed. He wouldn't make it halfway across before Orange caught him. The stake didn't make a formidable enough weapon for any kind of stand. One true thrust and wow, Agent Orange might need stitches. One swing from his machete and Adrian would need a mortician.

It left him with two options for any shot of survival—left or right.

Orange wielded the machete with his right hand so Adrian launched himself to the left, springing at the last as if from a diving board. His last words before the sprint seemed appropriate now too, so he employed them again at a louder volume—"*OHHH SHIIIIIIIIIIIIIT!*"

The whistle of the machete split the air behind him and a burning trail of pain opened across Adrian's back.

His arms pinwheeled like he could swim through the air. The nearest tree to the bridge stood at least twenty feet away and probably more, a distance he'd never reach with a jump on level ground, but falling forward it magically drew nearer as though the top of the tree were hauled back and sprung loose. In fact, it seemed to rise to meet him much too quickly.

Adrian somehow left his stomach back on the bridge and it spooled behind him to catch up, like the ring cord of a talking toy. He knew he should loosen as much as possible to brace for impact, but his body knotted up instinctively as he hurtled toward the pine tree, dimly aware if he didn't walk away from this landing his final words on this mortal coil would be *OHHH SHIIIIIIIIIIIIIIIT*. But that was probably a common sign-off in these parts.

He angled his body to the side at the last moment, rather than approach the tree as though trying to hug it. Whatever happened from that, it wouldn't finish too well for his balls.

Small branches jutted below the Christmas tree-like apex and then a row of larger limbs which didn't look especially strong. A bare patch opened to the trunk beneath those, like a passing giant tore out a clump. He counted on the longer row to break his fall without breaking him in the process. He fell so much faster than he expected. He tossed his makeshift spear to steel himself.

Adrian hit with arm and shoulder first, snapping through the frail branches up top and passing through them as easily as a subway turnstile. The thicker limbs offered the sturdier resistance of a heavy thump but he plunged through them as well, past the bare patch and into the next layer. A few of the broken branches came with him. The next row bounced him slightly to put him face up for a shaky view of shuddering limbs and spinning sky as he crashed through more needles and boughs until something stopped his descent with a jolt that punched the wind from him. He strained red-faced for the air that had been all around him a moment before. Pain flared in his bicep. He pictured an eventual bruise deep and wide enough to look like its own shirt sleeve. Several other areas complained in tandem along his arms, ribs, hips, legs, places where the tree blocked him or cut him on his way down.

His leg hung draped above him with the rest laid out in cruciform across a cradle of limbs. A particularly large branch formed the backbone of the "net" which stopped him. Adrian managed half a sit-up, mouth agape like someone laughing so hard no sound could come out. Finally his lungs agreed to function again and he breathed in, shallowly. His lowest ribs throbbed in protest; he probably broke a few. His body shifted like an accordion. Adrian cried out as he unhooked his leg from the limb and reached up to use it as a lever.

But I made it.

Broken ribs, cuts, and bruises aside, he hadn't killed himself with the jump or broken anything he needed to run. Never mind such an action seemed unthinkable at the moment.

He yanked himself upright, wincing, a small fire burning in his side. He angled his head to see through the haphazard collection of twisted branches to the bridge.

Though it would mean Erica and Sarah only received about a minute head-start for his trouble, some hopeful part of his mind imagined Orange forming a begrudging respect for him.

Whoa, didn't see that coming. That guy has balls of steel. Maybe I should let him g—

The shape exploded from the side of the bridge as if fired. No flailing limbs or *OH SHIIIIIT!* shriek of horror, just a silent missile with the machete raised as if he planned to split the entire tree down the middle.

Adrian made a pained gasp of despair. No reprieve after his full body concussion. Orange didn't want to make a stalking game of it. The movies were the movies and this was a sprint to the finish line.

With only a slight lead, he didn't want to use the branches like a ladder. After risking thirty feet of open air, a drop into any open passage seemed a negligible risk.

He grunted as he bounced off more branches. The tree sucker punched him in the worst of his wounds. He managed a good ten feet before the camouflaged form struck the treetop like a lightning bolt. Orange hit with a far greater velocity and something huge shattered overhead.

The tree hooked the worst sucker punch of all, sticking a branch in the fork of Adrian's legs. His weight crashed into it, and his previous balls of steel became a sorry rumor. Sickening pain erupted in his gut. He rolled off to keep moving, choosing the less splintered side of his ribs.

Curiosity got the better of him when he heard so much splintering and cracking overhead and he risked a look up. Orange broke the tree up top and followed when it snapped over, riding it down like the atomic bomb at the end of *Doctor Strangelove*. Limbs weakened by Adrian's passage effortlessly broke apart and permitted Orange to make up half of the lead. He hung on to the machete, which renewed Adrian's escape effort despite the volcanic waves of nauseating agony.

I have to get to the bottom so I can chop it down and kill the giant, he thought irrationally.

His stomach a rolling ball of acid, he deliberately

stepped out into emptiness where the nearest branch in the trajectory didn't look strong enough to support a well-fed squirrel. Sure enough it snapped underfoot and Adrian left his stomach behind again, the trunk flying past as he dropped faster and faster. He groped and another weak limb came off in his grip. He wasn't slowing down at all.

Adrian dropped the broken branch and clutched again. This time he gripped something wispy which drooped and splintered at its base, but did not rip clear from the tree. It swung Adrian into the trunk like a small vine.

He coughed from the impact and felt the world sway at the sight of tiny flecks of his blood on the needles. He wiped his lips with the back of his hand. It came away with a red smear.

He stalled for a moment, overwhelmed by the repercussions. It was more than the burning pain on his left side, he now realized. An invisible foot stood on his lung to keep it from filling. One of the broken ribs must have punctured it. Trying to run away would be futile.

A loud *whooomp* alerted him he wouldn't get a chance in the first place. Twenty feet below on the ground, Orange rose from a crouch, the blade in hand. He jumped all the way down and seemed none the worse for wear. The gasmask stared back at Adrian as if to say, *Your move, bitch.*

In the ensuing silence he finally noticed the sound of the rushing creek. He couldn't see it through the tree cover but would have been able to follow it to the others.

So close.

He coughed again, felt moisture on his lips and chin.

I'm dying.

He meant it as both process and inevitable conclusion—he could leap to the nearest tree, stay here, climb up to make Orange pursue him, or drop down and face the slayer, but each alternative resulted in death. As *Choose Your Own Adventure* scenarios went, it left much to be desired.

Something prodded his arm as he leaned back against the tree.

The stake!

Or what remained of it from Adrian's midair spear toss. Now snapped in half, it remained two feet in length with the stake itself intact and appreciably sharp, streaked with dried blood and a clump of stringy tissue.

Adrian returned his attention below. "You gonna—"

He meant to say *give me a chance to get down for a fair fight,* with some spontaneous and insulting profanity at the end, but his voice came out in a wheeze and something like reflux in his throat forced him to shut his mouth. He fought not to retch from the coppery taste.

He scaled down another ten feet. Orange closed in when Adrian reached a safe distance to drop down. He shouldn't have expected any kind of gentleman etiquette to a duel with a guy who snatched up a child and wrapped her in barbwire, but felt a streak of aggravation anyway. He wouldn't have apologized for the Jane Fonda crack even if he'd had the voice.

Adrian broke off a sizable branch and tossed it

down. Orange swatted it with the machete, cleaved it in half as easily as a sheet of paper. He used the distraction to drop the last ten feet, wishing he just aimed for this spot from the bridge in the first place to cheat Orange of the chance to butcher him.

Yeah, then he would have turned back and taken it out on Erica and Sarah.

Adrian stood up shakily. The stake seemed laughable in his hand, like a toy, though if he traded weapons with Orange, he'd probably still feel the same way.

Orange came for him. Adrian held the stake in front like a full spear, anticipating the agony that would result from any movement of his ribs. It had longer reach than the machete at least, so when Orange reached striking distance, Adrian lunged with both hands. Given his own mire of torment, he aimed for the balls.

Orange sidestepped and swiped the machete with mechanical reflex, a seemingly unmissable target now in profile. Adrian held on to the spear, a surreal touch to the sight of his hands and forearms in a bed of dead pine needles upon the ground while the remainder of his arms flailed helplessly above, soon saturating the ground with crimson jets. Despite the premium on air, Adrian tried to scream. He only managed a choking and coughing fit.

The stumps of his arms continued waving at their new diminished lengths. Blood jetted in buoyant bursts, alternating in intensity—the right side initially more vibrant, then the left—like he still had the hands to squeeze tubes of red paint on the forest floor. It leaked less urgently from the estranged forearms without a beating heart to propel it, but still formed an impressive puddle at his feet.

Adrian looked from his hands to his arms, the expression of his face seeming to repeat the same word over and over: *But . . . but . . . but . . .*

Orange observed the torrent and torment for a moment, some of it splattering his camouflage and anointing the ears of the necklace, standing close enough for Adrian to see the rapture in his eyes—a believer blessed with a front row seat to a miracle. If only to spare himself the sight, Adrian spat blood and bile at the gasmask plate. A scarlet starburst obscured a portion of the face, but the white of one eye hung in stark contrast, no longer rapturous. Now it held fury at the heretic who would desecrate his shrine and attempt to blind him from his glory.

Adrian tried to drop to the ground and hope Orange let him bleed out without further festivities, but a gloved hand snatched him by the throat and held him in place. His phantom limbs flew to pry the arm away but merely bled helplessly on his adversary. Orange's other hand whipped the machete through the air and slammed it into Adrian's flank, right into the point of impact from the tree.

The machete cleaved through his torso with surprisingly little resistance, a gray blur from the left that appeared to the right with pendulum-like efficiency. He watched in numbing horror as his legs folded beneath him and dropped away while he stayed upright, the gaping cavity of his lower half canting to the ground with a protrusion of spine. Wet sounds ensued, like a pile of banana peels slapping the earth. The innards not already evicted sluiced from the open gorge of the lower half, tubes and membranous sacs poured across the nettles as if from a burst garbage bag.

Numbing horror also because he didn't feel a thing despite witnessing the bifurcation, the plug pulled on his nerve centers forever.

But I led you away from Erica and Sarah, asshole, I—

Then he was falling, slung to the ground in the middle of the landfill of his own remains.

VIII.

I **JUST WANT** to go home," Shelly said. Her new mantra.

Tina folded her close, wishing their circumstances allowed Shelly to take more pictures. She established order that way. After the tunnel, she bounced back quickly from her meltdown by focusing on the camera. Even with the heads by the railroad tracks, the process distanced her from the horror through an alchemy of framing, control, and the illusion of observation numbing the reality of her participation. The JPEGs of their expeditions were less an archive than a calming mechanism, one Shelly herself might not have realized.

No one would condone the pictures now, like irate characters in a found footage movie demanding the chronicler *stop filming everything* and *get that camera out of my face!*

So Tina kept Shelly near and made assurances she believed . . . mostly.

Shelly sniffled. "My mom's going to kill me if he doesn't."

Tina squeezed her in a lumbering hug. "Same."

"They'll kick us off the team." She looked up sharply. "We might get expelled!"

"Oh, no way, don't think like that." Tina hadn't followed this path of logic to its grim conclusion, but Shelly needn't worry because she wouldn't be able to afford school anyway once they stripped her scholarship. Might as well fret over the spelling of her name on a mug shot.

"Do you think Erica's . . . "

"She's fine," Tina said, surprised this automatic lip service rang true on further inspection. "She always lands on her feet. We will too. You'll see."

Shelly nodded. "We just need a little luck."

Tina held in a humorless laugh. It sounded so simple, but after crossing paths with Orange and getting locked out of their escape, they'd have to start shitting four-leaf clovers to receive *a little luck*.

"I just want to go home," Shelly repeated.

Bryce bolted past them at the sight of Omar, who guided the little girl's mother. What was her name? Megan? She took measured steps, like a drunk on a sobriety test. The behemoth Grant followed close behind Bryce to lend his support to Megan.

With no further incident, they slowed a mile from the drainpipe to catch their breath and give the others time to catch up—hopefully sans pursuer. It seemed a good sign Omar had time to lead the woman in such a state.

"Where's Erica?" Bryce asked, obviously on the edge of panic.

"She and Clark went after Sarah," Omar said. "Orange took her up the hill."

"She went after *Orange*? That's insane!"

Tina tended to agree, but that was also pure Erica. Fearless and not more than a little reckless. She never understood Erica's attraction to Bryce. He adored her and his face looked ready to crumble at Omar's news, but as a good match for Erica? He may as well have been the key to the padlock they couldn't open on the drainpipe.

She deemed Clark a goner for sure, so that was a nice surprise, but he didn't seem to mind testing his good fortune.

Omar let Grant take over with Megan. She'd managed to put an arm around Omar's shoulders; she had to settle for Grant's waist.

"She's still a bit dazed," he told the giant. "Seems to be coming around, though."

"Is she talking at all?'

"She said, 'The boat can leave now, tell the crew.' But she started making sense after that."

"I can hear you," Megan announced.

"What about Adrian?" Tina asked.

Omar pointed up the hill.

"But a gun isn't going to do jack shit!"

"I've got the gun."

"Jesus Christ, they didn't even take it?" Bryce looked equal parts bewildered and terrified.

This is good news, Tina thought, though careful not to say so. "We need to go back. If you've got the gun, you can shoot off the padlock! We can get out of here!"

Shelly pulled out of Tina's arm to stand up straight, eyes brightened behind a veil of tears, a look somewhere between hope and zealotry.

Omar shook his head. "It's not as simple as it looks in the movies. And with that padlock on the inside, there's just as good a chance of blowing our own faces off."

Shelly reverted from newfound hope to desperate drowning victim. Tina took her hand and squeezed.

The sun reduced the fog to patchy wisps, all but eliminating it as a smokescreen. Orange could blend in with the terrain in his camouflage, might be watching them right now from above. Tina saw only columns of trees along the hillside like the quills on a massive porcupine. The babbling creek disguised their movements but allowed the same advantage to anyone creeping up on them.

"Let's keep moving," Omar said. "You good?"

He meant Grant, who nodded, but looked stricken over the news about the little girl. A good thing Bryce stole all the thunder with his fear for Erica. Better for Megan if they didn't dwell on the whereabouts of her daughter, whose condition just grew exponentially more terminal. Her terror must be near paralyzing, although Tina felt a good approximation of it with her own life and Shelly's hanging in the balance.

Shelly never would have come if not for her.

Erica's crazy! What if we go in there and he sees us?

But what if we go in and he doesn't . . . which he won't. We'd see one of the most secret places in the world.

Or we could end up on the registry. I went to school with a guy who got busted and he says he wouldn't have a job now if his uncle didn't hire him. That's happened to a bunch of people.

See, there you go. Lots of survivors who probably didn't even have a Stalker.

But most of them got caught before they made it in—

Shell, come on . . . there's three towns in there. It's huge. The chances he'll just happen to be where we're going are sooo remote. Robb Stark was still the King in the North on Game of Thrones *the last time someone got snuffed in there. It's been forever. We're not going to get caught. And we're not going to get killed.*

Yeah, that's what everyone who got "snuffed" thought too.

But they probably didn't have a Stalker. I bet it's safer than Funland. Didn't some kid get decapitated on a roller coaster last summer? Seriously, the chances of running into him are sooo remote. Besides . . . I'll protect you.

That cracked them up, the idea of Tina the protector versus the killer elite. She hadn't been entirely joking, though, and felt herself more capable than many would credit.

Now *sooo remote* felt more like the chances of everyone getting out alive.

She consciously loosened her grip on Shelly's hand before she started grinding the bones together. They trudged alongside the gurgling water, the steepness of the hillside diminishing beside them. A thick layer of leaves blanketed the earth, one more reason to stay near the creek—six people crackling through that would be a dead giveaway, emphasis on the dead soon enough.

Each step took them farther from the pipe, from one certain exit to an unknown that ultimately involved the military and the registry if it even paid off.

She flashed back to eight years old when she, her

parents and older sister Brittney went to the zoo. There were several exits, but they didn't find their way to one before somebody started locking up the gates at closing time. Her parents bickered as they tried gate after gate on the zoo map to no avail. Firmly in the too-cool-to-care stage of high school, Brittney shut them all out with an iPod. Tina followed along, certain they would have to stay in the zoo overnight. Her dad could not drop what he felt to be the salient point: *We came in through Gate C and we goddamn well should be able to leave through it.*

She understood his frustration all too well now. They entered through the pipe barely an hour ago, they had a key, but they were locked in the zoo all the same. More specifically, in the same cage as the star predator.

Tina wondered if that incident planted the seed for her fascination with exploring because despite all the trepidation, she recalled palpable excitement too...a thrill to be where they weren't allowed. By junior high she hung out at construction sites a few blocks from her house after all the workers packed it up for the day, wandering unfinished rooms without rails or even walls to keep her from plunging to the ground floor. Later, sneaking into her high school a few times and wandering the empty corridors, reveling in the thrill of the forbidden emptiness, like a haunting waiting to happen.

A car gave her greater access to such destinations, which forged a quick bond in college when she met Erica, who found the hobby tantalizing enough to the point of developing her own obsession. Abandoned factories, houses, strip malls, an old sanitarium once. All without incident but never boring, and lured them into a false sense of security that it would always be like that. So it hadn't taken long for one of them to say, *You know what would be really cool to see . . .* and the other knew the answer immediately.

This had been the year before Shelly enrolled, before Bryce met Erica, though she and Shelly would go to some of these places too in the service of adventure and Shelly's photography.

Now they were here in the ultimate forbidden place and holy shit, had it been amazing up until the peril skyrocketed. To that point they hadn't seen any buildings but the atmosphere absolutely saturated her, unmatched by any other trespass. She knew Erica felt something comparably seismic, and sensed they both privately pondered the same thing—how soon they could get back.

Now, though, she only cared about getting Shelly far away from here.

She wasn't ready to abandon the drainpipe discussion. "There has to be *something* we can use."

Omar gave Tina a tired look and seemed grateful when Bryce began a round of follow-up questions. "They went unarmed?"

"No, I gave Clark the rebar."

"Rebar?" Bryce repeated, on the verge of hysterical laughter. Versus Orange, it'd be like hoisting an umbrella in the shadow of a tsunami.

"*Rebar*?" Tina joined the chorus, her inflection a different sort. "If Clark comes . . . " She caught herself when she noticed another fog clearing—that of Megan's eyes. "*When* Clark comes back with that, we can use that on the lock. We should be going back there to meet him now!"

She went as far as to stop in her tracks, yanking Shelly's arm to force her into the show of solidarity. The others moved past like water around a rock.

Omar's tired expression turned to fire. "I tried to pry it open *and* I tried to break it off! It's not happening, so forget about that damn pipe!" He moved on without a look back.

An *ow* from Shelly alerted Tina that she reactivated the death grip. She intertwined their fingers so she'd be less inclined to squeeze.

Paranoia stirred the butterflies in her stomach. She wanted to point out nobody from her group officially died yet, so maybe Omar wasn't the best authority on what to do now. Not to mention most of his group wouldn't fit inside, and even if they rescued Sarah, she looked too weak to pull herself out of the daylight at the mouth of the tunnel, much less the full crawl ahead.

Still, if they went back and couldn't get inside, they might serve themselves to Orange on a platter with gunshots as the dinner bell.

If Omar's group hadn't put Orange on their trail, their odds of survival would be immeasurably better, but at least it alerted them to the tunnel sabotage. They'd have come back to find it waiting for them regardless and better to know now where they could figure out something before nightfall.

"I'd like to know who the hell locked you in here in the first place," Omar said.

They speculated while waiting for the others. No one else knew about their trip. They were blindfolded, but Adrian and Dusty must have watched for a tail.

It was probably the military, Grant said.

Bryce, who nearly wore out the ground pacing for news of Erica, snapped, *Bullshit! They'd never do that!*

Grant let it drop, though he could have bitch-slapped Bryce's head 360 degrees. His outburst stunned Tina, but she understood it better now. The latest Darwin Award nominee who scoffed at the danger of a place called the fucking Kill Zone hadn't trended for a few years, in the wake of a hashtag campaign discouraging just such recklessness called #stopthecarnage. What if it never truly stopped and the military covered it up? You didn't want to publicize it if you suspected a family member came to a gruesome end here, no more than admitting they died in a masturbation mishap from autoerotic asphyxiation—or the double whammy of both, since the KZ promoted all sorts of new psychological disorders and kinks.

This line of thought brought the G-Spot to mind. Tina hadn't counted on that particular consummation for their expedition knowing Shelly's nervousness, nor had she much wanted it herself. Screwing in the Tower had all the allure of eating someone out on a public toilet seat; the none-too-fine line between the high of the forbidden and sharing needles outright.

Erica privately downplayed the possibility with her and Bryce but she dressed accessibly enough. The thought of those two going up there to get it on? Gag City.

"Do you think they've reported us missing yet?" Shelly said.

"Babe, it's still morning. No one knows we even left."

"Ugh. Feels like we've been out here forever."

"Just a little further, Shell. We're getting there."

They'd dated almost a year, long enough to know her girlfriend didn't prevail as the coolest head in a crisis. She freaked out once after Tina tagged her in a picture on Facebook, worried her mom might see it and deduce their relationship went much deeper than "study buddies."

Tina's own mother was supportive. Her dad seemed uncomfortable but made a valiant effort at encouragement. The only friction came from Brittney, who dismissed it as "a college experiment you'll grow out of." The "experiment" began as early as middle school, but whatever. She brought Shelly home for Thanksgiving and it went well enough.

In Shelly's case, apparently Mrs. Creed would have shipped her off to a camp to pray the gay away if she diagnosed the symptoms early enough, and that sort of iron fist rule established a lifelong pattern of inhibition for her daughter. It sounded like dear old mom would have volunteered to warm up the tongs during the Inquisition.

Tina enjoyed pushing Shelly to overcome those little neuroses and face her fears. It brought them closer together, and she found it rewarding to see Shelly surprise herself. She intended today to be the crown jewel of achievement, the one where she could forever say, "Come on, Shell, you went to the Kill Zone and you're scared about doing *this*?"

This one might end up undoing all the prior progress.

"We should be getting close to the wall," Omar announced, a little breathlessly. Their strides became longer and quicker. He toweled the sweat from his forehead with a bloodless patch of his shirt tail. "He's supposed to stay away from there. We can check the map and figure out a Chicken Exit, maybe find a checkpoint. Get help for the others too."

Wall selfies on the way out, Adrian said at the tunnel. Following the creek wouldn't be the most direct route, but they must be close even if the stream would of course not run through it. Any minute now they should see it towering over smaller trees or they'd reach a clearing to find it waiting for them. All the taller trees were razed near the wall so Orange couldn't scale one and clamber over the top.

Omar echoed the optimism about the wall aversion as presented in the *Over the Wall* book—a glorified pamphlet, really Erica loaned her and Shelly last month.

Subject Zero avoids the parameters ("He means 'perimeters,'" Shelly said. "Did anyone even edit this thing?"). *There aren't enough outposts to cover all of it, but they can get there in a hurry. Electronic defensive measures would also be more reliable, allowing the military to send a tracker missile to greet him with a quick hello and goodbye.*

Yep. The wall. Safety.

Any minute now.

Her assurances to Shelly came back to haunt her. Yes, the odds seemed minuscule of running into Orange in an area so big. And apparently so big, the ends were no hop, skip, and a jump either.

"We can't leave the others behind," Bryce said.

Even though they pretty much already had, Tina noted.

"They have a Prowler," Omar said.

"Oh, come on, they weren't even together!"

"We can't offer better help than armed soldiers."

"You're not the only one who wants to go back," Grant added a little heatedly.

The one-two combo brought Bryce up short.

"No one's stopping you," Omar continued, "but we don't know where to find them. They know where to find us. Your best bet of seeing her again is to keep going this way."

"Clark's going to bring them back," Megan said resolutely. "We'll make Sarah well again. Everything's fine." She smiled horribly, broadcasting somewhere between shock and concussion.

Grant kept her trained forward with a wistful countenance.

Tina ached in a thousand places and could barely imagine running another step, but of course she would. After Orange's appearance back by the tunnel, she could have run up the side of a building and kept going into the sky.

Perhaps subconsciously, she brought up the rear like the initial foray with Adrian, this time locked in step with Shelly. Grant led Megan ahead of them, then Bryce, with Omar on point. She gave Bryce a sympathetic smile when their eyes met as he paid another forlorn look down the creek, another fruitless prayer for Erica.

Something changed in his face, neither horror nor hope, but Tina's pulse promptly spiked.

"Hey," Bryce said. "There's something . . . "

Not panicked, just uncertain.

Tina spotted it a moment before Shelly pointed at

something in the water about forty yards off. It bobbed closer to the opposite bank thirty feet away but the current pushed it closer to their side.

"Is that a . . . a bag?" Shelly asked.

That was Tina's own best guess. She discounted it as something from a tree immediately. While not as strange as a train rushing out of a fireplace, it still seemed a marvel of sorts. One didn't expect to see anything manmade like this discarded in an area evacuated decades ago.

Tina flinched at a high-pitched shriek behind her. Megan. Grant's barrel chest thankfully muffled her as she threw herself against him. Everyone went on red alert to take to their heels again, but since Megan stayed put, she obviously hadn't seen Orange.

"Oh my God," Shelly said. She took her hand from Tina's and covered her mouth.

It wasn't a bag after all. Its compact size suggested nothing human, but no mistaking now that it was part of a torso floating "waist" first, if that could be said of something that didn't truly have a waist. More like sternum first. The arms were tortoise-like where the limbs were hacked away. A stark white nub poked from the open cavity.

That's someone's spinal cord. The thought came from far enough away in Tina's mind it might have been the whisper of a telepathic voice.

The world's goriest flotation device rolled in a circle to reveal the ugly jagged stump of the neck with a matching vertebra nub.

If Megan hid her face for fear this detruncated piece belonged to Clark, it wasn't necessary. The flat, hairy chest left no doubt of a male origin, but much too slight and slender for her husband. No less awful for its unknown identity, though, and reason enough to turn away.

"I think those are the arms," Shelly said, her voice amplified behind her hands.

Farther back, Tina saw what looked like two branches peeled of all their bark. She swallowed back bile, overwhelmed by the madness of this moment. Forty-eight hours ago she flipped through the course catalog for next semester, her biggest worry the lack of literature courses in the later afternoon, and now this portrait of insanity.

Bryce looked absolutely gutted. He obviously expected Erica's torso next in the convoy.

Or what if it's the little girl?

Grant practically held Megan upright now, her legs bent and quivering. The torso nearly passed them, now five yards from their side of the creek, but the arms would need a few more seconds. They should at least let those pass out of sight before they tried to force her to walk. The sense of unreality threatened to consume Tina again, pontificating these finer points of the etiquette of mutilation.

Only Shelly turned her back. Tina automatically embraced her, as much for her own comfort as Shelly's, a little light against the wave of darkness crashing around them.

Over her shoulder, Tina saw something arc toward them like a strange featherless bird. Before her mind made sense of it, she tightened her arms around Shelly and tried to pitch them to the right, bracing for impact—both from the ground and the projectile she now understood to be an arrow. She heard the *thunk* of metal through flesh before she struck the ground with Shelly on top, the air pounded out of her lungs. She expected a burst of pain but felt only the torment of drowning with oxygen all around her.

Overlapping panic from the others.

"—down! The trees—"

"—come from—"

"—you see him?"

Tina shifted her head from side to side, searching for a magic pocket of air. Finally some of it accepted her invitation and hesitantly filled her lungs, hampered with Shelly still on top.

On top and motionless.

The others were far less inhibited, crawling, crouching, rolling, diving behind the trees flanking the creek. Megan flailed as Grant picked her up and carried her to cover.

"Shelly." Tina barely managed above a whisper. She tried to worm her way out from beneath.

The arrow jutted from Shelly's back like a flag pole. Tina noted the sting of a small cut on her arm, sliced by the arrow on its path to an involuntary human shield. The one she said she would protect.

With Tina halfway free, Shelly suddenly reanimated, her face contorted by agony.

Tina clasped her as though to absorb her pain, but only her own remained from the sense of crushing guilt. A mutilation of soul, not of flesh.

She hauled Shelly by the wrists, watching for another arrow.

I was supposed to protect her I was supposed to protect her I was supposed to—

She tried to shut down the news crawl of regret. Nothing would absolve this, not entirely, but she would have chances to make it up and it all started here.

Omar ducked out from cover to grab hold of Shelly too and they managed the last fifteen feet quickly, Shelly sobbing miserably. Omar used the opportunity to snap the arrow as near to the entry wound as he could without pulling it out.

"It won't get caught on so much," he explained, tossing the fragment aside.

"You're okay, Shell," Tina said. How easily one lie led to another—nothing will happen in there . . . I'll protect you . . . you're okay.

"Did you see where it came from?" Omar asked.

"Other side," Tina said. "But a long way."

"You're sure?"

She pictured the long descent of the arrow in a slope rather than a direct flight across the creek. She nodded.

Omar edged as little of his face around the trunk as he could for a look. Tina did the same on the other side.

She felt him before she saw him, the sharp awareness of an anomaly in the normal world of five senses and eternal death. An icy hand enfolded her stomach and clenched tight. She knew right where to look, back and beyond the creek where the slope of the hillside evened at last into level ground. He hit Shelly from a ridiculously long range, maybe two hundred fifty yards.

Agent Orange only reached the halfway point but he barreled forth at a reckless rate that would have surely face-planted anyone else into a tree trunk or sent them careening to the bottom in a broken heap. He exhibited no sign of the injury Omar's original group inflicted as he slalomed headlong between the trees, punctuated by dry and desiccated leaves crackling and crunching underfoot like small bones. He carried something she couldn't quite make out, but different from his appearance at the tunnel and definitely not a bow.

Omar shouted, *"HE'S COMING! MOVE!"*

They scattered like startled birds. Grant had to relinquish Megan before he ended up holding her back.

They had not discussed any new plan for dispersal, but when sanity returned they would remember the nexus of the creek. Tina's only allegiance lay with Shelly and she had her in hand now, intentionally guiding them away from the others in hopes they would all fan out and limit Orange's opportunity to reduce their numbers.

This strategy had one potentially fatal flaw—he had to choose someone at the outset, and Shelly provided the weakest link.

Playing Shelly's caretaker at least gave Tina a set of eyes for the oncoming obstacles of trunks, branches, stumps, and bushes in their path while she chanced a look back to chart Orange's progress. She didn't have a clear view now but saw enough between the trees to witness him stumbling, ironically tripped up by level ground after the near graceful dash through far more difficult terrain.

Tina willed him to fall and it seemed like she might get her wish as he flailed behind obstructive tree trunks, but he reappeared still upright as if a divine hand reached down and straightened him. *Deus ex hackina.*

He propelled himself into the air as he reached his bank of the creek. She thought he would somehow clear it and not miss a step on the other side. Thankfully he struck the water and sank like a stone less than a third of the way.

"Come on!" Tina turned from the creek and threaded them past a copse of fir trees, angling in a slant away from the creek and back toward the tunnel. She hoped to get them far enough away to double back and get behind him unseen, maybe on the other side of the creek.

She saw no one from their original group now. The woods swallowed them all, though she heard snapped branches and scuttled leaves. Live targets to lead him away, hopefully.

Shelly ran stiffly beside her, right arm limp at her side, trying to keep her back from twisting. They seemed to be in slow motion. When Tina pulled to move them along faster, Shelly whimpered with pain and their pace barely increased.

"Hold up," Tina said.

The terror escalated with Orange gaining, the thrashing of his limbs in the creek like the detonation of a string of land mines.

"We need to hide." She pointed to a pine with several low branches and a carpet of nettles littering the ground. "Crawl in there. I'm going to cover you. Come on, we need to hurry."

Shelly winced at slipping into the nest of pine limbs, but still seemed happier with any plan that didn't involve running with an arrow in her back. Tina pressed gently at her unwounded shoulder with far less patience than she felt. They didn't have long to do this and she still had to worry about herself afterward.

Shelly moaned and hissed, gasping when the underside of a wishbone branch nudged her arrow, but she wrapped herself into fetal position beneath the bottom row of limbs.

"Close your mouth." Tina swept long dead pine needles over her quivering form, still damp from the morning mist. The quick blanket effectively hid her from Tina crouched right beside her, so ideally Orange would totally miss her from even farther off. She brushed aside a few nettles from Shelly's eyes to give her a little bit of a view.

"Don't make a sound. I'm coming back but if I take too long, just go to the creek and follow the way we were going."

"Not without you," said the mound of needles.

Tina pressed a hand to her shape, wishing she could feel her without the cover in the way. It was a sorry last caress if it wound up being so, but good motivation to return for something better.

"I'm coming back," she said again, then sprang up and sprinted straight away from the creek rather than the prior diagonal. She moved a lot faster without Shelly, squeezing between trees and around bushes, hopping over logs, ever onward.

She developed an obtuse angle pattern—straight ahead opposite the creek, then zagging left away from Shelly's hiding place. She stumbled on the uneven terrain and once kept herself upright only by grabbing a branch, then had to stop to steady the limb so it didn't wave to Orange when she took off again: *Hey, she's over here!*

Then back to the pattern. Away from the creek, away from Shelly. Would she even recognize the hiding spot? Everything looked the same.

A stitch burrowed into her rib and when she checked behind her, she was no longer alone. Orange stormed between the trees with the same confident footing he displayed on the hillside, as if he would fell anything in his path.

No!

He vanished behind trunks and reappeared closer still, like a flickering image from a movie projector.

Had he found Shelly too? Would he be twenty yards from Tina instead of a hundred if he hadn't stopped for her? A despairing thought, though not to be outdone by another—he'd simply chosen Tina. He wanted her, with no concern for what became of the others or their proximity to the wall.

This revelation did not magically restore her to primary flight status, however. The stitch lingered, like a knuckle jabbed in her ribs. She pushed her body all morning and now it pushed back at the worst possible time.

Tina followed the slope of the hill, steering her course for overgrown bushes tall enough to conceal her and her path. It gave her the illusion of running in place while someone turned an environmental crank to loop another bush, another pine, another rock past her. A lot of energy for what seemed no true progress, like logrolling, moving her feet but going nowhere.

The sudden appearance of an actual log seemed like a mind trick of the environmental loop. *Logrolling, eh? Okay, try this.*

She wasn't thinking about stopping until she saw it, but her aching joints and lungs suggested maybe it wasn't a bad idea. She veered up the incline, careful not to leave footprints.

The log lay nine feet in length and hollow, though far from inviting; had this been the diameter of their entry tunnel, Bryce and Adrian could not have used it and Shelly's meltdown would have happened at roughly the second she stuck her head inside. An outcropping of rock protruding from the hill like a compound fracture wedged it in place. Better yet, mounds of leaves flanked the openings on either side.

Orange made no overtures at stealth. The snapping of twigs and sibilance of brushing branches drew nearer like a shadow minimizing to its source in fading light, but Tina had a window and a convenient formation of three overgrown bushes for disguise.

She held her breath and brushed aside the leaves. Nothing exploded in her face, and when she dug out her phone and aimed its light inside, she saw nothing but ridges.

The leaves were damp and mute compared to the desiccated crunches rapidly approaching, like snapping jaws chewing through the forest.

She slid her feet into the maw of her sanctuary and scooted inside, then reached back to rearrange the leaves into a deformed trapezoidal shape. The underside of the log rubbed against her back as she inched deeper, the bark scraping forearms and wrists. She stopped with her face two feet from the entrance.

Past the leaves offered Tina a view of the broken tree from which her log originated, and a natural arch of more trees lined up the slope. The pines shifted into a kaleidoscopic blur.

She closed her eyes and waited for the spell to pass, her lungs and the stitch still singeing as she breathed through her nose. No panting allowed, even if it seemed like trying to douse an inferno with a leaky bucket.

Her pulse sounded loud enough in her ears for Shelly to hear back at the pine tree.

Shelly.

The archway grew blurry.

Tina only needed to stay out of sight, then work her way back down the creek and guide Shelly out of here. It wouldn't absolve the sick feeling of guilt for bringing her here in the first place, but she would at least have kept the promise to protect her.

She wiped her eyes and continued to listen. She couldn't hear him. Maybe he veered too far down the hill for the sound to reach her.

Her ears played tricks in the prolonged silence. Phantom crawly things breeding in the carcass of a dead animal just below her feet, like the sound of chewing.

A hiding place hopefully worked for Shelly, but as seconds ticked by Tina debated the wisdom of her own. She would not be able to escape it if he found her, just like the girl in *Kill Zone Massacre 3* who ducked down in the back of an old car. Orange dragged her by the hair and repeatedly smashed her head with the door, a pun on her earlier comment that she needed to find some closure in the KZ. Tina rolled her eyes at the choice, but here she did the same thing. He'd have caught her by now if she didn't hide, though.

Not being able to see behind her creeped her out too much. She maneuvered as quietly as she could onto her right side and angled her cell phone to reflect the opening near her feet. Now she only had to shift her eyes back and forth to see ahead and behind her. After a few seconds on the cusp of a massive stroke, she convinced herself the silhouette at the base of the log only represented a configuration of leaves and not a gas mask peering around the corner as Orange mulled his options for killing her in such a tight space.

How much of this could she stand before it felt safe to find Shelly?

She worked the fingers of her right hand against a pins and needle sensation, extending and closing them in a fist, coaxing the flow of blood, like the creek off in the distance—

It hit her then. She heard the creek and the skittering of leaves and cones, but the birds fell silent. She heard them all morning despite the season.

Until now.

She locked her hand over her nose and mouth to mute her breathing.

He was here.

In the movies he struck down prey unaware, lightning from a blue sky, but she felt him back by the tunnel before she saw him. The same certainty settled over her now like a chill in the air.

Her eyes shifted—cell phone reflection, log, cell, log—like a tennis match. The phone shook in her hand, the reflected world shuddering in imminent cataclysm. She tried to stabilize her hand, certain he could still somehow hear it despite its soundlessness, same as he would hear her hair brushing against the log if she moved an inch.

The visibility through his gas mask must be poor, but if she left any signs of her passing out there, he would find them.

Passing. There was an unfortunate connotation.

She found control of her grip and steadied the phone. Ahead of her, camouflaged legs and black boots ambled past, halfway between the log and the dead tree. Now she heard the squish of socks in his wet boots. A crescent shape hovered beside them.

A pickaxe.

The temperature in her hideaway plummeted twenty degrees. He exited her field of vision, down the hill slope. His footsteps barely registered with sound, slight and methodical.

Not the hurried gait of someone who thought his prey must be far away.

He doesn't know, he doesn't know, he doesn't kn—

Something fast cleaved the air like the whirling of a helicopter rotor. The top of the log burst open to admit half the silver crescent blade of his pickaxe. Splinters sprinkled across her face as it embedded beside her head, almost level with her eyes. Six inches closer and it would have punctured her face.

Tina shrieked and snatched for it, operating on pure instinct with all organized thought consumed by the white noise of terror. She had little leverage in the tight confines and Orange yanked the crescent back through the log and out of her hands as though it were coated with Vaseline.

REINCURSION

She scooted away from the nearest exit, hoping he'd never expect it, and put her back to the opposite side of the log to minimize herself as a target. It shifted with her weight like it would tip over and roll, but the jagged bone of rock outside held it fast.

Tina pulled her arm from beneath her and dropped onto her back. She'd begun to tent her knees to help slide backwards when the pickaxe smashed through the side of the log. The intruding half of the blade worked at the cleft like a crowbar, followed by a big gouge as the other end crashed through the flank. The flat of the crescent pushed into her shoulder hard enough to hurt. He jostled it back through the hole before Tina thought to seize it again.

The pickaxe careened through the top again, and she had an instant to think she hadn't made enough of a gap, she was dead, but it only struck between her legs, close enough to nudge her groin.

He pried open a small vertical window as he hauled the pickaxe back through. She saw the gas mask through the split now, his manic eyes behind the transparent face plate. A limited view, and yet a total window to madness—both in his lust to kill her and the impossibility of his existence. He stood with his feet to either side, to easily slide along the length of the log.

His bulk seemed massive enough to blot out the sky. The necklace of severed ears hung in space and settled to his chest as he rose up to his full height, hands sliding to find the best grip for the next swing.

Tina screamed. He had her. She hid inside her own coffin.

He swung at her face. She scrambled right again

and this time the log shifted much less rigidly. The blow he struck to the flank created an aperture that permitted the outcropping rock which held the log in place. The crags painfully jabbed her as momentum rolled her across. She threw herself with it, knowing she'd be dead if it dipped back in place.

It didn't.

The log crested like a roller coaster entering the first massive plunge. Then she entered the void. The parting swing she expected to pin her like a butterfly never came. She continued downhill, hitting a stretch of open ground to pick up exhilarating, frightening speed.

Tina glimpsed a dizzying wheel of trees and sky through the nearest portal, then suddenly earth and darkness as she bounced around helplessly in a kaleidoscope of vertigo. She balled herself up as best she could, closed her eyes and ordered her head to stop its cascade free fall. In this state she would clamber out and face-plant in time for him to deliver the final bow, prolonging her death by a whopping twelve seconds.

A trunk nine feet in length had no chance to roll for long with so many obstructions, but blunt impact with a tree shed some bulk. The far end exploded into flying wooden shrapnel. The log scraped against the next impediment, bark shearing bark, shifting the angle vertically like a sled before gradually rolling back horizontally.

Tina screamed as she slammed something else, unleashing a series of tiny cracks. Smaller and weaker limbs this time, not a trunk. Nothing blasted apart. The log lurched upward among rustling sounds on a bed of splinters and breaks. Her momentum halted. The cylinder canted, seemed determined to keep going, but finally changed its mind and settled back into place.

The final collision opened several scrapes on her hands and arms, but nothing broken. Her ear and cheek burned—the fronds of a bush infiltrated one of the pickaxe punctures. It might have taken out her eye if she hadn't folded her arms over her head. Wherever she wound up, she wasn't flat to the ground but nestled in something thick enough to hold her.

She ignored the continued rolling sensation, a remnant of the vertigo, and reached for the rim to pull herself out. The weight of the earth plunged heavily to the right, and by all logic should have thrown her to the other side of the world.

Get out, get out, he's coming.

She struggled blindly. The cool open air on her face assured her of a solid, stationary reality, though her stomach didn't quite buy it since she threw up as she crawled into the world of daylight once more. Her bile preceded her in the copse of fir bushes. They shifted to the right, saturated in yellow vomitus, threatening to carry her off to another round of puking.

Providence guided her log into a thicket of bushes. The trunk seesawed with the distribution of her weight and coughed her out in a fashion. The fir branches met her and softened her landing but for the poke of several wood shards in her ribs. A massive snap threw her two feet to the ground.

She completed her roll away and scrambled to her feet, painfully aware of the ticking clock.

The boot falls of Agent Orange rumbled in her wake. Very near.

She ran without looking back. Past the bushes into the skeletons of trees. The first few steps felt uncertain, the ground meeting her feet too soon or not soon enough. She stumbled but pushed forward until the earth properly leveled once more. The air invigorated her, sharp in her lungs after the musty interior of the hollow trunk and that entombed feeling. She escaped the coffin, reborn, each step more assured.

Holy shit, the wall.

It stood a couple hundred yards away like a tidal wave frozen at its apex. Home base in the game of hide and seek. She could make it.

Oh God, let there be a patrol here, anyone who can get here in time.

"Help me!" she shouted, and then added, *"He's coming!"*

If they weren't in the business of saving, they might at least be eager for a crack at the killer elite.

No mistaking his pursuit, much heavier footsteps than her own and less human than elemental—a fissure opening a spreading void to swallow her up.

Still not looking back, Tina cried, *"The wall's up ahead, you fucker!"*

The footsteps of the fissure remained unimpressed by this revelation. The void continued to eat the distance.

Tina pointed at her talisman in desperation, hoping to see a squadron of soldiers rappelling down with enough firepower to liquefy a blue whale. She saw no one, though. No sentry pillbox with artillery, just loops of razor wire.

REINCURSION

Amidst the rush and collateral damage to brittle leaves and cones, she once more heard the heavy whoosh from when the pickaxe previously invaded her sanctuary. She threw herself to the left. The crescent pinwheeled past her to stick in a tree ten yards ahead. But for that trunk, it might have gone twenty more.

She rerouted to seize the axe. Throwing seemed desperate; the wall might bother him after all, and if its looming threat didn't dissuade him, maybe he'd stop for sure if weaponless. The next throw might not miss. She had to take it away from him if she could.

Tina looked back to see if she would have the time to claim it and keep running. Her blood turned to ice. Thirty feet away and would have been closer if he hadn't stopped to launch his projectile; so much faster than his bulk suggested, even in such sodden clothes.

She gunned for the tree, legs and elbows pumping. She stopped at the last second and grasped the handle just beneath the crescent, wrenching it backward with her other hand in the middle of the grip. The blade came free, but she had to jiggle it like a loose tooth.

As she spun away from the tree she let the momentum carry her back around into a sprint, time enough to see he narrowed thirty feet to fifteen. Despite the wall and her acquisition of the weapon, he wasn't stopping yet. Her heart sank somewhere in her stomach. She claimed the pickaxe, but there was no question which of them still needed to flee.

Tina screamed for help again to the faceless wall, not sure it would actually matter now if someone did respond. She worked the pickaxe back and forth in front of her to propel her faster. Fifteen feet had undoubtedly become ten, and in a few more seconds he'd be close enough to snatch her.

She had one option left and couldn't look back if she wanted to retain any element of surprise.

She counted to five then stopped and whirled, thrusting the pickaxe forward spike first.

Tina couldn't have timed it much better. She caught him with a hand outstretched to snatch her. The pickaxe pounded into his chest, and what force she didn't supply he supplemented with his momentum, impaling himself to the handle. No grunt of pain or outrush of breath to signify a sickle punched through his torso and out his back.

The blow failed to stop him short, however. He pushed forward, a grip of iron clenched around her arm. The other side of the crescent inched dangerously close to her chest; he wanted her to share in this ritual impalement. She relinquished her hold on the pickaxe and jumped back but his grip kept her locked to him. Tina spun sideways and backpedaled recklessly, a macabre dance where she trusted him to keep his grip. He failed her and felled her by letting go.

Tina slid in the grass, strikingly cool through her clothes. Orange's shadow fell upon her as he spread his arms and collapsed, intending to let his weight drive the pickaxe through her supine form. She rolled away in time, hauled herself up and broke away in a sprint.

The wall stood a mere hundred yards away. Maybe now he'd give it up with the added bonus of her zapping the spring out of the bastard's step. It probably meant no more than a bee sting to him, but might count as the last payment on her escape plan.

Tina began to round the first tree of stature to eclipse his view of her when something struck her in the small of her back with crippling force. Her arms flew up as her legs folded beneath her, the wind knocked from her lungs, so much pain she didn't get the chance to plant her hands. She hit the ground hard. The imperative of flight urged her to find her stride again, but agony held her fast to the earth.

I think he broke my freaking kidneys.

She hadn't been stabbed or tackled. A trap? It hurt too much to turn over.

His footsteps came patiently but inexorably, like heavy raps on her door from the reaper. She stayed flat, trapped in torment, afraid to move an inch and expand its dominion.

Orange gave her no choice. Her grabbed her wrist and yanked her face-up. As feared, the anguish renewed far beyond the walls of its initial appearance.

He stooped and retrieved the pickaxe by her feet. He'd brought her down with that, launched it and slammed the flat of the blade into her spine.

Tina screamed and held her arms up to ward him off. No strength accompanied the gesture, the spasms of pain making her rubbery. She was at his mercy, and knew he would show her none.

As he raised the pickaxe, she prepared to roll away. Anything for another second, another chance at intervention—divine or otherwise. He didn't swing it in her direction, however. He buried it in the trunk of the tree beside her, driving the crescent almost to the handle. The other half jutted like a strange new limb.

Oh God.

He easily slapped aside the shield of her hands

and forearms to clutch her by the underarms like an infant and lift her as effortlessly.

She flailed and kicked despite the wrenching pain to her back. The blows landed harmlessly. Even stomping directly on his crotch did not change the expression in his eyes. He appraised her with the delight and madness of a sadist—and pure hate. Perhaps that chilled her above all, the clear loathing he revealed, as if she were the aberration between the two of them, the deformity to be smothered.

The physicality of Tina's effort waned with its lack of impact. His body proved solid, unyielding.

Not everywhere.

She found the puncture wound from the pickaxe, obscured all too appropriately by a contortion of his soaked camouflage, and jammed two fingers inside. They were not an easy fit. A shudder rolled through her at the repulsive feel within; wet, slippery textures that made her want to yank her hand away. Instead she clawed, looking to slice or puncture whatever she found and widen the gap to permit more of her hand. Was there a beating heart she could stop?

Her intrusion had an effect the punches and kicks did not. He tightened his grip beneath her underarms and heaved her backward. She pictured the embedded pickaxe blade an instant before it pounded its way through her back. An instant later she beheld a new metal outgrowth from her abdomen.

The pain was everything in the world.

He ripped her away, crescent sliding back through her organs only to reappear once more from a different puncture. Brute force skewered her with no resistance. Blood spilled freely off the blade. She did not come off so easily when he attempted to pull her back. The axe caught on something it couldn't slide past—perhaps bone—until he shook her around a bit, a process of seconds which felt like eons.

The delay enraged him and he attacked in a frenzy, thrusting her back and forth, the punctures coming as fast now as a stabbing attack. The crescent grew slicker, petals of vital tissue adherent until close to the entirety of some organ sputtered away, as if evacuating an increasingly inhospitable environment. It looked like some creature of the sea born in blood with its yellow nodules; in a fading recess of her mind, she thought it might be her pancreas.

He let her hang, her feet twitching uselessly, too far above ground to gain any purchase. He did not seem tired from his efforts, only curious to admire this trapped, perforated thing. She tried to scream for Shelly to run, but her mouth filled with blood.

Orange seized her again under the arms. He did not pull her away this time but lifted her, the crescent stuck beneath the notch of her sternum gouging its way south as she went due north amidst the sounds of ripping meat and cleaving bone.

As she faded away at last, seeing the surreal spillage of most of her alimentary canal to the floor of the forest in a glistening, almost rubbery looking pile, she thought not of Shelly but that trip to the zoo so impossibly long ago as she wandered with her family, looking for the exit. That fear of being trapped and the relief of escape, though strangely she could not remember them finding their way back to the parking lot, only that it must have happened (hadn't it?).

And now, again, mercifully, that unknown escape.

IX.

IT WON'T WORK, Omar thought upon approaching the Chicken Exit, trying to keep his expectations measured. This mantra accompanied his inaugural Kill Zone visit too. *It won't work and I'm going to die. It is what it is.*

He hoped at first to find soldiers on the premises despite its decrepit state, someone shouting at him from the look-out tower with automatic weapons at the ready. It became clear as he jogged in that the last watch saw its day quite some time ago, though Agent Orange erected a new one in their place. What the line of heads lacked in anatomy, they made up for with a tireless refusal to blink. Judging by the advanced state of decay, they hadn't been relieved in a while.

The forsaken post radiated defeat—we thought we could contain him, but guess he just wanted it more. Well, he won the battle, but not the war. He took Morgan, Sandalwood, and Westing, but we double dare him to show his face in Marshallville!

He checked his path back toward the basin. Bryce and Megan were yet to emerge. Maybe he shouldn't have foisted the responsibility of Megan on the boy, but she came a long way since the attack by the tunnel; a little slow in her gait, otherwise able to advance under her own power. She could run in a pinch and they'd have plenty of warning as the basin offered no cover for Orange in pursuit. The nearest flanking trees were out of range even by his archery standards.

Omar splintered off to get the ball rolling ASAP rather than wait for everyone to stumble to the finish line. Every second counted.

The Chicken Exit wasn't like the ones he'd seen in pictures or news stories. Those were designed like payphones, convenient for Orange to sabotage. This simply said "Emergency Call Box." A foot wide by a foot and a half in length and fastened to a post anchored in the concrete, it didn't seem very resilient with Agent Orange's notoriety for disabling such devices or trapping them outright. Dingy silver and fluorescent orange with ample bird shit and spotted with rain stains, it contained simple instructions:

1. Press and hold button to speak.
2. Begin speaking after the beep.
3. Release button for instructions.

A red placard attached beneath the audio holes identified the coordinates with white lettering as C-13. Mounted on top of the pole, a rudimentary map of the Kill Zone with an inset of the immediate area proved too broad and ill-defined to help someone truly lost in here. Omar almost expected a question mark after the YOU ARE HERE icon.

He laughed when he remembered he had his own map and gambled his life to get it this morning . . . but hadn't looked at it one damned time since.

They specifically manufactured Chicken Exits to function in a dead zone, but he held every expectation of disappointment. It wouldn't work and his group would all die, as ordained from the moment Agent Orange emerged from the fog this morning.

He pushed the white call button and held it, leaning toward the grid of the speaker. The whole process seemed absurdly reminiscent of ordering tacos at a drive-thru.

Omar listened to dead air that might have been his own soul deflating.

His pessimism wasn't borne out his first time here as a scarecrow version of his current self—a withered husk down seventy-five pounds from his usual weight, barely able to eat from the medication side effect of nausea, and mentally unable to see the point. Like fueling up a car with no battery.

His family tiptoed around the prognosis, believers in the power of positive thinking. They spoke of a mythic time called When You're Better. Omar played along but he believed in a different eventuality— When It's Over. That blessed moment when the torture of breathing with pulmonary fibrosis would cease forever and him with it.

He hadn't wanted to go, wouldn't let himself spend what little remained of his life on false hope. He knew they'd take him to this bullshit "miracle spot" and do something like those fake healers he read about, running their hands over the sickly and pulling chicken livers out of their sleeve to toss in a bloody bucket—*I have removed the corrupt organ from you that you may go forth and walk with a clean bill of health and a new lease on life! Ten thousand dollars, please.*

But like so many times growing up, he committed

to one plan and then his mom informed him how shit would actually go down. She wasn't going to stand around and watch her baby die, not when they had Hope-With-A-Capital-H.

And When You're Better, you'll thank me for it.

He thought but didn't say, *Only thing I'll be telling you if I come back at all is* I told you so.

So he went with his cousin Lamar and a small unit led by a Stalker called Chan. Grant carried him from a much closer entry point than any he'd enjoy again, until stable enough road allowed for his wheelchair because the strain of simply walking it would have killed him. He expected them to say, "Okay, this is far enough," dump him to die of exposure, and high-five all the way to the bank.

Except Omar came back home cured of an incurable disease. By then they'd taken him home from the hospital to die anyway so his miracle recovery went unknown, though doctors would say they misdiagnosed him. He'd known immediately after the "Ritual" as they—and now he—called it that the void of his future would have to be filled after all, that the invisible man standing on his lungs all the time left for good. He walked back without Grant's help and ate two plates of his mom's cooking at home, well on his way to reclaiming those seventy-five pounds.

When his mother died only months later—an aneurysm, the kind of random lightning bolt of fate even the Healing Place still couldn't prevent—he vowed to get involved with the process that saved him as the best tribute to her imaginable. It carried its own failures—logistics worked out too late sometimes and people were more skeptical than he expected. Maybe that shouldn't have come as a surprise given his own cynicism before the process, but he'd have thought most would seize any rope thrown their way. He eventually stopped using his experience as a sales pitch because those who were going to go would go and the rest wouldn't be swayed by anything he said. He hated to leave them to their fates, but the triumphs were special with Omar in the function of Hope-With-a-Capital-H.

Now if he could just avoid Death-With-A-Capital-O.

Plink!

Omar jolted at the sign of life on the drive-thru menu. *I'll take a Quik-Escape combo, hold the Orange.*

"Hello?" He remembered to depress the button.

"Sir, are you in immediate danger?" A woman's voice, which couldn't have sounded more angelic to him right now.

"Damn, man, isn't everyone who calls you in here?" Omar said. Thankfully he'd forgotten to push the button to speak, giving him time to reevaluate his approach. He held down the button to say, "He's not here yet but we've seen him. We need help."

"How many are in your party?"

He pictured Megan and Bryce blowing noisemakers and wearing coned hats. "Three here, but our group split up."

And don't talk shit about us doing that. This ain't a movie and it was the right call.

Although he hadn't liked Grant's decision to run off after Tina and Shelly. A face-off with Orange seemed the more likely outcome.

"There's more," he continued, "uh . . . approximately ten of us. I'm sure some of them need an evac too."

Well, probably. Too late for some of them now, undoubtedly. He hated to take the hard line on Sarah by the tunnel but leading a charge to the grave profited no one, not their group and not the other ill people he could help by making it back. Such wisdom Erica probably understood now, too little, too late.

"Your name, sir?" Keys clacked through the speaker as she typed, though of course this would be recorded and stored forever.

He thought about giving Noel's name even though the gig would be up soon enough. But no point throwing him under the bus when they might never know of his involvement, especially when he looked like he *had* been thrown under a bus. It could mean trouble for his folks, who probably knew nothing about Noel's "career."

"Dexter," Omar said, noticing a blood spatter pattern on the pavement. He spelled it out while he looked around for inspiration, a new candidate per letter. Dexter Intercom . . . Graffiti . . . Staked Head . . . Barbwire . . . Bunker . . . Off in the distance, only trees. "Dexter Spruce."

No, there weren't spruce pines in the area, but it sounded better than Dexter Shortleaf. Somewhat.

His angel assumed the form of Doubting Thomas. "*Dexter Spruce?*"

He wondered if he accidentally gave the name of a famous person. Aggression seemed the best play to divert. "Don't worry about spelling it right, just come get us!"

"Mr. Spruce, I will require you to acknowledge that you are in violation of the Fraser Act, and extraction will require confessions from everyone with all applicable penalties up to and including fines, prison time, and registration."

The registration list would be a problem for a traditional career, but Omar's calling needed no background check or W-2. Grant, Megan, and the others would just have to deal with the fallout in their own lives, which had to be the least of Megan's worries with the likely fates of Sarah and Clark.

He looked again toward the basin as if he could see the entire path that brought him here, to the floating torso in the creek and all the way back to Doug and Noel.

"Yeah." Omar sighed, holding the button. "Acknowledged."

X.

"IT WAS ADRIAN," Bryce told her. Megan reluctantly looked at him. The movement made her head swim a little, her stomach swim a lot. A fall she couldn't remember gave her a hell of a gash, rendering most of the last hour (or two? or three?) a blur of frenetic movement.

Bryce continued, "Back at the creek. The body. It wasn't your—"

"I know." Megan said it with a huff of air; she still hadn't caught her breath from the climb out of the creek basin.

The looming tower played tricks on her mind. At first it appeared they were practically on top of it, now it seemed no closer for anyone but Omar, who proclaimed *Chicken Exit, I'll get this rolling!* and dashed toward the emergency telephone presumably installed there. Megan thought the military could be in the tower, but Bryce quickly set her straight. The outpost formed part of the original wall, abandoned in 1997 following the completion of a new wall encompassing Sandalwood that doubled the size of the Kill Zone.

It stood beside a wide opening where they removed the gate to give Agent Orange free access to the Sandalwood side of the vast enclosure. Better to allow him entry to the uninhabited space than risk him breaking through the wall at some other point to threaten Marshallville or another nearby burg. *If he wants to kill, he* will *find a way to do it,* her father said at the time.

Megan never understood why anyone would willingly live within a hundred miles of the KZ, and yet desperation for Sarah led her into the heart of the Kill Zone. There were no medical miracles left to be found in South America or Europe or from shady operatives in Russia. It left the Kill Zone their only Hail Mary pass, and the zombie psychopath intercepted.

We'd do it again.

"I was jealous of him. Adrian. Wish I could go back to . . . " Bryce shook his head.

Megan stumbled over a rock. Bryce grabbed her arm to steady her. He could have left her, run after Omar on some pretense or other, but he hadn't and she wondered why. His chalky pallor, downcast face, slumped shoulders, but wide eyes and rigid movements indicated some combination of shock and resignation. Prey in motion. The fact Orange hadn't come for them meant he went after the two girls, and Grant went looking for them half an hour ago so Grant was probably dead, too.

"Don't beat yourself up over it," Megan said.

"I was a dick when I thought it didn't matter."

"What we've learned with Sarah is that every minute matters. Every second. You don't take any of them for granted."

"Yeah, that's what Erica says."

Traipsing through the KZ for jollies wasn't exactly what Megan had in mind for living life to its fullest but she let it slide.

"She's seen some pretty messed up stuff. Sometimes I think she might be broken a little."

Ya think?

"When she was ten she was out with her dad and a tractor trailer creamed their car. He died in her arms. She held him while they used the Jaws of Life to get to her. She . . . uh, hasn't told me that yet. Tina did, to like, contextualize her one night after a big blowup. Someday she'll tell me herself, though."

"And in the meantime this is the kind of thing you have to do to prove yourself?"

"Something like that."

People were peculiar. They might subscribe to a philosophy of embracing every minute of life while still keeping those closest at arm's length. Maybe that's what happened here, with this boy wearing his heart on his sleeve while Erica kept hers under lock and key.

"She's a junior," Bryce continued, "but only nineteen. She skipped fourth grade."

But if she was so smart, why would she come to the Kill Zone? Erica and her friends' recklessness tempered her gratitude for the girl's help with her daughter. Sarah fought and struggled for life every day while this group squandered the gift of theirs, making a silly game of coming to this place of death.

Had Megan been so cavalier about her mortality at that age? To some degree, undoubtedly, but never to such an absurd extent. There were suicide attempts less effective than this. She wanted to slap all their faces but reality did the job for her, judging by Bryce. She only wished she trusted Erica not to put him right back in the line of fire if they escaped this brush with fate, or Bryce not to let her.

Auditing the foolishness of their motives proved quite helpful for not obsessing over the enormity of tragedy she may have inherited. Because if the worst were confirmed about Sarah and Clark—probabilities now wringing her heart bloodless in her chest—she might do the Gauntlet group one better for a death wish and simply lie down and wait for what would come.

Bryce looked back for approximately the thousandth time, which was fine by her; with him playing watchman she could keep her head steady and still, eyes toward the goal. Less strain on her head wound.

The tower loomed in the shape of a circular tube with a rounded observation deck enclosed in concrete and perforated with small windows guards once used to survey all approaches to the gate. A lone door at its base offered a promising opportunity to barricade oneself behind it and buy time for evac in the event of a siege, provided the Chicken Exit phone worked. If it didn't and they sought refuge there, it would be like sitting in a tree with a hungry grizzly below—only Agent Orange wouldn't get bored and walk away. An invasion to mutilate cornered prey would provide a rare challenge for a maniac probably eager for a change in routine. Maybe he'd done it previously; enough graffiti on the walls suggested frequency by Stalkers or Prowlers or whatever spray-painting thrill seekers called themselves these days.

The distant outline of heads on stakes meant Agent Orange did some tagging of his own. Megan didn't look forward to the smell.

She knew something of the game Bryce mentioned to her earlier in what played like a confession, unburdening sins and stupidities for absolution. When researching the KZ to prepare for the journey, she'd stumbled across the Gauntlet footnote and told Clark, who sarcastically replied, *So someone created a game to lure teenagers into the Kill Zone so they can have sex and die? Is that like life imitating art?* To which she'd replied, *I don't think slasher films qualify as art. That's like saying books about Agent Orange qualify as literature.*

Bryce's girlfriend dressed for the role of Gauntlet girl with her impractical thigh-high stockings, mini-skirt and thong everyone saw plain as day earlier; those sexy legs were probably taking a beating in her flight through the woods right about now. No doubt she intended the carnal payoff "bonus" with Bryce—maybe an orgy with the whole group for all Megan knew—and for what? Just to say they had?

But if the promise of sex lured Bryce's group to the KZ, actual sex brought Megan and Clark, eight years removed from the event. Perhaps there was a lesson in how irrationality and prudence ultimately herded everyone through the same chute of the abattoir.

Omar touched a large box fastened to a thin post. From this distance Megan couldn't tell if the thing worked, but at least it didn't blow up. He put his hands on his knees, leaned toward the post and looked toward Megan and Bryce as he spoke. Talking to a Chicken Exit operator or hurling invective because their latest hope evaporated like the morning fog? Time would certainly tell.

"Holy shit, it's Grant!" Bryce announced.

Megan kept her head still as she rotated her body 180 degrees. A couple hundred yards away she saw the shock of ultra-blonde hair and the ugly red and green sweater as Grant ran like hell through the creek, carrying one of the girls in his arms.

Too big to be Sarah, blast it. A fleeting, silly thought. How could Grant possibly stumble upon her? The logic failed to stave her tears. He saved someone's daughter, just not hers.

Bryce tented his hands over his eyes. "That's Shelly."

Had Grant somehow bested Agent Orange to rescue Shelly? A rich delusion for sure, but almost believable given the amount of time since they'd last seen the slayer. Grant's heavy footfalls launched sprays of water into the air. His frantic approach screamed *Pursuit!* and undermined the illusion he killed or maimed the enemy. Disheartening to see someone other than Clark or Sarah, but at least the trio became a quintet again. "Misery loves company," "strength in numbers," or a little of both, maybe.

"Should we wait?" Bryce waved excitedly to Grant, but his face betrayed the answer he wanted to hear.

"No, he'll catch us," Megan assured him as she rotated forward. She reached to the back of her head, drawn to the damage. Thick clumps of hair and coagulated blood surrounded the gash. It finally stopped bleeding.

"Tina could be lost."

Bryce left the more obvious implication unsaid as

if doing so nullified more sinister likelihoods and gave her something she didn't otherwise have: a chance.

"Maybe she fell behind." This Megan said with no conviction, but there were things Bryce needed to hear. He was in way over his head thanks to a girl who dragged several friends into trouble they weren't likely to survive. Erica was beautiful, out of Bryce's league to be honest, a queen bee that needed drones. Megan knew girls like her in high school. Self-centered. Superficial. Aware of her sexuality and only too willing to abuse its effect on those who wanted to be in her as well as the same sex who wanted to be her.

She assessed the chances at 50/50 Erica went after Sarah out of the goodness of her heart versus clutching her only straw for redemption. *I went after the helpless little girl . . . see, world, I did the right thing. If my friends weren't massacred, they would tell you we all begged to go there, it wasn't just me! #thoughtsandprayers*

She wanted to buy Bryce's portrait of Erica's sainthood, but all her money these days went to medical care.

Grant's motion proved contagious. Megan and Bryce started at a brisk walk, but soon ran toward Omar and the tower. The exertion and resultant hammering of her heart had the predictable effect in her cranium with the blood vessels throbbing so hard her head felt like exploding. Megan didn't stop, though. She kept pace with Bryce, no doubt surprising the hell out of him. She might have fifteen years on him but she kept fit, even when she didn't have to be so active for Sarah's sake.

As they approached, Omar stepped away from the Chicken Exit callbox to intercept them. His smile telegraphed good news.

"They're sending a rescue party," he said.

"Fuckin' A," Bryce gasped. He wiped his forehead with a hand. "Grant and . . . Shelly. They're," he paused to breathe, "coming."

Omar's eyes bulged. "What? Grant, really?"

They couldn't see the creek basin from here so Omar had to take his word for it. Clark would have joked about Grant missing the *Rescue 911* if he didn't hurry—another William Shatner reference. If he didn't say it, he would certainly think it, and Megan would roll her eyes at him so he'd know she knew and she might even answer *Better late than never* to elicit a smile. If in recent months she considered life without Sarah for the obvious reasons, she never considered life without Clark at all. It would be every bit its own hell.

"He's carrying Shelly on the run," she said. "No one behind him."

"Yet," Bryce added.

"So they're coming?" She meant it rhetorically, a way to test the sound of the statement, assess it as a realistic possibility. Could she leave without Sarah and Clark? No, she didn't think she could, but if they were still out there, alive, she would better serve them by making sure the military focused on additional rescues. A helicopter could cover the route back along the creek in minutes. The U.S. government wouldn't want the PR nightmare of abandoning a little girl to her fate in the Kill Zone. Megan wouldn't win any Mother-of-the-Year awards herself but her story would certainly contextualize their desperation once it came out—and who knew? Maybe their plight could accomplish some good toward long overdue "Right to try" legislation for the terminally ill.

The tower base featured a sturdy steel door, but its top half hung at a more pronounced angle than the lower half and wouldn't close all the way. To the left of the structure someone spray painted MR. DUNBAR TEAR DOWN THIS WALL. Such a casually stupid thing to write, no doubt someone who didn't understand the implication of the incitement, like a gamer who welcomed the apocalypse under the erroneous assumption mastery of post-apocalyptic video games would impart real-world advantages.

"No ETA," Omar said, "but they might get here before Grant does."

"Did you tell them we have . . . others who need help?" Megan couldn't bring herself to be more specific.

"Don't worry, they don't want to miss detaining anyone. They demanded a social when I gave them a fake name."

Megan looked at the tower door again. More graffiti scrawled above it, all of it rude, crude, and deeply obnoxious frivolity such as "G9" or maybe "69" given a crassly rendered penis. "G9UNTLET" and "KZ Krew" stood out for being so high up the "artist" required a ladder. Against her better judgment she leaned backward to see the top of the tower. The windows were still intact, likely constructed of bulletproof glass. Even if they opened they were too small to exit—nowhere to go anyway, except atop the tower or down to the wall on either side, provided you could land without falling—and falling was what she was about to do so she straightened and closed her eyes to let the momentary disorientation pass. The throbbing in her head intensified.

When the military abandoned the area, they left a standing checkpoint building large enough for two or three soldiers. The windows were removed, as well as the guts of the station. Some flagpoles and bollards remained, but nothing usable for defense. Telltale signs of former security measures marked the pavement where new concrete and asphalt replaced anti-vehicle spikes and other bollards so military vehicles could drive through the unobstructed gate. From what she read, they only deployed military ground vehicles upon the certainty of Agent Orange's death, and then only for routine maintenance, which apparently involved replacing/updating Chicken Exits to the new 2.0 model.

Bryce looked around uneasily. "So we just stand here in the open waiting? Is that safe?"

"Maybe not," Omar said. "Dispatcher said there was a bunker nearby."

He cautiously descended a concrete stairwell a few yards from the guard shack. The steps led to a steel door that hung ajar like the tower, but still looked functional, i.e., the thing could actually close. A door like this probably locked from the inside.

Megan heard machines. Blessed machines. Chopper rotors in the distance.

"Helicopters," she said.

Bryce grinned, eyes wide. "I hear 'em, too!"

But Sarah, Clark.

Omar shined the beam of a small flashlight

through the crack in the doorway. The concrete walls magnified the scrape of his boots and upper body as he reached into the opening. He pulled the door slightly, but enough to make it creak on its old hinges. The resultant metallic wail echoed from the stairwell, easy to believe it could be heard for miles and identified by their stalker.

It seemed unnecessary to explore the bunker with the helicopter(s) approaching. Shouldn't they stay in the open?

"Tripwire inside," Omar said.

The beam of light focused on the floor just inside the doorway, with enough of an opening for Megan or Shelly to fit through, but not Bryce, and especially not Omar or Grant. Sort of like the tunnel all over again, though no one would be in any hurry to slip through the crack to the darkness beyond. And once the helicopters arrived none of them would have to.

A vibration surprised Bryce.

"Holy shit! A text."

A curiosity, given the circumstances. Helicopter sounds, now a text? The outside world encroached as if their return to it wasn't outside the realm of possibility.

"What the hell, my battery is a hundred percent. It was almost dead by the creek."

"Fantastic, thanks for the update, Bart." Omar's sarcasm played quite well through the medium of a concrete passage as hollow as his sentiment.

"Bryce," he corrected absently. "Oh shit, it's from Erica! She met up with another Prowler—and she's got Sarah!" Bryce looked at Megan to reiterate "Sarah is alive."

Thank you, God. Thank you.

Megan looked over her shoulder to see Grant's distant form rising from the creek basin with Shelly in his arms. The successful rescue could only mean one thing: Agent Orange always intended to take out Tina alone and now abandoned the rest of their group to pinball back to Sarah's group.

"Is she hurt?" Megan asked, sobs halfway between relief and terror. "What about Clark?"

"Don't know," Bryce said.

"Warn them he's coming for them next!"

"Got it. Somebody named 'Prowlerman' wants to know about your healing place too, Omar."

"We can talk about it later if he gets them out. We'll be in the market for a new Prowler anyway."

Omar already had a second Prowler, though. Megan didn't know his name, but for whatever reason he hadn't been available for this excursion. *That doesn't bode well. First we can't book a hotel within thirty miles of Marshallville and now we get their second stringer?* Megan had told Clark, who replied, *We're getting in, aren't we? It's literally do or die for Sarah no matter who gets us in there. Besides, we still have T.J. Healer.*

Grant topped the hill now and took a breather, Shelly limp in his arms. His striped sweater bore a dark stain on the chest from either his blood or Shelly's, or maybe something as innocuous as sweat. Megan preferred the latter.

"Your boy looks like shit," Bryce said as his fingers and thumb worked the tiny keyboard on his phone. Megan remembered Clark's haphazard, halting, squint-eyed approach to texting; one of the many adorable things she'd never see again. The possibility of his survival seemed too remote to entertain with Sarah's life already one miracle too many, although she would be doomed too if they couldn't get her back in here within a week or two. Omar had the map to the Healing Place. A Prowler had Sarah. But there was a ritual, or a methodology, a way things had to be done there. Water, dirt (or mud), and a house, these were the only elements she knew. Probably no accident Omar brought a flashlight, either.

Text sent, Bryce stared at the phone, shaking it like it would hurry a response that couldn't come fast enough for him and Megan. "I hope Grant isn't leading Orange to us."

"Coz he wouldn't find us anyway?" Omar said.

Speaking of . . .

Megan pointed to the tower. "Shouldn't someone get up there to watch for him?"

"In a minute. If this bunker is trapped, so's the tower." Omar listened for a moment at the foot of the stairs. "Those helicopters aren't getting here with a quickness at all."

Megan cocked an ear. She had to concentrate to find the staccato rhythm which a moment ago sounded far more imminent. "It's getting further away!"

Bryce forgot all about the phone. "What the fuck!"

"Both of you chill," Omar said. "Megan, can you get through this crack in the door? There's an axe in there."

Bryce apparently missed the chill memo. "You've got a gun!"

"And what do we do when we pump him with the

last bullet and he keeps coming? Pistol-whip his giant ass? We need the axe. A motherfucker can't run you down if you chop off his legs. Megan?"

She looked off in the distance toward Grant. Head down with a slow limp-walk, he appeared in worse shape than they thought. The courtesy of adrenaline granted his prior spryness through the creek, like the original Marathon runner; maybe he'd succumb to wounds from Orange and drop dead when he finally reached them.

As she turned back to Omar she caught a glimpse of the callbox. Something off . . . The C-13 tile tilted sideways, something she hadn't noticed before.

"I know it's dark in there," Omar continued, "but there could be other stuff we need. He has stashes all around."

The phone. The map. Sarah.

"Give me the map and I'll do it," she told him.

"What?"

"Give me the map if you want the axe."

"We don't—"

"Dude! Give her the map! Grant could fuck him up with that axe. I can't even hear the helicopters now."

Huffing, Omar pulled the map from his back pocket and passed it to Megan who'd taken the steps two at a time to reach him. "Hang on," she said as she unfurled it. Passing Bryce, she grabbed the cellphone from his hand.

"Hey!"

She plopped the map on the dirty concrete and took a picture. It came out as a blur. She took another with the same result. Another. Another. The fifth time offered a human readable image, but she noticed a peculiarity about the map—the marked milestones were encoded with a five-character alpha-numeric system. These could be approximations intelligible only to the Healers. Even another Prowler might not understand the coding and—

Oh, that's clever.

—the destination could be *any* of the marked milestones! Only the Healers would know which one, or, perhaps, which combination of them would be required for the healing process. It made sense. The Healing Place wasn't a pro bono operation, it was their livelihood. Although they hadn't gotten much money from Clark and Megan (who'd just about tapped their resources and were looking at bankruptcy no matter what happened with Sarah), Omar and his pals recouped losses through more lucrative clientele.

"We'll get you and Sarah back here, Megan," Omar said, although he sounded perturbed enough to reconsider the proposition at a later, safer, time.

Regardless, she tapped the image to send it in a text to her and Clark's cellphones, which their Prowler forbade on the journey. For good measure she forwarded the text to Erica's phone—maybe Megan wouldn't even need Omar and his back-up Prowler.

"Map's no good if you don't know what to do when you get there," Omar warned. "And if word gets out the place'll be ruined—it won't work for anybody. Now will you please get the damned axe?"

Megan returned the phone to Bryce and headed down the stairwell. Phone calls notoriously couldn't be made in the Kill Zone and she didn't trust the texted image would reach its intended recipients, either, so she stashed the map in her front pocket for safekeeping.

"Flashlight?"

Omar handed it over. "You're not getting the gun."

Megan pressed her back against the wall and peered through the opening. The axe hung on the wall, supported by two nails driven into the concrete. Two inches from the floor a tripwire stretched end to end across the doorway. Another wire stretched from the inside handle into the recesses of the dark corridor beyond. Omar held the door in place as Megan squeezed through the crack, right foot well above the tripwire. As she crossed the threshold she saw the wire strung from the door handle stretched to a pulley several feet down the passage. From there it extended toward the ground where it looped another pulley and came across the doorway at the floor, which meant this was one wire, strung to a trap somewhere behind her. Megan kept her back against the door frame and cautiously lifted her left foot over the floor wire.

Heaving a sigh of relief, she spun to face the opposite direction. The beam of light found the wire at the floor and she traced it to its terminus: a spool. She looked for something amiss, but it was truly just a spool. Opening the door caused it to wind and unwind. The wire strung across the threshold was for show, not a trap at all. She smirked.

"While you're waiting for that text you might wanna give Grant a hand," Omar said to Bryce.

The periphery of the beam caused a glimmer in the darkness, flushing her giddy relief through a tight funnel of terror. The abruptly raised flashlight brought a gasmask lurching out of the darkness.

XI.

I T LEAPED AT her, a specter from the place where she kept hidden things.

Gantry Road.

Cool air breezed around Erica's bare legs, tendrils of winter reaching from the forest into the surprise December warmth to exert its mastery over season and fate. A beam of pre-noon sunlight broke clouds to spotlight the sign for Gentry Road. White letters against a green background, tilted at an odd angle as if the world were upending.

Gooseflesh bloomed.

"What do you do before you cross the street?" Erica asked.

Smiling loudly, little Sasha left no doubt she knew this answer. "Left, right, left!"

Erica puzzled for a second. Left, right, left? March across the street? Sasha's straight-laced mother Elaine (who also happened to be Erica's much-older sister by 21 years) would not have taught something so reckless. Tight control over the television and internet made the internet an unlikely origin so Sasha must have gotten marching orders from a kid at school.

Sensing Erica's confusion, Sasha made a

production of slowly turning her head, saying "Left" before looking the opposite direction to indicate "Right" and then to the original direction again, "Left!"

Erica laughed. "Okay, I was gonna say 'Look both ways,' but I guess you give one side extra coverage."

Thirteen year-old Erica led her six year-old niece across the quiet residential street in a tony suburb of Green Bay on a pleasant summer day. Exile, an imposed reading list, summer school, babysitting, and family dinners with austere Elaine and unyielding hubby Curt weren't how Erica envisioned the summer before her sophomore year of high school, yet here she was, two hours from her Milwaukee home serving a sentence of Boredom. The epic sickness of June 19/20th would have been punishment enough, but her mother hadn't seen it that way. Whatever category fell beyond "hangover," well, Erica reached it. She didn't remember the cops breaking up the party, or drinking too much for that matter, but both things happened and she awakened in the hospital with alcohol poisoning and an angry bedside mother presiding over her immediate future, blaming everything but the obvious. Mom seemed willfully oblivious to the notion the third deathiversary of Erica's father might be a factor. Nah, nothing to see there. Trying to hold her dead father's brain inside his crushed skull while he sucked occasional breaths like a beached fish had absolutely nothing to do with it. To defend her mother's obsessive micro-management, her gray-haired father had just gotten to the part about Erica being a "miracle baby" when a tractor trailer came along to prove his point; she suffered a single scratch in an accident that killed both drivers.

Sasha walked the bike as they crossed. Erica heard the deep rev of a large vehicle some distance off. A little loud for a residential street, a little too fast, but the truck would have to exceed two hundred miles per hour to catch them in the road. Still, she couldn't take any chances with Sasha's safety.

Erica took hold of the handlebars. "Let's hurry."

"Okey-dokey." She smiled with no self-consciousness about the gap in her teeth, as bright as the sun overhead and its stark reflection off her bicycle spokes.

At least only-child Sasha would file this visit away as a good memory. She deemed Erica the coolest person ever and dubbed them "summer sisters," a more extensive relationship than any afforded by Erica's real sister. The hundred miles between her and Elaine were presently suspended but the twenty-one years remained. Elaine moved out before Erica's birth, leaving her to grow up alone with a mother almost resentful over this surprise child erupting from her uterus at forty-five. Her father seemed conversely delighted and appreciative of the opportunity, and his presence leavened everything until his absence shadowed it. Darker times followed.

They reached the sanctuary of the sidewalk well before the imposing pickup reached the intersection. If Elaine were around, she'd be ready to take the license plate and report the driver. There were rules, after all. Things you did not do because when the mores and morals of society were violated the center would not hold—or some shit.

So far the two weeks were pleasant enough. "Yes, sir" and "Yes, ma'am" went a long way to securing

Elaine and Curt's good will. She'd hoped Elaine might have kept something of their father's from before Erica was born, but only found an old wallet that wasn't even Dad's. Maybe a half cousin thrice removed or something, but a weird keepsake regardless.

Erica stayed on her best behavior. The reading and chores weren't overbearing—loss of all electronic devices meant she would be bored otherwise. But she knew the repercussions would extend beyond summer—her mother already decided to Say No! to MPS as if the public school system or older classmates were to blame for her daughter's bad choices. A litany resulted: *I never should have let you skip a grade . . . you're too immature.* All things considered, Erica thought she dealt with things remarkably well. And she wasn't an alcoholic—the merest thought of ever, ever, EVER drinking again made her nauseous.

The pickup continued to barrel toward the intersection behind her and even Erica couldn't abide the excessive speed. She whirled with a ready glare. The truck careened toward her so fast she had but one reaction: run. She didn't get a single step before the pickup bounced the curb and threw a warm wave of air against her legs and arms. It never honked, never squealed tires in a last ditch effort to stop before it battered its way into the rear corner of the house. Between ugly tire gashes in the lawn lay the broken, twisted frames of bicycle and girl.

Erica ran to her. Fell beside her. A broken mouth drew a slow, halting breath. Glassy eyes saw through Erica, beyond Erica, to something not of this existence.

She had to call this in, get an ambulance here, Erica turned and looked for the street sign.

Gantry Road.

She blinked.

Gentry Road.

"Erica?"

Erica adjusted Sarah. Held her closer.

"Hey babe, you okay? I can get her," Billie said.

It was the third or fourth time she'd offered. This time Erica gave up the little girl, who might be safer with someone else anyway.

But hey, at least you didn't have to worry about oversized speeding trucks and epileptic drivers in the Kill Zone, right? Then again, maybe she'd met her lifetime quota for freak road accidents.

"Are you sure we shouldn't take her to Sandalwood?" Erica whispered.

Relinquishing the weight left a lingering sense of imbalance. After being overly taxed for too long her left arm came back to life with the soft burn of pins and needles. Spine and back muscles were out of whack from counterbalancing the load. Add the myriad aching muscles from the tunnel crawling, hill climbing, endless hiking, frequent running. When the time came she'd probably be ready to die.

"Not a good idea right now. We'll check into this healing thing once we're safe," Billie said. She opened her mouth to say something else, but stopped short.

"What?"

"Got a weird question," Billie said and, prompted by Erica's nod, she added, "What's your mother's name?"

"Rhonda. Why?"

227

Billie smiled. Shook her head. "You remind me of someone."

"I get that a lot. Usually from guys." But once from the girl who would become her best friend, Tina.

"Bet you do."

Erica didn't want to say, but Billie probably saw her on the news. The local stations reported heavily on the volleyball championship a couple of weeks prior. A big deal since Marshallville typically aspired to no greater than perennial doorstop in basketball and football.

Erica reached to Sarah's wrists and checked the makeshift bandages fashioned from Adrian's T-shirt, later supplemented with Erica's second legging when the left wrist bled through. The barbed-wire gouges were swollen and weepy, but the monster otherwise spared her. For the moment.

"Too tight?"

"I'm okay," she reported, voice as soft as the breeze. "Thank you."

"You're welcome." Erica kissed her forehead.

"So what's a Gauntlet?" Billie asked.

Erica squirmed. She couldn't describe it in front of Sarah; rather, didn't want to describe it at all. The still-unnamed Prowler guy took one look at her outfit and said, *You're a Gauntlet girl, but where'd she come from?* Gauntlet girl. It sounded so demeaning in that context, reducing her to the kind of stupid *girl* who'd drag friends into the Kill Zone to die.

OSnap me, guilty as charged.

It wasn't the worst nickname ever given Erica. Her senior year of high school everyone turned on her because of a bastard boyfriend named Roger Boone.

228

He thought she'd cheated on him (she hadn't) and her pictures conveniently ended up on a revenge porn site. When her mother filed charges against Roger, Erica's friends abandoned her and backed the football/basketball double-threat phenom who could (and did) have his scholarship offer rescinded. When she ran from a mob of these former friends, they bestowed a nickname for the remainder of the year, the hurtful, dehumanizing, and rather simplistic double entendre The Pussy.

"It was just a way to get my boyfriend in here," Erica said.

Once doubled with Tina and in particular Shelly, the group bloated into something too large and slow to stand a chance of completing such a mission impossible. Prowler design provided an unforeseen bonus as Adrian slowed them so much they'd never reach the second station before midday—and by extension never get back in time for the G-Spot—which played to Erica's true goal: Sandalwood.

"Let's just say, confronting danger isn't his thing," Erica added.

"So he doesn't challenge you?"

Erica smiled. "But he'll never betray me, either."

Bryce didn't know about the Roger Boone betrayal. She doubted he could handle the snaps floating out there in the dark recesses of the interwebs. He enjoyed Erica the sexual libertine but he'd tear himself apart if he knew how she'd become that way. She chose her wardrobe today less for his benefit than a continued oath that Roger Boone would never ruin that part of her. The instinct in the wake of seeing her naked body online (and God, the comments—*o u bitch gonna fap all day* offered the most Shakespearean of the proffered sentiments) was to cover up every inch of herself and hide from the world forever. The staunch disapproval of Sarah's mom today provided a gutting reminder how few attributed any motives beyond "free lunch."

The Prowlerman, who told them not to run, now ran along the ancient asphalt, zigzagging around the brittle, fallen leaves. Billie, if that was really her name, told Erica fresh destruction would be a telltale sign for Agent Orange—wisdom initially imparted by this guy comparable to Adrian, only older and nameless and self-serious in a way Adrian would never get the chance to master.

To hear Prowlerman tell it, nothing supernatural enhanced the inhuman killer's ability to track someone; he might be endowed with an endless number of restarts, but he hunted humans simply by the disturbance they caused in his domain. To that end, he sent Erica, Sarah, and Billie to the intersection of Gentry and Fortuna while he created a couple of false trails that might buy them a little time when they needed it.

"He went after the other group," Prowlerman announced. "Thinks you're going nowhere without a Prowler."

The way Agent Orange keyed on her and Sarah before Adrian's sacrifice convinced Erica she wouldn't be long in following him into the thereafter, but he'd already missed three opportunities to kill her to prey on someone else instead.

It was happening again.

I'm going to live and they're all going to die.

Because she brought her friends to this place. She facilitated it all, same as leading Sasha to her appointment on Gantry Road. Tina wanted to go in, but she wouldn't have come if not for Erica. Her excursions to abandoned sites were enough for her. Erica tried, but whatever attributes they offered were nothing compared to the need for here, something almost ten years in the making.

Erica Jensen Smith! her mother yelled as she snatched the *Newsweek* magazine. *Where did you get this? This stuff is of the devil!* She shook the forbidden fruit in the air. Special Issue: "The Event." Ten-year-old Erica found the magazine by accident, tucked inside an old box of her father's things. Her mother ripped it in half. *Wait until your father gets home!* Though when he did, she realized he was in just as much trouble as she.

Prowlerman snapped his fingers.

"Huh?"

"You there?"

"Sorry. Was thinking about how my mom tried to keep me away from here."

"She didn't try hard enough."

Erica laughed humorlessly. "You have no idea . . . but the more she tried, the more I needed to do it." It could have been a case study in one of her psychology textbooks as a demonstration of how parents can make you what you are by trying so hard to prevent you from becoming what they don't want.

"Save the navel-gazing for later," Prowlerman said. "Stay with me. Focus. Right now you're the furthest thing from his mind, which gives us the best chance we'll get."

"But he looked ready to . . . " Sarah trained her sad, sleepy eyes on Erica, who offered a wan smile and left the sentiment unspoken.

"Plans change. Soon as you think you know what he'll do, he does it differently."

Unpredictability, thy name is Orange.

"Was your mom from Sandalwood or something?" Billie asked.

"God, no. She's barely been out of Wisconsin."

Prowlerman gave Billie a look as if he alone could initiate conversation.

The Special Issue hadn't been the only interesting discovery in her father's things. He owned a Glock that should have been her exit from the hell of senior year. She did her part. She put the gun in her mouth and pulled the trigger, only to find she was no longer the only broken thing at hand—the firing pin on the Glock jammed. There had been no sense of divine intervention and no relief at her stay of execution . . . except from Roger Boone, her shocked audience, whom she'd hoped to traumatize forever with her final act. The only exit was stage left back to her car, appropriately enough, since he undoubtedly thought the whole episode the scare tactic of a drama queen. Somehow after that she kept going, unfortunately so for the friends she lived to bring to the altar of sacrifice today.

Ironically she felt almost spiritually restored now, Sandalwood for her like a religious person's pilgrimage to Mecca. Even in those trips with Tina, that omnipresent thought in her mind: *I could come back here alone and finish what I started. No one would ever find me until it was too late.* That temptation seemed farther away now.

Erica checked Adrian's phone. No reply to the text she sent Bryce at Prowlerman's behest. The strength of his feelings far overpowered hers in the relationship, but of course she cared. She just didn't know if she could again risk that vulnerability she'd shown Roger anytime soon, maybe ever. It hadn't seemed like a conscious choice then. She knew better now; if you let someone in, they could run wild and carve you up. Bryce seemed the safest situation she could hope for, but even then she felt compelled to push it to riskier territory, both emotionally and physically.

Please be okay.

No reply to the text she sent her mother, either. A simple "This is Erica. Borrowed phone. I love you," so out of character her mom would have to know she intended it as a final communique. Something she'd never be able to explain if she made it out of here. *Why did you send that out of nowhere, Erica? What was happening? Did you go THERE?* But it seemed like bartering with fate, as if escaping the KZ unscathed could only be offset by willingly presenting another difficult challenge. Silly thoughts, to be sure, one fate so unlike the other as to be laughable, but desperation did strange things to one's reasoning.

Her mother forbade Erica from going to Marshallville State University, refused material or financial aid. But then MSU extended a volleyball scholarship and the academic achievement grants made it financially possible anyway. A September baby, she entered school early and later skipped a grade, which made her a minor entering college. She had to threaten an emancipation lawsuit to get her way. Leaving home undeniably helped her, not only to start anew without a single person around from the prior scorn torrent, but a rescue from her mom's passionate ideologies, too.

Although now she'd allied with someone who could teach her mom a thing or two about control.

"Okay, radio silence for the next bit," Prowlerman said. He'd carried Sarah the previous ten minutes and didn't look tired, certainly not in the intensity of his stare. "Don't fall behind. Follow my trail step for step as close as you can. Mind on the now."

A quick downhill pavement dash followed with the quartet making up for lost time while they could travel at full speed. Five minutes later they were deep in the woods again and twenty minutes after that they reached the wall.

"Don't get your hopes up," Prowlerman said. "Westing is on the other side, not freedom."

Erica soon understood the disclaimer. Either the ground had settled or erosion from hillside run-off washed enough soil through loose rock that a fissure opened beneath the wall, with the resultant crevice large enough for people to fit through without even having to crawl.

"Shortcut," he said.

Though Erica stood closer, Prowlerman handed Sarah to Billie as though only the adults could play a role in the little girl's fate. Erica felt a surge of possessiveness like she'd come out on the losing end of a secret custody battle.

Prowlerman descended through the hole and immediately reached through for Sarah. Odd woman out, Erica looked around with unsettling dejection.

She dared not consult her KZ map for fear Prowlerman or Billie would see the clearly labeled Gauntlet stations. She didn't feel self-conscious often, but when it happened it threatened to become a relentless downward spiral of depression and dark thoughts. This wasn't the time or place for it. Or maybe this was the perfect place for it.

Chin up, chin up, chin up. Don't go there.

She focused on the What Next. They would cross here and gain time. The alternative would have been to enter the Westing portion of the Kill Zone through an open gate at a decommissioned military outpost. There were two such places along the Westing barrier built at pre-existing roads to Sandalwood closed off by construction of the wall in early 1997.

Once Prowlerman reached the other side of the wall he turned to help Erica climb through. He kept his face neutral, unlike his initial assessment.

You're a Gauntlet girl.

Well, his sense didn't hold up to scrutiny either, did it? At least her visit counted as a one-off and not a career in a shark tank.

Erica looked through the hole to the place she left behind, a lot like the Westing Annex she'd entered, but different somehow. She couldn't understand or quantify the feeling this place gave her. The moment she set foot in the direction of Sandalwood she felt something she'd never felt before. Like "home" but with a deeper emotional resonance, like revisiting a hug from a long dead father. Agent Orange ruined that shit in a hurry, though. Erica had always been exceedingly, unnaturally lucky where general health was concerned, so assumed this would be an uneventful trip— uneventful except for the psychic benefits of forcing Bryce and Shelly to face the dragon of the unknown. And it would have worked, too, if it hadn't been for the actual Dragon.

She noticed Prowlerman staring at her, almost aghast.

"What?"

"You're not even out of here yet and you want to come back?"

"How did—"

He turned his back on her to help Billie with her descent.

—*you know?*

There seemed to be something between Billie and Prowlerman, but their interaction confused the hell out of Erica. In some ways they seemed like strangers, yet the glances they shared hinted at a much deeper relationship. She wondered if they'd had sex here. A stupid thought, but this place had been inextricably linked to sexuality for Erica. She knew why. She'd been fourteen the second time she saw the *Newsweek* special issue. A friend's brother had it hanging on his wall in a Mylar bag, the exalted centerpiece of a trio of fifteen-year-old magazines chronicling the Sandalwood Massacre. To its left an issue of *Life* with a boy carrying a cat through a military checkpoint, to its right an issue of *U.S. News & World Report* with what seemed like a thousand squares containing the faces of victims, a yearbook page of the slain. She used her budding feminine wiles to get the mint condition prize into her hands, but he'd used his masculine guile to get his hands onto her prizes. Her body wasn't a passive participant in this process; deep below the surface hormones danced magically—a magic she'd never recapture with him. *I thought you liked me!* he complained. *I thought I did, too, so sorry.*

The specter of sexuality with the Gauntlet led to its derision among KZ enthusiasts as a somehow inferior pursuit, though, and no doubt informed Prowlerman's distaste for the endeavor. If you stopped at G9 and ate a sandwich in the tower, no one would really care, but carnal pleasures invited finger-wagging from the Mayflower crowd. It hadn't been her motive anyway, with the prospect of sex merely a carrot for Bryce, who didn't realize his Brave Face landed somewhere between "animal in trap" and "deer in headlights."

The implications of the Gauntlet Girl dismissal hit closest to home with her prior ridicule as The Pussy.

Hey Pussy, I got a flip phone with a cam, why'onch you gimme a nice spread?

Nice tits, biiiiiiiitch, I just about jizzed on my keyboard last night.

Roger says it was so loose he wasn't even sure he got it in . . . yo, after seeing those pics, I believe that shit.

Not just guys, either.

Way to ruin it for Rog cuz you're too big a slut to keep your cunt to yourself.

I can't believe you thought your ass was worth sending to anyone but Planet Fitness.

She tried to mute the awful cascade of echoes.

They didn't trail the wall on the Westing side. Prowlerman said they needed to take the shortest distance between the two points. A long, quiet hour later they reached the portion of the Westing wall separating them from the real world. Prowlerman whistled as he approached, a strange warble like a familiar bird. A distant answer came in response. Prowlerman relinquished Sarah to Billie so he could text.

"I can take her," Erica said.

"Soon," Billie whispered.

"Try to follow my steps," Prowlerman said as he followed the wall from a distance of several feet.

Large rocks and dead vegetation formed the landscape between the wall and the forest. A dead zone air patrols could survey easily and likely a mirror image of the other side of the wall.

Prowlerman whistled again. Another answer, this time closer. Someone trailed them out there, closing the distance fast. Stalkerman, possibly Adrian's contact, Rad C.

Memories of Adrian provided a fresher torment to drown the old soundbites from school. She thought he'd have made the same sacrifice for others, but she'd always wonder. Had it been Omar or Bryce in her place, would he have tried to trade Sarah to invite the crosshairs? Unlikely. Regardless, he wouldn't be here today if not for her. She belonged on the Cause of Death right there with Agent Orange.

They followed a downward trajectory. Wall plates were not aligned along this route due to the steep grade. Some jutted up to a yard higher than the next plate. As if this may invite attempts to scale the walls there were extra spools of concertina wire atop them. Hybrid creek stone and concrete foundations embedded the bottom to guard against erosion.

Prowlerman stopped, took a breath and cocked

his ear toward the woods. Excitement filled Erica. This felt like the culmination of their journey even if she couldn't see how or why.

He whistled.

The answering whistle outside came louder than before. Stalkerman caught up to them.

"Here's what you wanted," Prowlerman said, but not to them. "At the base. A Cabot."

Erica didn't understand the lingo, but he bent down and pulled away a well-disguised piece of paneling made to look just like the surrounding creek rock. Beneath it, a thick, sickly-yellow foam filled what had been a tiny egress. The stuff hardened into a solid form that sounded rock hard when knocked with a knuckle. A piece of rebar jutted through a gap in the surface.

His face said it all.

"Ah, shit!" Stalkerman grumbled from the other side. "Visions of greensleeves disappearing before my very eyes."

Prowlerman turned and slammed his back against the wall. His hands went to his head.

"Plugged," Stalkerman said. "And recently, too."

Prowlerman's basket had landed, all eggs obliterated upon impact.

"Someone's cock-blocking us, boddy!"

Erica looked at Sarah who wept softly in her sleep.

XII.

GRANT DID HIS best to stay shielded behind the trees—not easy with his size and urgency. The girls ran back toward the direction of the tunnel when they splintered off, and he watched long enough to see Orange follow.

Omar didn't want him to pursue.

"What do you think you can do?" Omar said.

"I can bring them back."

"It was too late the second he turned left. You know it."

He shook his head. *"I can bring them back."*

Omar sighed, returned the head shake when he assessed Grant's sweater. "Still can't believe you wore that thing. He could see it through a brick wall, man."

He grinned slightly. "Hey, it's got me this far."

Omar held up a hand as if to arm wrestle in midair. "Good luck."

Grant clenched his hand to Omar's.

"Don't play martyr. Get your ass back if it's hopeless."

He nodded absently, his mind on the closing distance between Orange's steps and Tina and Shelly's.

"I mean it," Omar said. "We need you for this." He

held both the stare and grip to signify he meant the Healer Group, not the home stretch to rescue.

"I know, brother. We're only getting started."

This satisfied Omar enough to release his grasp.

"Get to the exit. We'll catch up." Grant ran and didn't look back.

He moved at a speedy clip by his standards. Of course he did—no excuse not to without Sarah to carry. He lamented not going after her the second Omar told him what happened. Even now he entertained the foolish hope he'd somehow cross her path while pursuing Tina and Shelly. If he avoided Orange and gathered everyone, great, but he didn't mind the prospect of a confrontation with the killer either. Hopefully the others rescued Sarah—he refused to accept she might be dead, not with the Healing Place within reach, that just wasn't fair at all—but if not, he wanted a piece of that bastard.

Grant didn't need the sweater now and hated the extra heaviness, but he kept it on. Terrible for camouflage, as Omar said, but if that helped the girls see him, so much the better.

As he hurried along, he listened like someone who flipped a pebble into a deep hole to determine its depth, waiting for wrenching screams. He remembered the ungodly anguish this morning of Noel and Doug. If not for Sarah, he might have made a stand there, but he considered her the priority in all of this, even now.

Grant could commiserate with Clark and Megan over losing a child. His nephew Daniel lost a soul-crushing battle with non-Hodgkin's lymphoma, and while that had been bad for him, it absolutely destroyed his sister Paula. A divorce and suicide attempt followed in the ensuing two years. Of course Grant's pain did not compare to hers, but he still knew the helplessness of sitting in a hospital room day after day, witnessing the deterioration of the boy's condition as every treatment option failed miserably. He also spoke with other families in waiting rooms with similar stories and comparably dire or even worse prognoses. Sometimes they pulled through, but far too often they did not. Eventually came Daniel's time, and bitterness rushed to fill the void left by hope.

He still had plenty of that. If they just knew four years ago this place held miracles and not only abominations . . . He never disclosed it to Paula as he thought it could push her to a second attempt to know a cure existed all along. Grant might soon find himself in the unenviable position of explaining what brought him here if the military evacuated them from the Chicken Exit.

Maybe it was par for the course of the universe to strike Sarah down within reach of a cure, but he wouldn't concede defeat yet. They had to keep fighting, same as she.

It didn't magically fix his grief, but it helped immeasurably to have a role with the Healing Group and a purpose these past two years. Most people went through life like buoys rocked by the currents, always reacting, never changing, but he helped facilitate the greatest work imaginable. Like chemotherapy, a lot of risk went with this option but at least it absolutely cured as long as you made it past the Orange guard. They always did until today. He knew a handful of children who owed their lives to a stopover in

Morgan. One of those families sent him this godawful sweater last Christmas and he considered it a talisman of good luck. He might have to rethink that.

Grant possessed no advanced tracking skills and trusted providence to put him on the right path, but maybe the sweater hadn't exhausted all its good luck after all because someone called his name. He stopped and looked around fruitlessly.

"*Grant.*"

This time he saw her, or at least the huge mound of pine needles from which the voice originated. It seemed obvious once alerted to it but if you weren't closely examining the ground, you could easily miss it. He crossed the ten yards of distance and crouched down beside her. Not bad—only searching for a couple of minutes and already found one of them.

"Tina?" he guessed.

"It's Shelly." She made no effort to crawl out from cover, but he spotted the opening for her eyes.

"Do you know where Tina is?" He checked around for any movement between the trees. They seemed to be alone.

"I don't know." She sniffled. "She hid me and ran that way." The nettles shifted slightly as she lifted a hand and pointed off past Grant.

"Did you see . . . him?"

"Yes." Her voice came out as a squeak, then a sob as she said, "He went the same way she did."

He winced. Too much to hope they hid close by one another and just waited for the coast to clear. "Okay, Shelly, I'm going to try to find her. You can meet up with the others if you go back and follow the creek. They regrouped."

The pine needles shook back and forth above her head, clearing enough to reveal strands of hair. "Not without Tina."

He hoped she wouldn't say that, but she might be too badly injured to go it alone anyway and at least Grant could help her on the way back, maybe with everyone in tow. He took stock of the surroundings as best he could to recognize it on the return trip. "Okay, you watch for me. I'll be back as fast as I can."

He spread some more needles to fortify her disguise in threadbare places. If she'd managed to elude Orange, Tina might too. He just had to hope again she saw him if he couldn't see her.

Grant followed in the direction she pointed, trying to intuit Tina's escape strategy. She obviously wanted to lead Orange away from Shelly. Would she have foresight to plan for a way back?

He plotted a diagonal course which fulfilled the qualifications of distance from Shelly and Orange alike. He'd give it fifteen minutes or so and return to Shelly if he didn't find a trace. If Tina doubled back first and they took off together, he'd decide whether to go for the Chicken Exit himself or split off and look for Sarah.

Omar's point that the search group knew how to find them made sense, but that was before a torso floated past—most likely Adrian's, which begged the question how Orange could dump it with the arms in the creek and somehow get far enough ahead on foot to ambush them at the intersection point (a lot of moving parts involved in this equation).

Fucker moves fast for a dead guy.

If Tina didn't duck her ass out of sight, Orange already had her.

Grant felt a tug and his heart jumped into freak-out mode when he saw a thread spooling back toward a tree branch. He assumed a trap, suggested by the ominous hollow opening in its trunk, but he only snagged his sweater in passing to draw out a long green strand. He snapped it from his arm, pulse pounding in his temples. The inside of the trunk caught his eye and he peered closer.

Something lay within. He found a stick to poke inside, expecting some kind of motion-activated censor to clamp down like Noel's bear trap. Nothing triggered. He examined every available angle, finding no wires attached to the object, which appeared mounted on nails. When he peered around the other side of the tree he spotted the driven heads.

Grant counted to three and snatched the handle, intending to pull it out as quickly as possible. Its unwieldy nature caused it to bounce off the rim until he found the right angle for extraction. He held a rubber-gripped tool with a dual blade. One side featured something like a sharp chisel, the other a four-pronged rake for gardening.

He patted the arm of his sweater. "Good looking out," he whispered. He'd be tempted to start wearing it year round. He would have never found this thing, which an old sticker on its handle identified as a flexrake hand tiller.

If I went after Sarah I'd probably find her and a brand new place to heal her in no time, he mused, and never mind he wore the miracle sweater when bad luck befell their group all of ten minutes after arrival today. Its good luck recharged and now he moved on armed with something from an Agent

Orange weapons cache. It made sense; AO couldn't just lug around a sack full of weapons like some kind of kill-crazy Santa Claus. He'd stash them all around. This one smelled faintly of WD-40. Orange kept his toys in top condition.

Grant resumed his hurried gait, assured by the weight of a weapon in his hand. He hadn't made it twenty more steps when he heard screams. They were faint and sounded farther uphill and to his left than he expected. He broke into a run and hadn't gone far there either when a massive crashing sound thundered far back to his right.

What the hell? Did he throw a tree trunk at her?

Grant changed direction once again, pushing back to his original angle. The terrain did not allow the quickest path where he needed to go, forcing him to run several yards to get around copses of trees unpassable for his size. For all his upper body strength from the weight training he maintained for his role as a transporter, he wasn't light on his feet at all. The chase left him way behind and only Tina screaming off in the distance clued him where he needed to go. Orange would catch up to her before he would if she didn't get a chance to hide.

The flexrake seemed to weigh far more than it should. His lungs smoldered. The dampness of the ground sucked his boots in like a marsh. It took him a moment to realize Tina's shouting became actual words. Too far off to understand her but a minute later he hypothesized when he saw the enormous structure blocking off the horizon.

Holy shit, that's the wall.

Had she found an outpost to help her? There

hadn't been an explosion of gunfire, but maybe Orange turned tail first.

He had to see either way so he pushed on, hoping not to run smack dab into a fleeing psychopath. He kept the flexrake held at shoulder level, ready to bury it in Orange's skull if he popped out from behind a tree.

A series of thuds sapped his optimism for Tina and the potential safety of the wall. The closer he drew, the wetter the sounds became, like a boot stomping through an icy pond and now splashing in the water beneath. Tina hadn't shouted in the past few minutes.

Because she can't.

Sick despair became a giant hand at Grant's back, propelling him faster toward the sounds, flexrake whipping back and forth as he pumped his arms. Orange overpowered a petite young woman, but it would be a different story against an armed man equal in size.

The trees parted to bring him to the site of a grisly tableau which turned his stomach even in the thrall of adrenaline. His fears for Tina were confirmed, her body torn into a V shape and stuck to a trunk with jettisoned organs piled at its base. This last humiliation must have just occurred as Orange still had his hands fastened to her legs, preparing to step back and perhaps admire his handiwork. He didn't get the chance.

Grant never stopped, charging with his flexrake poised high. Orange turned to meet the new threat. His gloved hand stopped the blade's descent easily but the collision pushed Orange up and back and his throat sprouted a strange curved shape which came dangerously close to puncturing Grant. Orange added his own darker concoction of blood to the already slickened metal as it oozed from his throat wound, bubbling around the opening.

Grant wrenched his weapon away from the gloved hand still locked around it. It sailed somewhere behind him as he stumbled back and landed on his ass. Orange shuddered on the pickaxe, his feet kicking a couple of inches above the ground. Grant didn't hesitate while he had him pinned, ignoring the flexrake to lurch forward on his knees and cinch his arms around the flailing legs. He hauled downward with all his weight, hoping the head would pop back like a Pez dispenser.

The one solution no one dared suggest—kill him and potentially restore all their options with Sarah, as well as an exit that didn't involve incarceration and registry. It seemed the most unlikely scenario, yet here Grant knelt on the verge within seconds of attacking.

Metal unsheathed to alert him that victory wasn't within easy reach after all. He dropped his grip and rolled away an instant before a machete split the air. He went for the flexrake, seizing it in time to see Orange push himself away from the tree with his feet, the slope of the blade retracting into his throat; no worse for the wear after an injury that would have killed anyone else.

Tina's limbs swayed like drapes behind him.

Grant backed away from the machete and to lead Orange away from the pickaxe. He shook the flexrake to call attention to his theft.

"You want it back, bitch? Come on! You're going to die for what you did to her!"

Orange glanced back at Tina, a chilling affirmation the slayer understood language and didn't continue his body count on autopilot for no other reason than because he died doing it in the first place. Easy to think so when the gas mask made him faceless and alien.

If Grant thought the acknowledgement a coincidence, Orange dispelled the theory when he snatched a handful of Tina's blonde hair from her scalp and ripped her forward. The body jackknifed to the ground, face-planting while the limbs struck impossibly akimbo.

Orange tilted the mask up as if saying, *Oh, you mean her?* He stepped on the back of her head as he advanced, pivoting to grind her face in the dirt.

Grant roared and swung the chisel blade at Orange's head. The gas mask dipped beneath it. He backhanded and the four prongs of the rake side ripped across Orange's sternum. He sidestepped a lunge with the machete and struck at the wrist, burying the chisel blade in the crook of Orange's arm. Orange fumbled the machete as he ripped his arm away. Grant planted a boot in his gut and pushed him back. He did it mainly to keep him away from the machete but as an added bonus Orange stumbled over Tina and hit the deck.

The fall put him uncomfortably close to the pickaxe still jutting from the tree. Grant rushed him, seeing his best opportunity yet to open the sonofabitch's skull. Orange grabbed something in the grass, slightly turning as he stood and swung forth with both arms extended and hands clamped. Grant gained almost half the distance when Tina's wish-boned body unfurled. The side with her left hand and arm struck him hard enough to knock him off his feet. He held on to the flexrake, barely, arm throbbing from the impact. The surreal sight of a moment ago prepared him for the next—Tina's head barreling face-down at his own as Orange swung her overhead by both ankles.

Grant slid to the right on his back. Her face thumped on the ground simultaneously with the snapping of her neck. It drooped at a sickening angle as Orange flipped her up like a bedsheet. He failed to parlay it into the momentum needed for another dive bomb and the body slumped to the ground. Grant scrambled up and sprang over her torso, stepping between the split halves, swinging the flexrake. Orange turned his face up so the chisel blade met the plate of his gas mask instead of the top of his skull. The plate gave in but sapped the power of the swing. The blow intended for his skull punctured his face and the momentum pushed him backward.

Gravity yanked the flexrake out of Orange's face. More blood seeped from the wound, almost black. That Grant could reach down and touch his face did even more to demystify him than the sight of the blood. He swung at the eyeballs with the prongs. They punctured Orange's forearm as he threw it over his face. Grant pulled the rake back, twisting it again to the chisel side.

Orange clutched a fistful of Tina's entrails and slung them at Grant. They smacked his face like a pile of wet towels, one coil draping over his arm. The world went red and black. He staggered back, trying to make sense of the sounds around him, flinging his arm to shake off the hanging entrails. He struck out with the flexrake as he wiped his eyes, convinced Orange would deliver a deathblow he couldn't see coming.

Life came back into focus. He'd ended up near the machete. Orange still stood a safe distance away by the tree but claimed the pickaxe from the trunk like Excalibur. Grant traded the flexrake to his other hand, grabbed the machete, and took the offensive.

He trusted to instinct in lieu of experience with hand to hand combat. He slashed overhead with the machete as he approached, thinking more about where to strike with the flexrake if he missed. Orange deflected it easily, hoisting the pickaxe to use the full expanse of the blade as a shield. Grant swung the flexrake from the left to bury it through Orange's ribcage.

He didn't get the chance.

Orange's block became a fluid motion with the pickaxe a falling spear. He drove the sickle through the instep of Grant's boot. It passed through leather, skin, and bone with a dull thunk which did no justice to the resulting eruption of horrifying agony that compressed the entirety of the world into a few inches on Grant's foot. Orange withdrew it as easily as a knife from butter.

Grant's mouth dropped open as a tortured scream burst from his lungs. He pitched backward, as much to take his weight off the foot as any attempt at survival, and screamed again as his weight returned a step later.

Orange arrested his momentum by hauling him back by his sweater. Red and black consumed his vision again. He saw only flickers as Orange swung the pickaxe at his face, but everything cleared as the blade filled his open mouth and pitched down his throat. His screams terminated in a *culk!* sound. His esophagus and voice box ruptured. The opposite slope of the pickaxe blade seemed impossibly large, a slide that reached all the way to the sky. Blood burbled around his lips, spilling down his face and chin. He couldn't breathe.

The long protruding crescent drew nearer, driving into his upper teeth as Orange slowly pushed up the handle before jacking it up in one rough motion. Two of Grant's teeth cracked in the sockets as his maxilla bone shattered. The crescent lodged in his esophagus bulged the skin and then burst through his throat far enough for him to see it curl past his chin. Orange relinquished the sweater and let Grant drop. Orange towered high above him now like an ant he'd crushed beneath his boot, massive and unknowable.

Grant writhed face-up on the ground, choking on the blood pooling and trickling through the puncture. A whistling sound emanated periodically from his shredded throat like the beat on a heart monitor. He thought of Sarah at first, with the half formed idea in his mind that once freed his soul could fly to protect her if he just focused on her face, when that whistling sound stopped forever. When he no longer had the strength to move his own fingers, though, he thought more practically of the path he stomped through the woods to get here—the one Agent Orange could follow right back to Shelly's hiding place.

XIII.

BRYCE MOVED HIS phone around. Bars appeared, disappeared, reappeared.

Service.

No Service.

This wasn't at all how he envisioned his visit to Gauntlet station ten. The G-Spot loomed nearby, practically mocking his impotence in the face of fate's grand design. As a destination for sexual activity, this tower predated the Gauntlet itself, probably inspired EXTREMEDEAN69's much larger quest.

Instead of blasting off with Erica on its upper floor he feebly reached out to her on an intermittent cell connection. They couldn't even sext each other.

He glanced into the stairwell where Megan slipped through the cracked doorway, chancing a trap so she could fetch them another weapon—provided *it* wasn't trapped.

Giving up on his phone, Bryce pushed it into his pocket.

A metal plink drew his eye to the Chicken Exit callbox. The identification placard fell from the unit to the pavement below. "Real high tech piece of equipment right there," he whispered.

Where the hell are the helicopters?

"While you're waiting for that text you might wanna give Grant a hand," Omar said.

Bryce already considered it, but it meant leaving the guy with the gun. Now he couldn't feign the ignorance of not having had the thought himself. It would scream cowardice.

"Ah, yeah, of course." Bryce practically rapped the side of his head to acknowledge insensitivity over spinelessness.

Grant, with head down and shoulders slumped, lumbered like a man ready to drop. Shelly dangled from his arms, her face toward Bryce, but almost upside down. She slowly gasped like a fish trying to draw breath from waterless air.

Megan screamed. Bryce turned back to the bunker.

Omar bolted halfway up the stairwell.

"Megan?" He had the gun out and aimed at the doorway in case it blasted open with the force of an Orange explosion. He looked professional in his stance, like ex-military or ex-police.

"It's . . . oh my God—it's just a mask!" Megan yelled. "He's got a spare mask stowed down here."

Omar tilted his head back to look heavenward as he returned the gun to his waistband, stopping just short of genuflection. He headed down the steps to fetch his prized axe.

Damn, jump scares are for the movies.

Bryce hurried toward Grant, hoping Shelly might have recovered enough by now to walk under her own power. He wasn't the carrying type.

"I'm coming," he told them. *Not a coward, see?*

Shelly looked horrified. Her mouth continued to

move and Bryce remembered the arrow in her back when he saw its jutting broken end. She could be suffocating on her blood, something easily remedied with a puncture-the-lung maneuver he'd seen in so many movies. Maybe Omar or Megan knew how to do it because Grant didn't even know how to carry her, which surely contributed to the agony. Shelly's pain gave him a twinge of guilt for shirking his obligation as a friend. She needed evacuation immediately, but the helicopters were no closer.

And then the significance of the fallen placard occurred to him with all the subtlety of the spray-painted G9 amidst the plethora of graffiti. They named the Gauntlet station for the Chicken Exit location. This wasn't C-13, it was G-9—Agent Orange swapped the placards.

Fuuuuuuuuuuuuuck!

No wonder the helicopters were no closer. Erica would have known this—*he* would have known this if he hadn't dwelled on the G-Spot nickname. Bryce had to call the dispatcher and let them know the right location or there would be no rescue.

"Grant, hang on, I'll—"

Something in Grant unsettled. As if regaining his lost composure his slumped shoulders broadened; his slow, halting steps became assured, gravel-crushing stomps; his head rose to reveal a ghastly, frozen rictus of an expression. Grant's face, Grant's hair, but not Grant.

Translated through a new lens, Shelly's gasps for air became the warning: "Run."

Bryce stumbled back a step—*the monster was only five yards away*. His mind flashed to a movie

Erica made him watch because it came from her father's collection. He blurted a nonsensical warning to the others.

"Keyser Söze!"

Agent Orange made a projectile of Shelly, and Bryce's hesitation between dodge or catch defaulted to the latter when Shelly struck him face-first in the chest with such a powerful impact it knocked him off his feet. In desperation he sucked air to scream a warning so Omar could put the gun in play, only to have the breath stolen when his back collided with the pavement, his scream of alarm a wheezing whimper. The impact jarred his neck so hard it felt like several vertebrae snapped. Reeling and powerless, the large shadow overtook him, but it kept going.

Bryce's left leg worked, but most of Shelly hung as dead weight on his right leg. The remnant of the broken arrow shaft jutted erect against the blue sky. He scrambled from beneath Shelly, who coughed and choked against his chest.

"Omar!" Bryce screamed, so high-octave he half-wondered if he heard himself or Shelly.

Bryce grabbed her hands and jerked her upper body off the pavement. From the waist down she dragged concrete as he backpedaled toward the open tower door. It was a suicide gambit to seek shelter there, but he couldn't leave her in the open.

"Oh shit!" Omar shouted.

Bryce glanced to the right and saw Agent Orange tossing aside Grant's red-and-green striped sweater as he barreled toward the stairwell. The gas mask slapped at his back.

The gunfire came too little, too late. A quick

succession of reports echoed from the stairwell as Omar beat a retreat to the bunker. The resounding shots sounded like cannons, but the maniac ran toward them without fear. He hurled himself into the stairwell, disappearing from view as the steel door clanged shut.

Bryce pulled Shelly past the call box. She scraped the ground like an anchor, leaving a curious trail of blood, pine needles, a boot. Would Orange stay occupied long enough for him to inform dispatch of their correct location? He'd gamble Shelly's life with such a—

Orange burst from the stairwell, target locked. "Ohshit!"

Ohshitohshitohshit

Bryce looked over his shoulder at the open doorway. He could fit through the space without stopping to open the door further. It had a latch, but if it didn't lock from the inside he and Shelly were doomed sooner than later.

Sooner, after all, for when he snapped his head around to see how much time he had to reach the tower he found he had none.

"Omar!" he screamed as he stepped backward through the doorway with Shelly. His foot hitched the threshold and backward momentum did the rest, tossing him to the floor, Shelly atop him.

Agent Orange slammed a boot into the broken arrow in her back with the force of a sledgehammer driving a 60-penny nail through Jell-O. The arrowhead pounded through Bryce's groin deep and hard in a searing flash of fire, erupting in starbursts of agony.

Shelly spurted a gob of blood on his stomach as Orange yanked her up the remaining protrusion of the arrow, the bulk of which remained embedded in Bryce. Orange slung her, gurgling and wheezing, beside him. A particularly forceful exhalation sent a sputter of blood from her chest wound.

Bryce rolled to his side and dared survey the damage below. The bloody shaft projected from his crotch, blood dribbling from the tip to the tower floor. He grabbed it but the merest touch sent a shockwave of pain that short-circuited his willpower and knocked him on his back again, gasping for air. A world of vivid, wild color flashed through his mind, not a side effect of trauma but of the spray-painted tower walls. Coupled with the pain, this sensory overload nearly blew his mind.

Agent Orange stood in the doorway for a moment unmoving, a lurker at the threshold, with Grant's wild mop of hair silhouetted against the daylight outside. From the angle Bryce couldn't see the face, which was just as well. Then the calm before the storm passed.

Orange dropped upon Shelly like a penitent to his knees, dragging a serrated knife across her throat in the same motion. The trench went deep enough for the teeth of the blade to rattle across bone. Blood burst through the shredded flesh, joined by a pool filling Shelly's mouth and overflowing her lips. Orange sank one knee into her chest and pressed. The steady crimson stream sloshing from her throat blasted up again in rejuvenated fountain sprays. He withdrew the knee, allowing it to ebb once more, and then eased forward again to summon the geysers.

Bryce watched in stark terror over this Sergio

Grueletti style special effect brought to splashy life—
or death. Shelly choked all the while until the struggle
for air ceased and blood passively seeped across her
cheeks and into her nostrils.

He understood then, at last, the revelation
momentarily denied by the immediacy of his pain and
now displayed in arm's reach. Some part of him had
still believed a reprieve would be granted from this
fate. The Chicken Exit seemed less a miracle than
foregone conclusion because of course he would
survive, he *had* to. Bryce must go on, he had family
who loved him, a whole life ahead of him, and though
this may be true of everyone else, he fancied some
loophole mandated his survival with only the scars of
a harsh lesson about the frailty of existence . . . an
existence, though, which still continued for him. Now
he saw his true future embodied in Shelly's vacant
stare.

Bryce reached out to her, covered her eyes with
his hand as though to thwart the prophecy. Then he
closed his own eyes and cursed his failure to dissuade
Erica, as well as his involvement of Adrian when the
whole thing might have died before it ever got off the
ground. Instead he enabled her and brought Adrian,
Tina and Shelly along for a death ride.

Why? Why? I didn't even want to fucking do this!

With his eyes already closed Bryce feigned death,
hoping Orange would pass him by. Instead a knee
pressed to the side of his head, crushing him against
the floor so hard he divulged his status with an
involuntary cringe and groin-agonizing body twitch.
His eyelids snapped open as he awaited the snapping
of his skull. Instead, Agent Orange put a gloved hand

upon Shelly's forehead as he slid a knife through the skin at her temple. Blood pooled at the incision point, became several racing streams.

Sickened by the disgusting mutilation, Bryce closed his eyes.

No no no no no no.

A sharp jab on his forehead inspired the desired reaction: reopened eyelids and a scream.

With Bryce's renewed attention, Orange inserted the knife into the slit at Shelly's temple. The cold blade slid into view through her ear canal. A wash of blood spilled through the concha, filled the scapha, overflowed the helix and dribbled to the gritty floor.

Horrified, Bryce shut his eyes again for the merciful blackness. Two sharp jabs of the knife into his forehead and they parted again. Hot blood trails ran along his smarting brow.

He grabbed Agent Orange's powerful leg with both hands, squeezed so hard it hurt his fingers. Orange jabbed at Bryce's forehead several times, crisscrossing in a random pattern of punishment. Head pinned, he couldn't dodge but kept hold of the leg through stubborn determination.

"Omarrrrr!" he pleaded. "I've got him!"

Orange flicked the shaft of the arrow with the knife blade, sending an incapacitating burst of pain through Bryce and a blast of blood from his rectum.

"Ah-ahhhhh! I'm sorry, I'm sorrrrrrrryyyyyyyyyy!" Bryce held his hands aloft, palms-up, a show of contrition. He opened his eyes comically wide, an exaggeration to prove his full attention and cooperation. *I'll watch* The Mutilation Hour with Richard Dunbar, *just please don't touch that arrow again.*

Orange continued with the excision of Shelly's left ear and the hair that came with it. He dropped it in front of Bryce's face, then worked on the other ear, which Bryce blessedly couldn't see, though he heard the nauseating soundtrack of blade notching bone and snapping flesh.

Abruptly, Orange turned Shelly's face toward him. He recoiled from the blank stare, but dared not close his eyes. His stinging forehead ached enough already.

Raised voices echoed from a chamber below. In addition to steps leading to the upper deck of the tower, Bryce glimpsed a stairwell that led down. Did it connect to Omar's bunker? Could there still be a rescue somehow, his reprieve allowed only because he abandoned all of his arrogant hope?

The knife plunged into Shelly's neck. Bryce cried as the blade sliced its way through the original incision to form an asymmetrical cross, skewering the trachea with a splash. Shelly and Bryce's blood mingled in the puddle between their faces, her left ear an island in the crimson sea.

No rescue, just another massacre if the others weren't warned.

He grabbed Orange's forearm, a futile effort the butcher easily cast aside to continue his craft. Not dissuaded, he clutched Orange's leg and squeezed as though sheer force of will could crush the muscle and bone beneath. The lone effect was in supercharging Bryce for a massive strike with his legs. Defying the screaming nerves, his feet plunged toward Agent Orange and struck their target with every bit of the epic force he had mustered. Though certain he struck his target in the head or left shoulder, he bounced off as if he collided with a brick wall. The effort hadn't been in vain as the pressure against his skull released, freeing Bryce to roll to his back and trade one dead countenance for another. Grant's expressionless face hovered above Bryce like a rubber Halloween mask, darkness through the slack mouth, but the eyes . . . Bryce glimpsed something in the dark chasms, feral glints in the inky shadows. A line from last semester's philosophy class surfaced like the punchline to a horrific joke. "And if thou gaze long into an abyss, the abyss will also gaze into thee . . . "

Bryce opened his mouth to scream.

The knife plunged into his abdomen at the navel, striking so deep it chinked bone. The edge tore upward, slicing through viscera and strafing the vertebral column. His breath hitched when the blade struck sternum, powerless to close his gaping mouth or suck a precious gasp for his starving brain, mute from the mutilation. Worse, he stared into the abyss, unable to avert his gaze.

Orange unpaused the moment with a forceful flick of the wrist. The blade rent ribcage and its hilt dealt a final crushing blow to Bryce's chin, slamming the door on a silent scream and shattering teeth into dozens of gum-slashing shards.

XIV.

AMPLIFIED BY THE confines of the bunker, the steel door crashed into its frame. Omar grabbed the latch and threw his weight behind sliding it into the wall. A stunned Megan stood with axe in hand, wondering how things took a turn for the worst so quickly. Gunfire. Omar racing to seal the bunker. But what about the others?

As if reading her mind, Omar said, "It wasn't Grant!" The terror on his face seemed too raw and personal so she aimed the flashlight beam at the ceiling.

"But Bryce? Where's—"

"Might as well've been shooting a locomotive."

"But Bryce!" Megan protested. The words sounded too harsh, too loud in the confined space, essentially a corridor with closed steel doors at either end; doors which could be locked or trapped, making this a tomb as easily as a sanctuary. The door at Omar's back offered the only sure way out and they already knew where *that* path led. This could be a dead end for them, implications obvious.

He still carried the gun and an uncertain amount of bullets. Megan had the axe, but didn't think her odds any better for wielding it. And how would it

263

work in here? She couldn't swing it overhead without the ceiling obstructing its path. In the bunker only the gun mattered.

"Gotta find a way out." He took the flashlight from her.

The closest door in the corridor proved a bust. No handle, and the puckered scars of welding surrounded the door, forever sealing what lay beyond.

"We're so screwed if the other door is welded," Omar said.

He knocked aside the hanging gas mask with an angry swipe—*take* that, *effigy*! It gave Megan such a start before. Backlit by the flashlight, the mask swung menacingly from its hook. Part of her wanted to destroy it as if doing so could damage Agent Orange himself; attack the mystique, harm the man.

"Thank God. Locked from our side," Omar announced.

"What if there's a trap? What if he's there?"

"If he's on the other side, you run like hell. I'll hold him back as long as I can."

"And leave you?"

"Megan. I should've been long gone. The Healing Place gave me two and a half more years. If you get the chance, haul ass."

The dim glow from the flashlight provided only a faint and shadowy view of his face, but it seemed like the first time she'd ever truly seen him. So many questions which had to wait for a precarious later.

Omar disengaged the lock with a creaking scrape.

Megan let the head of the axe touch the floor so she could hold its handle with one hand. With the other she felt along the steel door for the window.

When she found the knob she stood at an angle and readied to slide the metal shield aside, assuming it would budge.

"Be ready for a worst-case scenario," Omar said.

The door wailed on ancient hinges, but nothing leaped at him.

She'd opened the window at the same time and light entered the bunker. No shadow on the other side, so she pivoted at a safe distance from the two by five inch glassless opening. The outside stairwell appeared empty.

If Orange was busy with Bryce and Shelly, he wouldn't be much longer. Megan lifted the axe with both hands. The metal head made for an awkward balance.

"Light at the end," Omar said.

Given their location upon entering the bunker, the direction of the tunnel, and the distance to the source of light, Megan guessed the other end led beneath the tower, which made this underground passage a below-ground shelter for either reinforcement or retreat. The tower door hung crookedly and wouldn't close, so no way to shut off Agent Orange's access from that end.

"Omarrrrrrrr!"

A heartbreaking plea or warning or both from Bryce, either from the tower or close enough for his scream to carry. Megan blinked away tears. Mothers were losing sons and daughters and they didn't even know it. They would find out later; disappearances followed by creeping dread and tragic confirmations. Nothing would ever be the same for those families.

A shadow shifted across the light at the end of the tunnel.

The creak of a slowly opening door bludgeoned its way through the corridor, the soundwaves battering the concrete walls around them. Through the fear Megan made sense of the sensory input—Agent Orange stood at the threshold to the tower door, the lingering darkness within the increasing source of light.

Omar's outline showed a steady, side-to-side cadence as he walked backwards to put himself on the right side of the door. His boots crackled the grit on the floor.

The distant light momentarily brightened, then dulled just as quickly, followed by a loud shuffle and thud loud enough to reverberate through the tunnel.

Megan felt along the wall for the axe.

The shadow crossed the light again.

Grabbed by the hair, Megan almost screamed as she shook free. Just the damned gas mask, punishing her for conspiring against it earlier.

"Think he left," Omar whispered when she drew close enough.

They waited, listening.

A violent impact stormed through the bunker—Agent Orange at the stairwell door behind them. Megan and Omar ran toward the light, their urgent, thudding steps echoing like a herd rather than a duo.

"Hold up, hold up," Omar whispered as they approached the open doorway. "He could've played us."

Another loud thud at the stairwell doorway indicated Agent Orange didn't flush them in this direction just so he could double-back and intercept them at the tower. Megan bolted ahead of Omar even though he had the gun.

"You don't have the axe?"

She ignored the comment and barreled up the concrete steps as lightly as she could. There didn't seem to be traps anywhere, but at her rate of speed she might notice one too late to stop. She reached the doorway safely. The door itself stood further ajar than before, enough to permit even Omar to easily slide through the opening.

A simple plan coalesced in her mind: if Agent Orange stayed in the bunker stairwell, they would make a hard left outside the tower and exit through the open gate. With the wall shielding them from view they could get a head start before Orange discovered their escape route. Find another Chicken Exit, set up a second rescue attempt.

Another loud thud came from the tunnel behind them. Orange went all-in on his stairwell door assault. This time she heard it coming from outside the tower, too, only it sounded more distant, more contained, less apocalyptic. Had they been trapped in the bunker awaiting his grand entrance, they would be cowering in abject fear. Perhaps he thought both interior doors welded shut.

When Megan approached the last few steps she turned to Omar and raised a finger to her lips. With an incredulous, puzzled look he pointed to the gun as if this were an expedition he should lead. She couldn't risk an argument or the time it would take to hear a plan potentially inferior to her own so she turned her back on him and hurried the last few steps, only to hear the slap of her boots against wet pavement.

Halfway to the door Megan found herself standing in a wash of blood. She would have cursed her carelessness had there been a way around it. A deep red flood filled the entire floor. Now she heard the pattering of dripping blood and took another step to peer into the stairwell leading to the top of the tower.

"Ah, shit," Omar whispered.

Bryce atop Shelly. The bodies were stacked on the steps with the stumps of their necks downward to facilitate exsanguination. A channel gaped open in Bryce from his abdomen to his neck, a crevasse with torn, ragged entrails inside and out. No one could exit the tower without taking a trail of blood with them. Her surefire plan foiled from the start.

They couldn't get through the gate without Orange knowing what they'd done, but the blood would eventually wear off. If they made it far enough ahead they could elude him.

While she considered the implications, Omar passed her and went to the door to look outside. Orange's beating of the other door ceased. Either he got in or gave up.

Megan heard a vibration from Bryce's body. A glow through the front left pocket of his pants verified he'd received a text. Grant's face lay on the floor beside him like a discarded Halloween mask.

"He's coming," Omar reported.

He tapped Megan's shoulder and nodded toward the steps to the tunnel. Megan nodded, too, but didn't follow in retreat.

The angle of the tower door prevented Agent Orange from seeing her so she hurried to the bodies. She reached into Bryce's pocket. A wound between his legs glistened with blood, meat protruding from a tear in his jeans where something was ripped out with such fury it pulled a gob of genital with it.

The helicopters grew louder, suddenly much louder. Were they finally coming?

Megan tugged the phone, but it caught on the inside of Bryce's pocket and his body shifted. He slid off Shelly until he wedged against Megan's left forearm. Another tug and the phone came free. She immediately shoved it into her own pocket. Without Bryce to unlock it she wouldn't be able to reply to the texts, but she could at least read them from the lock screen—a one-sided interception of information without the ability to reply beat knowing nothing at all about her daughter's fate.

Fresh blood filled many of their tread marks, but enough footprints remained for Agent Orange to know they were here and returned to the bunker. They would be trapped with helicopters and possible rescue hovering above them.

Megan untied her boots. The withdrawal of her arm caused Bryce to slide to a rest beside Shelly's body. She removed the left boot. Still no sign of Orange. She set her foot onto a concrete step unsullied by blood. Gripping a handrail, she shook her right foot free, then leaned backward and clutched both boots. She shook them twice to knock free as much blood as she could, then held the treads against her sweatshirt to thwart dripping. She hurried up the steps to the landing and glanced back before heading up the next set of steps. Still no sign of Orange. And no telltale signs anyone used the stairs. She reached the top floor landing just as the tower door began to creak.

Black socks trampled words and images left by previous visitors. Surrounded by a Technicolor tapestry of spray painted messages, Megan stood in the gallery of the graffiti gods, where a thousand tags and multilayered messages covered the circular wall, ceiling, floor, with names and dates scrawled on the railings. The disorienting mix of imagery and styles overwhelmed the senses. Only the windows were spared, but the decades-old safety glass became practically opaque, like eyes afflicted with milky cataracts.

Remembering how Agent Orange's presence in the tower affected the shadows, Megan squatted to make herself a smaller obstruction to the natural light. Boots next to her, she stayed perfectly still. Someone left a crumpled blue blanket against a wall beneath pornographic images of the Peanuts gang. There were several "Banksy?" and "Banksy where are you?" pleas. The recurring combination "G9" appeared on ceiling and wall, often rendered to look like "69." Then she saw the disgusting, crusty remnants of dried bodily fluids on wall, floor, even ceiling, slung there by creepy, sick fools who'd risk death for reasons of sexual insanity.

From the squatting position she couldn't retrieve the phone, which pressed painfully into her thigh. She kept her arms crossed and listened.

Through a window she saw two low-flying helicopters approaching with the quickness Omar had awaited. Agent Orange stood sentry between her and them but she couldn't help feeling a sense of elation at their advance. Their presence introduced new variables to the doom equations, if nothing else extending the time it would take for Orange to figure an answer.

She felt him in the foyer below. He'd be standing in Bryce and Shelly's blood. Silent. Unmoving. Would he bide his time? Wait for the helicopters to give C-13 a cursory check, write this off as a false alarm, or crank call, and head back to base? Surely he wouldn't attack. There were limits to what a solitary, ground-based zombie Rambo could do, weren't there?

Attack the choppa, freak! Do it.

She welcomed the thought of him disappearing into a .50 caliber red mist.

She hadn't heard Omar close the door as doing so would have echoed through the basement tunnel, channeled into the tower by the concrete walls, but surely he heard the rotors and knew how close they were to rescue.

A Black Hawk led a larger, wide-bodied helicopter with a helpful red cross so panicked victims would know the rescue chopper. The Black Hawk spun sideways at a slight angle, surveying the immediate area. It flew low enough to kick a swirling mass of dust and loose debris through the air. The rescue chopper circled at a higher altitude, possibly to avoid ground fire should it come to that.

Land! Land!

Despite the military presence, Megan felt a rapid drop in her prospects for survival. They weren't landing. She and Omar left nothing outside to indicate their presence, no different from all the other stations already bypassed.

Omar, do something!

If only Megan had the flashlight, she could send

bursts of light through the windows. Dot-dot-dot-dash-dash-dash-dot-dot-dot, an SOS to the pilots.

She did have the phone.

And it vibrated an incoming text.

Too loud until she could crush it against her sweatshirt.

Shit!

Crawling on hands and knees to the nearest window, careful to make no noise even though the thundering rotors would likely mask it, Megan prayed the helicopters stuck around long enough. She withdrew the phone and scrolled through several texts from the same number, pleas for answering texts, apologies. Finally she found a lengthier text. Agony and relief—Clark died, but the Prowlers who found Erica and Sarah were taking them to a nearby exit.

Megan held the phone to the glass as the helicopter circled around. She activated the screen, locked the phone, activated the screen, locked the phone. She repeated the pattern, hoping the light bright enough to penetrate the cloudy glass.

The scent of the dust wafted through the air along with something else, something earthy and dank. The shadows moved. A reflection appeared in the window beside her. And then she heard the sticky sound of boot treads leaving footprints of blood on concrete.

Megan spun and saw him climbing the stairwell, now wearing a different gas mask to the one hanging in the tunnel, perhaps obtained in a stronghold here.

It's the demon.

"Omar! He's in the tower! Run! *Run!*"

Agent Orange neared the top of the stairs, his speed completely nonchalant.

Megan pocketed the phone. She hurried to her boots and stepped into them.

Orange topped the stairs and only eight feet separated them, if that.

She hurriedly tied the left boot, unable to look at him but immobile in her peripheral vision. Megan shifted to the right boot, tears forming in her eyes. This thing killed Clark. So many others. Her turn.

The helicopters were leaving; with them, hope.

Orange looked to his left. An explosive concussion rang from the stairwell, another, then another, deafening. He turned and staggered backwards. Megan lurched out of his way, seeking refuge where the railing met the circular wall, behind it the chasm of the stairwell. Omar charged up the steps, tossing the gun away when each trigger pull earned a click. He whipped the axe into the air with his left hand and added his newly freed right hand to the handle to wield it with maximum force.

"Get out of here!" Omar yelled.

But she couldn't escape because she'd get between Agent Orange and Omar as he readied to swing the axe. Lurching, he swung it overhead, barely missing the ceiling before Orange stepped forward to intercept it with one hand in its downward arc. Omar gritted his teeth and tugged with both hands. A quick flick of Orange's wrist and the handle flew upward, the axe head downward where it struck a glancing blow against Omar's forehead. Stunned, Omar staggered backward a step, blinked twice, and threw his hands to his face as the four inch gash above the bridge of his nose unleashed a river.

Orange stepped back and swung the axe so hard

it knocked Omar's head against the nearest window. The axe handle exploded into splintered fragments, leaving the axe head buried in the glass with snaking, zigzag lines radiating from the impalement. Omar's body struck the floor. The only attachments from his head were his broken lower jaw and a tongue that seemingly licked the floor in the spasms of his death throes. A large remnant of his crushed skull slipped backward off the axe head and smacked the floor near the blue blanket.

Megan jumped over the railing and managed to hit the mid-level landing feet-first, but tipped forward into the concrete wall, striking her forehead. Her instinctive need to flee sent her feet moving before she'd quite figured her bearings. She spun and put her right heel onto the edge of the second step; her left foot landed in Bryce's chest incision. She slid forward, shoving a glut of entrails through Bryce's neck hole so hard some of it spattered through the doorway. A crushing blow to her right knee on a concrete step halted her momentum. With a scream of pain, she let herself tilt backwards to get her leg beneath her.

Agent Orange's footsteps thundered behind her.

Megan stumbled through the doorway. Her right knee and hip sent torturous needles of pain with each limp. The helicopters were leaving—no, they *had* left. So recently all of the dust hadn't settled. She frantically looked above, side to side, and saw the shapes of their salvation ever diminishing toward the horizon.

Nearby, just off the pavement she saw five stakes that weren't there before—two of them topped with Bryce and Shelly's heads, a third some sort of sack with hair or maybe a drooping mask of some sort. There were two open spots in the gallery and she knew one had been reserved for her.

Did the choppers call off the rescue because of these fresh trophies, judging it a lost cause?

She hobbled toward the Chicken Exit call box. A sharp pain in her back flushed the air from her lungs mid-breath. A projectile protruded from the right side of her sternum, a long, asymmetrical piece of blood-soaked wood Agent Orange used to hoist her into the air.

She reached backward with clawing nails and found purchase, tearing at his head with all her might. She tried to rip it from his shoulders and shocked herself when it came free. With a primal surge of hatred and anger, she hurled his head as far as she could. It flew past the Chicken Exit box as Orange dropped her to the ground. Somehow she landed on her feet.

Bastard! You bloody bastard!

Megan staggered toward the head and dropped to her knees before it, pounding it with her fists in primitive triumph. She opened her mouth to scream but only sprayed droplets of blood against the black face, glassy eyes and the strange tube coiling from his mouth.

And then, blessedly, the obstruction to her breathing reversed itself. The broken axe handle disappeared into her chest, exited her back, and she arched backwards to draw a much-needed breath . . .

Only no breath came. She filled up with emptiness, drowning in open air. Her body felt horribly wrong, numbness settling in all over like frostbite.

RYAN HARDING AND JASON TAVERNER

Head tilted, she saw a shadow eclipse the sun. The hazy features of a distant face blurred into shapeless blacks and greys. Her eyes caught a fixed point beyond the head, hovering above—the dripping tip of the axe handle. The jagged point abruptly descended. It pierced her right eye and shattered her eye socket in an explosion of light that folded her backwards.

XV.

WHILE EVAN AND his charges skirted the inside of the Westing Annex he considered the implications of their next destination. Since he put all his faith in the blocked exit, he hadn't taken very good care of their trail on the Westing side of the wall. If Agent Orange didn't fall for the false trail on the Sandalwood side, he'd get to them without much delay. Because of this, Evan opted for the closest possible exit instead of the nearest military checkpoint.

Carlson's whistle paced him on the other side of the wall. Although Carlson probably didn't need Evan's reply given the noise Billie and Erica made, Evan did it anyway.

Erica carried Sarah because Evan would need all of his upper body strength for the task ahead; Billie, too. This, of course, presupposed the scaling station supplies weren't purloined by the bastards who cut off the previous exits. To Evan's knowledge, only five people had known about the fiercely guarded secret crawlspace created ten years ago by a Prowler named Cabot, part of a trio who stuck to themselves. Two of the three were dead and the third married, moved to Colorado and started a family. Before moving to the other side of the country, he entrusted Evan with the day-to-day running of his security business as well as the existence of several egresses.

Evan wouldn't have told a soul about this one except he used it to evacuate a severely wounded Prowler named Bryan Starling the previous summer. More recently, Starling joined a company that wanted to "professionalize" forays into the Zone. Via Starling they made overtures to Evan—overtures rebuffed because doing this strictly for the "greensleeves" seemed a bridge too far. Every entry into the Zone tempted fate; making an assembly-line, cookie-cutter process out of it would get people killed.

And sooner or later you'd have to eliminate the competition, either competitively . . .

Or through other means, like shutting down the access points of other Prowlers. Starling also happened to know about the tunnel exit Erica's group used.

Starling, you greedy bastard.

Evan shook his head, a symbolic gesture to shake off the anger and frustration that would only distract right now. The ruined exit was an issue for another time. Three lives depended on the scaling station right now.

A murder of crows took flight. Judging by the distance they were on the Sandalwood side of the wall. If this signaled Agent Orange's approach Evan had less than thirty minutes to complete the evacuation.

He glanced up and saw one of several openings the size of holes in notebook paper.

"We're here!" Evan called, loudly enough for Carlson to hear.

278

"So we're screaming now?"

"See the holes? In the wall?"

Billie and Erica looked, but it was Carlson who needed to find them on the other side of the wall.

"Yeah."

"Line up with them and put your back to the wall."

"Got it."

"Now you'll go straight to the woods. About . . . " *Was it twenty or thirty?* "Uh, twenty-five paces into the tree line turn left and in fifteen paces there's a stump with a supply box stashed underneath. Get the bag."

Please let it be there.

Carlson whistled.

Evan turned to Billie and Erica. "To the woods," he said.

A nearby copse of pine trees would have to suffice as a hiding place.

When they reached it Billie appeared flushed, but not from the exertion. Evan recognized the look, what an old Stalker called "Buyer's Remorse." He'd once seen it in a fifty-something investment banker certain he'd never get out of the Kill Zone alive, their "near-miss" courtesy of an encounter with another Prowler. After leaving the Kill Zone the banker threw up and kissed the ground—well to the left and downwind of his chunder, of course.

This wasn't me. I—I'm not this kind of person. I honestly don't know what the hell brought me here. Why I needed in here so badly. It—

Seemed like a good idea at the time? Evan offered.

The guy vigorously nodded. *Yeah. Yeah.*

Billie's MacGuffin had been her father's ashes,

but, really, everyone who came here fit into a larger, overarching category called Moths to the Flame.

"Got a text," Erica said. She showed Evan the phone. "Will this help?"

It looked like a coded map of Morgan, useless to an outsider and only marginally useful to a Prowler unfamiliar with its iconography. Wherever the other group planned to take Sarah for "healing," this map likely showed it. Through trial and error Evan felt reasonably certain he could decipher its locations. Bella's life may depend on it, Sarah's definitely so.

"Forward it to the number I gave you," Evan said.

"What about . . . ?" Erica showed him texts from Rad C asking for updates.

Evan shook his head.

They were near the junction of the Westing wall and the original Sandalwood wall for the scaling station. They essentially put themselves in a corner, limiting their escape opportunities and making for a most unchallenging stalk should Agent Orange find them.

"I'll get Sarah to the top of the wall and down to my partner." He looked at Erica. "Stay here until you see the ladder, then hit it fast as you can. It won't be an easy climb. You got a problem with heights?"

"I, uh." She paused to look at the wall.

"Never mind, most people would have a problem with this." He turned to Billie. "The ladder can't hold you both so stay here until she's over the top. If Orange comes after me first, you two run. A couple ridges over there's an old road that takes you to the highway. Go left and you'll eventually hit a military checkpoint. If you see signs, ignore them—he likes to switch those around. And for God's sake, announce your presence and approach the checkpoint with hands in the air."

"I'm not—" Billie started.

"You protect her. Don't worry about me. And if Erica's climbing the wall when Orange gets here, protect yourself. You go for that road. When I get them out I will come for you, I *will* find you."

"All we need is a waterfall," Billie said with a smile.

"Okay, I don't get the reference but I'll take it as a yes."

Although she nodded, Evan figured she'd do something stupid if the moment came.

"I'll need to fasten Sarah to my back for this. Your shirts should suffice." He pointedly looked at Erica. "You *are* wearing something underneath, right?"

"Yeah, but Billie should go before me and I go last."

"No," Billie said. "Absolutely not."

"I'm faster. He's had two or three shots at me and—"

"Elaine, you're not—"

"Erica."

"What?"

"You called me Elaine."

"Did I?"

Carlson whistled.

"You did," Evan told Billie. "Cut the chit-chat. The order is what I say it is. Wait here."

He ran back to the wall, screaming inside. Every part of the process seemed to take so long, minutes they didn't have. The pin had been pulled on the

Agent Orange grenade and they were scrambling to toss it out of their bunker before the blast.

To Carlson he called, "I need two of the spikes. Throw them over."

A moment later a gleaming metal bar spun end-over-end as it cleared the top of the wall. It landed several yards away with a loud ping that echoed between the wall and woods. The next spike pinged off the other side when it ricocheted off the wall, again when it struck the rocky ground. Carlson cleared the hurdle on the second try. The pings were a necessary evil and they'd be on Agent Orange's radar, confirmation of his quarry near the Westing wall.

"You want the bag?"

"Not yet."

Each spike had a hand grip with a four-inch long protruding shaft designed to fit into the holes burrowed into the wall. There were several such entrances around the perimeter created by mountain climber/Prowler George Rassimov. He survived countless forays into the Kill Zone only to die climbing the north face of the Eiger in the Bernese Alps.

Evan left the spikes at the base of the wall, hoping this wouldn't be *his* Mordwand.

He listened for any telltale signs of Agent Orange's approach as he returned to the woods but heard only Billie and Erica's whispers and the shuffle of their feet through pine needles and soggy ground. All the recently melted snow made them imminently trackable. If Evan could do it over he would put more effort into covering their route on the Westing side and/or creating more false trails. Now they were running out of time too fast for any exit but the most dangerous one.

Without her dirty sweatshirt Erica looked like she'd taken a wrong turn on the way to a rave. To complement her miniskirt she wore a black silk shirt that reeked of expense. She crossed her arms like Evan caught her naked in the Garden.

Billie helped fasten Sarah to his bare back. Her black long-sleeved shirt with Erica's sweatshirt crisscrossed Evan and Sarah at the shoulders with his long-sleeved shirt wrapped around their middle. When he stood Sarah didn't slide down his back, although it felt like a little too much slack in the binding. No time to redo this. Given Sarah's weight, she wouldn't drop through because of gravity—he'd worn empty backpacks heavier than this little girl. It painted a foreboding picture of the possible future with Bella. Getting older yet getting smaller. Wasting away.

"Eyes and ears open," Evan whispered. He held his stare with Billie, aware these may be his last words to her and the inadequacy of the moment to communicate everything that mattered. Like the fever need of the Sandalwood sickness, however—this apparent in Erica too, strangely enough—he thought he saw the unspoken enormity reflected in Billie's face too. The reunion of days but bound by a lifetime. "Be safe. Stay in cover."

He hurried back as low to the ground as the extra weight allowed, both on his back and in his chest. At the base of the wall he grabbed the climbing bars and thanked Rassimov for the exit. A left-hand hole at six feet in height provided the first slot with the right-hand hole roughly two feet above it diagonally. The left and right slots alternated like this for twenty feet and then there were extra holes so every level had a parallel counterpart in case of arm fatigue. Evan slid the point of the bar into the aperture and lifted as if climbing the pegboard back at the Sandalwood Middle School gym. With his right hand he lined up the second bar with little effort and slid it in. Errant scrapes marked the concrete surface around the hole from previous climbers with a harder time getting the pin into the slot.

"I've gotta pee," Sarah said.

Evan took their weight with his right arm so he could pull the left pin from the wall.

"Can you hold it?"

"I think so."

The right-handed chin-up brought him within range of the next gap. He reached upward with his left hand and slid the pin home. He lifted with his left arm to remove the pressure on the right pin and pulled it out.

At his back Sarah moved vigorously.

"You . . . okay?" he asked as he prepared for the next grab. This was harder than he remembered—and he was just starting.

"Waving at Billie and Erica."

"Whisper, okay?"

"Okay."

He slid the pin into its next hole and lifted.

Pace is the trick.

Withdraw.

Insert.

Evan had to assume Orange gained close enough

proximity by now to see them making this climb. He would have to anonymously report the exit for the military to disable. It wouldn't be beyond Orange to fashion climbing rods of his own once he'd seen it done.

Withdraw.

Insert.

Rassimov's achievements included several speed climbing records. Some of them still stood, although someone bested his Mount Rainier time two years ago. Evan wondered how fast Rassimov scaled this wall. Probably less than a minute. If only Evan had such speed.

"Will I be able to see my mom when we get to the top?"

"There are lots . . . of trees."

Evan reached and had more trouble mating the pin with the slot this time.

"You'll see her . . . "

Withdraw.

The pin scraped around the hole.

Come on! Damn! Rassimov would laugh at my ass.

Finally it slid deep.

" . . . soon."

He could only afford a temporary respite before the next lift. Sarah had ceased to be the light, airy load from before and become more like an anchor whose chain someone tugged from the ground.

Carlson whistled a question. *You still there, brah?*

"I've really gotta pee. This is tight," she whispered.

"Go if you . . . gotta."

Withdraw.

Insert.

"I don't pee in my pants. I'm not a baby."

The concertina wire at the top of the wall posed the next challenge. There wasn't standardization in these crossings and Evan never used this one before, only verified the existence of the supplies outside. It would suck to get to the top and not be able to disconnect the spiral wire. What if Starling and his pals immobilized the concertina wire? No, that was something a sadist would do; let some poor sucker climb to the top only to discover *ha HA, no escape for you!*

Insert.

Evan shakily withdrew the climbing bar with his right hand. If he dropped one of the bars he'd be doomed. With only one bar he'd be stranded and would eventually fall; a drop from this level would break one or both legs, to say nothing of Sarah if he dropped the wrong way. One should always carry a reserve bar. He'd made a climb like this before but only thought of such a thing now. Strange.

Insert.

A loud crack echoed in the forest, the sound of wood snapping. Distant, but on *this* side of the Westing wall.

He noted several scrapes around the upper holes where tired climbers faltered at connecting their bars. He contributed several new scuffs.

Six levels left and he felt compelled to skip the parallel holes due to the lack of time.

Five.

A loud cacophony erupted to his left. Three horses burst from the woods, charging with reckless abandon. Near the wall they turned as a group and disappeared where Evan's peripheral vision couldn't reach. Behind him. Now to his right. The thunder of their hooves rolled off in the distance as they fled something horrible.

"Wowwww," Sarah gleefully whispered.

Four.

Three.

Two was a struggle, the spike nipped the opening several times before he slipped it inside.

One slid home with unexpected ease. He spotted the connection band which held the concertina wire together. Every four feet were connectors that snapped in the event Agent Orange slung something up here like a grappling hook to haul himself up or to tear down the wire and climb it, barbs and all—the military considered things a crazed, undying psycho might do that sane people would never attempt.

"So high," Sarah said.

"Tell me if you see anything moving in the woods. Or if you're slipping."

The pins were parallel to each other, several inches from the apex. He grasped the top of the wall with his left hand and grabbed the pin on that side with his right hand, now within reaching distance of the left-most band of concertina wire. The band was tight, but came loose with Evan's insistent tug. No sabotage. He tossed the wire upward. The bolts holding the section slipped their grooves and momentum rolled the spiral of wire outside of the wall. It cleared a segment around four feet in length. He heard the metallic stretching of coils as they dangled out there, suspended by the fastener to his right, barbs scratching the concrete.

More animals took flight. Birds. Deer. Too much movement to be coincidental. An inhuman wrecking ball hurtled through the woods. Agent Orange didn't usually do it this way, startling animals into the role of emissaries for an imminent unnatural disaster.

You saw one of my false trails, didn't you? You know there's a Prowler in the game.

Or he wanted to get inside Evan's head. Maybe both ideas had validity. Either way, Agent Orange knew he wasn't tracking two lost girls but their Prowler.

In a few minutes he'd find their original attempted exit and follow them straight here. Evan's stomach tightened. He couldn't get all of them out. There simply wasn't the time.

Don't panic. We'll all get out.

On the flat wall top were two holes for the climbing bars. Evan found the first one and stuck in his pin. Water and displaced gunk squirted out. Using the bar for leverage he threw his left leg onto the wall, carefully avoiding a snag on the nearby concertina wire.

"Watch your legs," he warned Sarah. "Let me know if I get you too close to the wire."

In his peripheral vision her right leg swung wide and he assumed she did the same with her left. How comical must this look from the ground?

It didn't take much to get on top of the wall, which contained sufficient real estate to maneuver with a rectangle of concrete forty-eight inches in length and eighteen inches in width. Thirty feet off the ground, though, so the squeamish need not apply and, in fact, might feel paralyzed at such great heights.

"Evan go in Zone," Carlson said in an affected monotone. "Find him papoose."

Evan held up his hands as if to receive a pass from below and called, "Bag, man."

"Who's he?" Sarah whispered.

"He's *Rod*, since we're apparently using names."

Carlson used both hands to swing the supply bag in Evan's direction. Legs clamped to each side of the wall with his right hand gripping the planted climbing bar, Evan leaned far enough to catch hold of the bag at the apex of its ascent. An inch lower and it would have been unreachable at a time when every second counted.

The exchange garnered a fist-pump from Carlson. He hoarsely whispered, "Adrian over there?"

"Not with us. There's a second group."

Sadly, Rad C had no idea his nephew likely made the ultimate sacrifice. Evan felt comfortable enough with the lack of definitive proof to field questions with calculated ambiguity, even though Erica's story meant Adrian had a distinct disadvantage. Every Prowler knew the odds of escaping Agent Orange decreased significantly the nearer your proximity at the point of retreat. Adrian also hadn't tried to escape so much as lead Orange away from others. Doomed from the start.

"Hang tight back there," Evan whispered.

"You made a joke," Sarah said in the same hushed tone.

Evan smiled. She and Bella would be the best of friends and they could certainly meet. Until they accounted for Sarah's mother, Evan and Billie could provide shelter for her. In the meantime, he'd find out everything Sarah knew about this attempt at healing her—provided she knew anything at all. This brought its own host of complications, but he needed that straw to clutch if all else failed.

"I need you to close your eyes. Just hold on loosely, but don't let go. Tell me if you need to move? Okay?"

"Okay."

Evan rose to his feet. Sarah's grip tightened beyond his "loosely" mandate but not enough to choke him.

"How do you do that?" Carlson said. "Unders are my thing, never Overs. I'd retch."

"If anything happens to me make sure this gets decommissioned."

He took a couple of steps backward and squatted to insert the second climbing bar in its wall-top slot, unleashing a slurping gush of water and dirt. He unzipped the bag. This scaling station had the worst ladder, made of rope. The others offered sturdy three-story fire escape or wooden rung ladders. In the case of the fire escape brand they were heavy enough to require a rope to hoist them. Evan would have preferred reeling that up versus the difficulty of Billie and Erica climbing a rope ladder flush against a flat surface; well, if he'd had more time.

A movement, tiny, almost negligible, almost overlooked, in the direction from which they'd come.

Far distant, midway between forest and wall stood the Minotaur.

Despite Evan's innumerable forays into the Kill Zone, he'd only ever seen artists' depictions or actors' portrayals or questionably-reliable photographs or post-mortem images of the monster slain. He'd never seen the real thing, the real *live* thing, until now. Blood-curdling. Spine-chilling. Hair-raising. A thousand clichés couldn't describe the 200 proof distillation of dread.

At least I can get Sarah out.

And then the impossible happened. Agent Orange calmly walked to the forest, as if his quarries' trail dead-ended at the wall.

He saw me. Had to.

Evan closed his eyes and recalled his Kill Zone mantra, the one passed on to him by his father through the gift of a book.

Don't panic.

Two rings at the top of the ladder fitted snugly around the climbing bars. Evan tossed the ladder over the side and it unfurled neatly, stopping a foot shy of the ground. On the inside. With Orange too close to successfully evacuate everyone, the best hope now would be to save Erica and Sarah.

But Billie . . .

Stay back in the woods you sonofabitch, leave us alone.

Unprompted, Erica sprang from the woods and raced across the open expanse. She ran like an athlete, which gave Evan hope she might fare well against the rope ladder.

"He's coming, but he's looking for three of us," Evan announced. "Three sets of prints, but we've carried Sarah the whole way so he'll see three of us on the wall. You need to stay put, Billie. Don't fu . . . *freak*ing move no matter what. I will come back for you . . . "

Her waterfall comment finally clicked. Hawkeye's speech in *The Last of the Mohicans*.

"No matter how long it takes," he added so she would know he finally understood.

While Erica climbed, Evan hung the supply bag on the right-hand climbing bar.

"Where are Mommy and Daddy?" Sarah asked.

"We'll meet them later," Evan said with the surety of an adult who knows certain lies must be told to children.

Could he risk bringing Bella here if this healing place truly existed in the Kill Zone? Was it hubris to think he'd fare better than the Prowler who brought Sarah? He blithely exposed Billie to this, without expectation of these consequences. Perhaps he'd grown jaded, like a driver who'd lasted a lifetime without a crash only to see the lights of an oncoming car, no time to react.

Erica stalled three quarters of the way up the ladder. Twisting her body, she tried to draw the ladder away from the wall so she could get the tip of her boot onto the rung. She succeeded and raised another couple rungs. She wasn't taking them one at a time. Far better instincts for self-preservation than he expected from a Gauntlet type.

Come on, come on.

A rush of movement caught Evan's eye.

"The bad man!" Sarah screamed.

Agent Orange burst from the woods like a passenger racing to catch his flight. He came with two stakes already prepared, but he cast those aside and they clattered along the rocky ground. Why stake two, three, or even four heads when you've got a ladder to freedom dangling in front of you?

XVI.

ALL WAS QUIET on the western front until an inhuman bomb exploded from the woods. Though Billie watched and listened for him he'd still appeared out of nowhere, perhaps because Billie was distracted by her last conversation with Erica.

How do you know Elaine? Erica had asked when Evan began his journey to the wall.

She's your mother, isn't she?

No, she's my sister.

We were evacuated together. The day after the Sandalwood Massacre. Elaine Jensen. I'll never forget her face. Billie touched Erica's hair. *Or this. You look so much alike.*

Erica, with the strangest smile, whispered, *That bitch.*

In the here and now, Evan seized a climbing bar to steady himself and reached to Erica. Grabbing her by the wrist, he hoisted her off the ladder toward the top. As she threw her right leg high to gain purchase, her boot swung into the concertina wire and several quick shakes couldn't free it. Evan grabbed the left-most climbing spike, the one closest to him, and slid it from the wall, letting the left side of the ladder fall over the edge. Unfortunately, Erica was partially draped around the other climbing spike so Evan replaced the left spike and began to tug the ladder up hand over hand.

Hurry! Hurry!

He managed to pull it about ten feet from the ground as Agent Orange closed in. Orange threw himself into the air and snagged the last bit of rope, bouncing off the wall. The ladder jerked downward and snapped taut, initiating a chain-reaction that knocked Evan into Erica and Erica off the wall.

And then Evan tumbled from the wall when he tried to grab her.

Billie stood in stunned silence as Sarah screamed.

Evan threw a death grip on the climbing bar and caught himself with a loud grunt, dangling from the edge. He dug for the knife on his belt. Nearby, Erica swung upside-down like a pendulum, her right boot snagged in the concertina wire. Her palms swished against the smooth surface of the wall to slow the swing of her body.

Orange planted a foot against the wall and scaled using the collapsed ladder the same as he would a simple rope. He moved so fast it seemed like an optical illusion where he must be on a horizontal platform. He'd reach Evan before Evan sawed through the rope.

Billie ran for the poles Agent Orange brought with him. She grabbed the one six feet in length and sharpened at both ends, its purpose obvious. The other had only been sharpened at one side as if he'd been interrupted during his whittling project.

"He's coming!" Sarah screamed, her ashen face twisted by the horror of his approach.

Billie jumped and swung the pole, but only struck the wall beneath him.

Damn it!

She didn't have the strength to throw it with enough force to damage him so she had to hope Evan's rope-cutting ploy succeeded. She wedged the base of the shaft into the ground, clasping the stake and pushing with all her weight to drive it deeper into the earth until confident it would stay that way. Billie backed away to evaluate Evan's progress.

Orange was almost within range of Evan.

"Your legs!" Billie warned.

Evan spread them, putting them out of reach, but Sarah's legs still hung within his grasp. She tried to swing them away, but he reached—

The rope snapped.

Orange dropped.

But not before snagging Sarah and tugging her violently through the clothing straps. The force of the extraction seemingly tore her in half, a horrifying illusion created when her sweatshirt wrenched over her head and came down a second after her fall.

Agent Orange landed in a heap, snapping the stake with his weight. Sarah landed on his chest and bounced off. Billie ran for her as the dazed giant extended his leg to assess the broken three foot section of stake that entered the back of his thigh just above the knee joint and protruded near his hip. He adjusted his gas mask to better see the impalement.

Billie gave wide berth and approached the unmoving Sarah from Orange's blind side. Nothing appeared awry with the little girl's limbs, but it had been a hard landing. The skin of her back presented as a ghastly, inhuman white except a red streak that ran along her spine from Evan's belt. Billie had to hope she'd sustained no neck or spinal cord injuries because a snatch and dash was the only option. With any luck, adrenaline alone could get her halfway to the military checkpoint. Grim determination would have to suffice for the rest.

Overhead Evan moved hand over hand along the top toward Erica. He couldn't mount the wall with the shirt that once ringed him and Sarah at the waist pulled halfway to his feet. Whipping his legs back and forth, he attempted to dislodge it so he could get a foot atop the wall.

Abruptly Agent Orange rolled to his side. Billie recoiled with Sarah in tow, but Orange seized Sarah's leg and jerked her out of Billie's grasp as he hopped to his feet. Sarah's head swung downward, hair sweeping the ground with her skull barely missing a large rock. The stake still jutted from his right thigh, but if it hurt he didn't show it. He held Sarah high in the air, dangling her by her right leg as if in parody of Erica's plight. With a tilt of his head he presented her as a curiosity.

"Let me have her," Billie said. "She's just a girl. People brought her here. She didn't come willingly."

Orange dangled Sarah toward Billie as if he were contemplating a magnanimous act, wholly out of character. Or did he recognize Billie? Did he sense her as a rare one who got away? Did survivors matter to him? In a couple of the movies, the fictionalized version mysteriously escaped the Kill Zone to claim the life of a survivor from the previous film; one such scenario gave Billie recurring nightmares about an icepick through her temple (and cured her of ever watching another of those things again). Although no documented cases existed, it didn't stop hundreds of survivors from fearing they would be the first. Billie wondered if she was the only one dumb enough to bring the opportunity to him, but then she considered Erica unwittingly following Elaine's footsteps. What hope did anyone have if the lure could be in one's very DNA?

"Billie, run and don't look back!" Evan yelled. "Erica, look away."

She backed away from Orange, but really, if he lurched forward she'd still be well within his range.

"You did this, but I got away." She lifted the bottom of her T-shirt to show him the scar. "It's me you want."

She put the distance of another step between them as Evan finally kicked away the shirt that bound his legs. It dropped through the air unnoticed behind Orange.

"Run, damn it, *run!*" Evan's voice cracked as the sound of his struggles echoed lightly from the forest.

Orange grabbed Sarah's left leg and rent her like a wishbone. She tore as effortlessly as wet paper, the burst inside of her cascading to the earth in a torrent of tissue and crimson thick enough to rush up Billie's shoes and seep through their tongues. Orange jettisoned both pieces to either side in the same motion, arms outstretched as if to say *voila.*

Billie reeled on her heels, screaming her horror, shock, disbelief, rage as she ran to the other stake.

Evan above, voice climbing in pitch: "No! He can't catch you with that leg! You run, Billie! *You fucking run!*"

RYAN HARDING AND JASON TAVERNER

With the stake she ran—at the child killer. He stood his ground, waiting. Rearing back as though to take a swing at him, she raised her left elbow high and at the last moment brought it down and swung her right elbow out, plunging the stake toward his torso. He moved to the side, grabbed the stake and slammed her into the wall.

XVII.

BILLIE CRACKED HER forehead against the wall so hard it dropped her where she stood, a likely concussion to go with her unconsciousness; Evan didn't want to consider it could be any worse than that. Nearby pieces of the little girl he couldn't save were testament to the prospect of tragedy.

"You can't wage a war up there!" Carlson shouted. "Exit stage left!"

"Call in a breach!"

"Seriously?"

"Do it!"

The odds were maybe less than fifty-fifty, but if the military dispatched a helicopter to stop an imminent Agent Orange escape, it might give Billie her only shot at survival.

Evan tried to undo the knotted sleeves of Erica's sweatshirt while the hanging Erica watched Agent Orange pull the wooden stake from his leg. It clattered across the rocks, sprinkling blood as it went. With any luck Billie damaged the femoral artery and Orange would bleed out.

As long as Evan stayed atop the wall he remained top priority—at least Evan thought it worked that way. Billie obviously wasn't going anywhere so it made sense to focus on those in danger of escaping. He could very well butcher her for the shock of it like Sarah, though, as a psychological tactic. Evan acted like she wasn't important, didn't even look for signs of life. It may afford her the opportunity for escape previously ignored if he kept Orange's focus up here.

If she had mere unconsciousness to awaken from.

Erica made a token attempt to get to her boot by trying a hanging sit-up. She might be lean and athletic but she lacked the core strength necessary for that maneuver. The tautness in her limbs slackened noticeably after what happened to Sarah, like she wanted to just pour out onto the ground in a boneless puddle.

"Don't," Evan said, "you're more likely to dislodge your boot. You'd need abs of steel for that."

Tears ran in reverse from her eyes, sliding down her forehead. "He can't jump this high anyway . . . right?" On the face of it the question seemed ludicrous; after all, Erica hung over twenty feet from the ground. Assuming such a leap within the realm of possibility for a monster with inhuman strength, the leg wound would prevent it anyway.

"No." He removed his Leatherman tool from its snap holster. "I think his grab for the ladder was his best shot."

"Well, it was a pretty fucking good shot." Her breath hitched. "If I got up faster, even a few seconds—"

"Don't."

He knew you could walk *if* back forever, in his case to no Agent Orange at all, but Billie leaving town thinking of him as only a "neat kid" if she ever thought of him at all and Evan growing up in town with his parents and so many different triumphs, regrets and failures, a different life and a different world altogether.

If just this instead of that.

"It wasn't you," Evan continued, "it was him."

Orange stood below in a puddle of blood, none of it Sarah's because hers weaved around rocks in a different direction, headed downhill. He wrapped the fallen shirt around his upper thigh—Evan would have caught the thing before it slipped off if he'd known it would aid the bastard.

With the help of the Leatherman pliers he managed to unknot the sweatshirt. He needed it intact to be of any use and a perfunctory search yielded no tears.

After cinching Evan's shirt, Orange wrapped Sarah's sweatshirt around the entry wound and tied it off.

Evan braced himself on the climbing bar closest to Erica and leaned over the wall, hoping the sweatshirt had enough length to connect them, enough strength to support her weight without tearing.

"Grab this." He swung it over to her.

Erica pushed against the wall with her right hand and reached with her left.

Bereft of the weapons he needed for a wall encounter, Agent Orange picked up the stake Billie used to lunge at him. Limping backwards, he put space between himself and the wall. He tossed the stake into the air and caught it with his right hand so he could launch it like a spear.

The first time the sleeve arced toward Erica she missed it, but the second time she pinned it to the wall with her palm and closed her fingers around it.

"Get hold with both hands."

Orange slowly backpedaled, gauging the distance, the optimum angle.

"Don't let go."

She placed both hands on the sleeve, knuckles white.

He'll go for her. If he misses me he loses his javelin.

It was a hell of a gamble to put himself into a position where he could not dodge, but something made this feel strangely personal, as if Agent Orange held him accountable for daring to interfere with his hunt so he must show Evan he alone was the master of fates.

Orange reared back and as soon as he lunged Evan tugged on the shirt. Unexpectedly Erica's weight disappeared and the sudden slack sent him backwards so hard he nearly tumbled off the wall. The stake glanced his abdomen as it whistled past and sailed through the trees outside the Kill Zone, splintering its way through distant branches.

"Whoa! Shit!" Carlson yelled. "Nice dodge!"

It wasn't a dodge and Evan fully expected to see Erica on the ground, but she readied her left hand for another try at the sweatshirt.

"Soon as you think you know what he'll do, he does it differently," she said.

Evan looked at the blood seeping from the scratch on his stomach, knowing he could have a stake poking through his back right now.

"That was a hell of a risk!"

Evan swung the sweatshirt. She caught it again and wrapped both hands around it. Anchoring himself with one leg inside the wall and his hand on the climbing bar, Evan stretched as far back as he could, pulling Erica higher.

"Can you . . . reach the . . . "

The new angle of her foot broke the boot free, leaving a hunk of black leather on a razor-sharp piece of metal. Her body dropped, but she maintained her grip. For Evan, it felt like twenty more pounds added to the load. Sucking air through gritted teeth, he lifted her again.

"Not sure they believed me," Carlson reported below, "but fair warning, if I hear a chopper, I'm outta here!"

Erica took one hand off the sweatshirt and gripped the top of the wall. Evan clamped the shirt in his teeth, slowly releasing the slack until confident it wouldn't rip his lower jaw out of his skull, then dropped it to seize Erica's free hand with his own. It disturbed him that somewhere below Orange wouldn't merely play passive observer and might be launching some other strike this second while they were unable to monitor his movements. He pulled Erica's wrist toward the climbing bar and made a vise with his elbow outside the wall to brace himself, then released the climbing bar and replaced his grip with hers.

"Hold this tight as you can."

Something slapped Evan across the lower back. He glanced over his shoulder and found the rope ladder draped upon him.

Oh no.

Agent Orange jerked the rope. Instead of ripping Evan from the wall it slipped off and ineffectually fell into the Kill Zone, seemingly no purpose behind the maneuver. Without a grappling hook or some other way to catch hold of Evan—

Oh hell! He's fishing for the loose wire.

It hung on the outside of the KZ, but if he snagged it with the rope he could pull it over the wall. When stretched, each four foot coil would more than double in length. If that didn't drag Evan and Erica to their deaths the barbs might make them wish it had, and with so little protection for their skin the razors might be lethal on their own.

"Hang on a minute." Evan got to his knees.

Orange let the rope fly. Evan swung the sweatshirt into the concertina wire, hooking multiple barbs. Moments later the rope landed next to it. He yanked the wire straight up amid the sounds of shredding fabric and stood as Agent Orange pulled the rope taut. The sweatshirt lurched away and the coil of wire snapped from its mooring, glancing off Evan's left leg and barely missing Erica's shoulder. The redirection sent the coil flying right at Agent Orange.

Eat that, asshole!

Orange's brute strength coupled with the puncture wound left him unable to dodge the barbed serpent. He turned and it struck him in the back. Part of the snake coiled around his front, hooked his necklace of ears, tangled with the rope ladder, snagged his jacket. Arms in the air, Orange looked down at the mess he'd made.

Evan's left calf stung beneath a ragged three inch

tear in the back of his jeans. It felt like a deep cut. Hot blood coursed down his leg, into his boot.

He took the opportunity to evaluate Billie with Orange distracted. She hadn't moved.

Please be okay.

Orange's current predicament would keep him busy a little while, but once he extracted himself he'd have a cat o' nine tails on the end of a very long rope at his disposal.

"We've gotta move," Evan said.

He took his climbing bar from the wall and plugged it into the hole on the outer wall. A symbolic first step to the outside world with no corresponding sense of relief; instead, a complete, soul-deadening dread over who'd be left behind.

With no belt or even belt loops to grab hold of he had to reach for the fanny pack band around Erica's waist. Soon she was on her hands and knees in front of him, trembling from the effort, exhaustion, shock.

"You're doing great," he said. He reached around her to get the spare climbing bar from the bag. Inserting it into his back pocket, he checked Agent Orange's progress with the wire removal. Not much so far, though. The monster's sole focus had been delinking his ear necklace. He gave it a careful two-hand toss toward a large, flat stone to get it out of the way. Protect the trophies! Unbelievable. Evan envisioned someone tossing the necklace high into a tree and escaping while Agent Orange dropped everything to retrieve it.

Backed against the next section of wire to allow Erica space on the wall, Evan lost any room to maneuver. The same predicament waited if he stepped over her. She inched her knee away from dollops of his blood.

"You've gotta stand up. Think you can do it?"

They were losing their head start. Orange tore his way out of the wire, showing little concern for the damage he sustained in the process.

"Erica, I can't get around you like this and he's almost loose."

Groaning, Erica began to rise.

"Is that Helen of Troy, his McMuffin?" Carlson hollered.

Hitchcock spun in his grave while Evan reached around Erica's boots to pull the other bar out. The supply bag dropped to the ground outside.

"I don't understand Prowlerspeak, what's he mean?"

"No one knows, especially Prowlers. Focus on the wall."

Clots of Orange's flesh stuck to the barbs like torn fabric as he ripped more away down below. After he extricated his leg he'd only have to untangle the concertina wire and the rope ladder.

"Can I drop down now?" Erica asked.

The phone in her fanny pack vibrated in staccato bursts as Carlson furiously tapped missives to a nephew who hopefully hadn't gone to his grave equating futile Kill Zone quests with a breakfast sandwich.

"I need you to walk forward, okay?"

Erica moaned. "You ask a lot, Prowlerman." She shuffled away from Evan with slow baby steps.

He leaned forward and plugged the climbing bar outside the wall, then shifted sideways to take one more look inside. Orange worked diligently on separating the razor wire from the rope ladder. Definitely a cat o' nine tails on its way. Billie still out cold, but no puddle of blood around her. With luck, military would intervene before it was too late and Evan would see her soon. Probably when she cracked under the pressure of questioning and the military hauled him in, but he wouldn't blame her, he wouldn't blame her at all.

"Okay, you can lower yourself now." He let himself hang from the side of the wall. "You're going to have to get on my back, though."

"I . . . " In case talking somehow affected balance, Erica paused to get on her hands and knees. "Don't know if I can."

"Ease yourself off the side and hang onto my back. Use the shirt as a strap. Whatever it takes. Don't let go of me and don't relax your grip because it'll jar you each time I drop a level."

Erica peeked over the side at Carlson and a 30-foot drop. "Ugh. I can't believe I'm doing this."

And she did it more quickly than Evan would have believed possible. It also hurt like hell. Evan gasped at the sudden addition of her weight and the treads of her boots raking his sides and eventually the sweet spot of the barb wound on his calf. She draped an arm over his and clamped a hand over his on the climbing bar.

"Okay, you . . . reach under and get hold of the shirt strap. Need my hand."

She did so and Evan promptly set the descent in motion, left hand first.

"I'm sorry," she whispered. "This should be Billie."

"I'll get her out," Evan said.

Evan seated the left pin and eased himself downward.

I can do this. Only twenty-eightish feet to go.

But would he be able to get out of range before Orange launched the razor wire over the wall? He feared the whistle of metal whipping their way. He needed to get at least ten feet down to avoid that particular danger.

Withdraw.

"Looking good from here," Carlson said. "Looking *real* good. No wonder he jacked."

Insert.

His biceps and triceps ached from the strain. He'd only just begun. How the hell would he make it all the way down? He wondered how low he had to be for Erica to drop safely. Ten? The rest of the descent would be much easier.

Descent? Then I could go back up. Go back for Billie.

Suicide mission. And . . . completely selfish. He couldn't risk Orange getting these climbing bars. If anyone could best Rassimov's time it would be the killer.

Withdraw.

Insert.

Billie began to scream.

Evan put his forehead against the wall. Tears filled his eyes.

"I'm sorry," Erica said, sobs imminent. "I'm so sorry."

Withdraw.

Insert.

Searing pain flared in his left arm. He'd torn something, likely from the extra pressure exerted by Erica's arm over his shoulder. He couldn't slow his descent by using parallel holes, though. The wire would come any second now.

It always did, over and over the whips of the world.

Scrape marks ground into the concrete from his belt buckle formed primitive etchings before his eyes.

The screams from the other side of the wall were the worst thing he'd ever heard, worse even than Bella's and Danielle's sobs from the chemotherapy sickness, because he'd done this to Billie, *he* put her in this position. *And I couldn't wait to do it.* To get her in the Kill Zone and show her. Oh, yeah, I just preserved your house like a historical artifact from thieving bastards, no biggie. He could have insisted on getting the ashes himself. Those with the compulsion to enter the Kill Zone were seldom dissuaded, but he knew the psychology well enough to make a reasonable argument against and, given that she had children to consider, he might have talked her out of it. If only he could take it back (and there it was again, if only this instead of that); he wished he could look her in the eyes and tell her it wouldn't be worth it—

A strange whistling presaged the cat o' nine tails and a shower of blood signaled its arrival. What slammed the concrete above sounded far more substantial than wire. Evan looked up, straight into Billie's horrorstruck eyes. That made a fortuitous sense, but for an instant he couldn't reconcile the sight as a whole. It was her, but it *wasn't,* something effectively communicated by Erica's scream in his ear. Before it tapered off, he finally understood.

In a sadistic parody of Evan's rescue attempt, Agent Orange fastened Sarah's headless body to Billie's back, then wrapped them in the concertina wire.

None of it seemed possible, even within the parameters of Orange's outlandish lore. But the evidence hung above him, a woman and child somehow lassoed over thirty feet.

"Billie!"

She opened her mouth, but her face abruptly contorted in pain. A spray erupted from her neck, freshly opened. Cascades of blood rained upon Evan and Erica as Billie slid through the wire, drawn toward them by gravity in a slow, winding corkscrew that shredded flesh and fabric alike.

A razor barb slid through a goose-egg on her forehead, opening a skull-deep laceration over her left eyebrow before slicing across the pupil of her eye. Numerous rifts opened throughout her body, her skin the ravaged canvas of a psychotic artist. A gaping hole in her shirt revealed a puckered scar yielding new fruit. Her arm slipped from the coil, a barb hung on her left patella, another lodged in the jeans binding her and Sarah and their descent momentarily stopped. The rain of blood, however, flowed freely. A piece of flesh dropped to Evan's cheek and slid across his wet face like the burning trail of a tear.

"HOLY SHIT!" Carlson bellowed, recoiling from the wall to avoid the downpour.

Erica began to slip.

"Hang on."

Withdraw.

Insert.

He lowered again, madly gripping the stainless steel climbing pin. The grooved metal prevented slippage from sweaty hands, but now blood covered the instruments and the hands wielding them. Erica's death grip became a more immediate threat, now lubricated by blood, sweat and tears.

The rotors of an approaching helicopter were a mockery. Survive and go directly to jail!

Carlson took to his heels immediately, true to his word. "I'm went, boddy!"

"We need help!" Erica pleaded.

"No shit!" He didn't so much as pause to look back when he said it.

The next drop was too rough; Evan switched to every other hole to expedite the descent. Erica's arm came loose. Despite the desperate grappling of her legs, she slid down his back. The shirt crisscrossing his torso suddenly bore the brunt of her weight when she snatched it out of desperation.

"Put your arm through."

Metal scraped concrete as Agent Orange hauled Billie back toward the top of the wall, apparently wishing to reclaim his prize. Or about to drop a bomb.

Withdraw.

He blinked as blood crept into his left eye. He frantically searched for the next hole, desperate metal scratches against concrete.

Insert.

The concertina scrapes became a litany of screeches. Orange let go of the rope and Billie plummeted towards them.

"Hold on!" Evan yelled as he withdrew the left pin and tried to swing to his right to take them out of range of the falling bodies.

Abruptly Billie lurched to a halt, momentum thrusting her harder into a net of razor teeth. Her abdominal tear gaped wider to a full rift where a bulging purple bubble burst into an outpouring of bowels. A steaming deluge struck Evan in the act of reaching for his left-hand slot. The wet gush knocked him sideways, swinging Erica and twisting them away from the wall. He clawed for the bar again as Agent Orange let go.

Though certain the trajectory of the bodies would have to collide with Erica, somehow they missed her to slam into his arm and shoulder. The shirt tied around him ripped free. She dropped. The rope followed like a slithering snake chasing its prey. Wet flesh and wire slapped the ground and somewhere in the discordance came the solid ping of a climbing bar hitting rock.

A hundred and twenty pounds of weight caught on Evan's belt. Stinging furrows on his back and abdomen marked the trails left by Erica's fingernails.

"You okay?" she asked, still hanging on, spared another direct hit.

Some had Lady Luck on their side, but Evan had her draped from his legs.

He stared at his empty left hand, an open gash running from the knuckle of his index finger to his wrist. Another laceration arced around the opposite side of the wrist and stretched to his elbow. His dark blood mingled with Billie's and Sarah's. He flexed his hand and cringed from the pain, but everything seemed to work otherwise. A stinging sensation at his shoulder blade and warmth coursing down his back indicated at least one more wound.

I'm okay.

He found a dry spot on the wall and tried to wipe the blood from his palm.

They were still fifteen feet from the ground. Too high a fall with all the rocks and uneven ground below them, not to mention a mess of concertina wire.

Evan retrieved the spare climbing bar from his back pocket.

The descent slowed to a crawl. Became a blur of step-by-step movements. Deep concentration. He tasted blood, he didn't know whose. More of it leaked from his arm than circulated to his fingers and soon the whole thing turned numb. Somewhere along the way he lost Erica, heard her land with an "oomph!" Then came the sickening sounds of wire strafing rocks, the smack of wet parts sliding, the gurgles of displaced blood and entrails.

"Rad C!" she screamed.

When Evan hit the ground blood erupted from his boot, a hot flow that surged over his ankle to join the earth. He turned and put his back against the wall, but didn't dare let his legs slide out from under him; if he sat down now he'd never be able to get back up.

When he tried to assess the damage to his left arm he found a mess of different fabrics wrapped with boot laces. A crimson face hovered in front of his, talking vague nothingspeak, but her ethereal white eyes and teeth were strangely mesmerizing.

An Apache helicopter appeared in the distance, following along the wall, just near enough to see rocket packs hanging from its stubby wings. Dizzy, detached, Evan watched as though it came for someone else, someone not him, the boy from The Picture maybe.

If they left now, they might escape whether or not Agent Orange retreated on the other side to distract the military. But maybe this would eventually be another in a long line of ifs for Evan to wonder about.

"Come *on*!" Erica tugged him.

Evan trudged to the woods in what felt like slow motion, weighed down by his exhaustion and the blood of Sarah and Billie.

They were deep within the forest when several rapid, explosive reports brought Evan out of his stupor. The AH-64 fired its 30mm cannon. No sooner did the firing stop and the echo fade did the civil defense sirens begin to wail.

Ten minutes later, they reached the dead-end street long since vacated by Carlson. Red and blue flashing lights in the distance signaled a roadblock so they crossed the street and took to the woods for cover.

"Unlock the phone," Evan said, swaying on his feet. He tapped a message to Rad C.

The next half hour became a blur of non-stop movement through wooded terrain amid the din of helicopters, police sirens, civil defense alarms, and intermittent cannon fire. They approached a highway where slow-moving traffic rolled toward a distant, out of sight roadblock. Staying inside the woods, they trekked alongside the procession until Evan saw the white Impala Carlson called the Radmobile. When Carlson saw them emerge from the trees his hand fluttered like a bird as he beckoned them rapidly behind the window.

Carlson squealed into a U-turn and Evan closed his eyes against the blur of outside motion. The car spun Evan back to the wall where he'd stood with an expectant Billie.

"Look, we don't have to do this," he told her.

"Are you backing out on me?"

"No, but if you've changed your mind . . . if you're having second thoughts."

If . . .

THE END
OF
REINCURSION

SURVIVORS FROM THIS
NOVEL WILL RETURN

(H)ACKNOWLEDGEMENTS

The authors would like to say thank you and ki-ki-ki-ma-ma-ma to Jarod Barbee, Patrick C Harrison III and Death's Head Press for unleashing this bloodbath of a sequel, and Alex McVey for the gruesome cover art. We also extend our appreciation to Brendan.

We remain indebted to the work of Arkady and Boris Strugatsky, as well as the slasher classics of the 70s and 80s. We are also indebted to the legacy of David G. Barnett, whose Necro Publications laid the foundation for hardcore horror as know it. RIP Dave.

Ryan thanks Kelly Robinson, Lucas Mangum, Chandler Morrison, Kristopher Triana, John Wayne Comunale, Edward Lee, Bryan Smith, Brian Keene, Jeff Burk, Christine Morgan, Regina Garza Mitchell, Mike Bracken, Geoff Cooper, Philip LoPresti, Jeremy Wagner, and Brent Zirnheld.

ABOUT THE AUTHORS

Ryan Harding is the three-time Splatterpunk Award-winning author of books like *Genital Grinder* and collaborations with Kristopher Triana *(The Night Stockers)*, Lucas Mangum *(Pandemonium)*, Jason Taverner *(Reincarnage)*, and Edward Lee *(Header 3)*. Upcoming projects include the collection *Transcendental Mutilation* from Death's Head Press, a novel with Bryan Smith, and a Splatter Western.

Jason Taverner is . . .